PRAISE FOR THE NOVELS OF JULIET BLACKWELL

THE WITCHCRAFT MYSTERIES

A Cast-off Coven

"If you like your mysteries with a side of spell casting and demon vanquishing, you'll enjoy the second title in Blackwell's Witchcraft mysteries."   —*Romantic Times*

"This awesome paranormal mystery stars a terrific heroine."   —Genre Go Round Reviews

Secondhand Spirits

"Juliet Blackwell provides a terrific urban fantasy with the opening of the Witchcraft Mystery series."
                                 —Genre Go Round Reviews

"An excellent blend of mystery, paranormal, and light humor, creating a cozy that is a must read for anyone with an interest in literature with paranormal elements."   —The Romance Readers Connection

"It's a fun story, with romance possibilities with a couple hunky men, terrific vintage clothing, and the enchanting Oscar. But there is so much more to this book. It has serious depth."   —*The Herald News* (MA)

continued . . .

HEXES AND HEMLINES

A
Witchcraft
Mystery

Juliet Blackwell

AN OBSIDIAN MYSTERY

OBSIDIAN
Published by New American Library, a division of
Penguin Group (USA) Inc., 375 Hudson Street,
New York, New York 10014, USA
Penguin Group (Canada), 90 Eglinton Avenue East, Suite 700, Toronto,
Ontario M4P 2Y3, Canada (a division of Pearson Penguin Canada Inc.)
Penguin Books Ltd., 80 Strand, London WC2R 0RL, England
Penguin Ireland, 25 St. Stephen's Green, Dublin 2,
Ireland (a division of Penguin Books Ltd.)
Penguin Group (Australia), 250 Camberwell Road, Camberwell, Victoria 3124,
Australia (a division of Pearson Australia Group Pty. Ltd.)
Penguin Books India Pvt. Ltd., 11 Community Centre, Panchsheel Park,
New Delhi - 110 017, India
Penguin Group (NZ), 67 Apollo Drive, Rosedale, Auckland 0632,
New Zealand (a division of Pearson New Zealand Ltd.)
Penguin Books (South Africa) (Pty.) Ltd., 24 Sturdee Avenue,
Rosebank, Johannesburg 2196, South Africa

Penguin Books Ltd., Registered Offices:
80 Strand, London WC2R 0RL, England

First published by Obsidian, an imprint of New American Library,
a division of Penguin Group (USA) Inc.

First Printing, June 2011
10 9 8 7 6 5 4

To Jane Lawes
Thank you for the magic—
I miss you so.

Acknowledgments

Thank you to my wonderful editor, Kerry Donovan—and congratulations on the new human, Reed! And to my literary agent, Kristin Lindstrom, who is unflagging in her support.

Special thanks to R.G. for allowing me to witness your spell casting and to glimpse a bit of your world. And to Renna Santini for answering my numerous (and no doubt obnoxious) questions about the Rom and traditional healing spells. *Muchísimas gracias a Cathy Romero por enseñarme en las tradiciones mexicanas.*

We authors require many supportive shoulders on which to lean, and ears in which to whine. . . . I couldn't manage without my fellow writers. Many thanks to my fellow Pens Fatales (www.pensfatales.com). To Mario Acevedo, Rachael Herron, Nicole Peeler, Cornelia Read, Steve Hockensmith, and so many more for promoting my witchy ways. And to Sophie Littlefield for putting up with all my secret nastiness . . . and making it seem like a feature rather than a failing. You are amazing.

And to the long list of friends and neighbors that I thank in almost every book—you know who you are, and you all serve to make this life an adventure. I am privileged to know you, and it's no exaggeration to say I could never be what I am without your love and support . . . and cocktails! You are my family.

To my mother, Jane, and father, Bob, and sisters, Susan and Carolyn. Thank you for giving me the kind of start in life that everyone should be lucky enough to have. And for continuing to be there for me, even when I'm crazed. Your support means more than you know.

To Jace, for making me laugh just about every day—and for whipping the next generation of schoolchildren into shape. And to my guy, Sergio . . . you are, were, and always will be an inspiration to me.

And finally to Oscar, my neighbor's little black cat . . . I put "smoked ham" on the grocery list.

'Tis the night—the night
Of the grave's delight,
And the warlocks are at their play;
Ye think that without
The wild winds shout,
But no, it is they—it is they.

—ARTHUR CLEVELAND COXE

Chapter 1

It didn't take a witch to figure out something was very, very wrong on the thirteenth floor of the Doppler Building.

It wasn't called the thirteenth floor, of course. It was the penthouse, and Malachi Zazi lived there. Or . . . *used* to live there. At the moment his body was splayed atop a long banquet table, a jagged shard from a shattered mirror protruding from his chest. Deep red blood spatter created a gruesome Rorschach pattern on the snowy white Belgian lace tablecloth.

I took a deep breath and concentrated on not losing my lunch.

Most days I deal in vintage clothing, not corpses. I may be a natural-born witch, but I'm no more comfortable around violent death than any other mortal merchant on Haight Street.

I was here only because SFPD inspector Carlos Romero had asked for my help. I now understood why.

"When was he found?" I asked.

"This morning," said Inspector Romero. "By his housekeeper."

"Time of death?"

"Medical examiner hasn't determined that, but the victim had guests for a midnight supper. The last ones apparently left around two thirty."

"The body hasn't been moved? The legs were pointed toward the door like this?"

The inspector nodded. "Everything's as it was found. Including the bird."

"What bird?"

As if on cue, a small brown sparrow swooped past me and landed on the table near the corpse. It chirped and hopped about, then flew away. I jumped when a black cat sprang onto the tabletop and gave chase. Feather and fur disappeared into the bedroom.

I clutched my medicine bag and whispered a quick protective chant.

Romero scoffed. "I didn't think witches were scared of black cats."

"I'm not. But a sparrow trapped in the house is a sign of death at hand."

"Yeah, well, we got a dead guy on the table."

"But the bird . . ." I shook my head. "Death is still lurking. It's a bad sign."

"That's nothing," the inspector snorted. "So far we've got a ladder positioned in front of the door to walk under in order to pass into the room. There's a broken mirror over the fireplace, an open umbrella in the corner, and a black cat. Even *I* know these are alleged signs of bad luck."

"Don't forget the thirteen chairs at the table," I mused. No point in mentioning that lying atop a table is considered bad luck, and lying down with one's feet pointed toward the door is referred to as the corpse position. "And we're on the thirteenth floor. Not that there's anything unlucky about the number thirteen; quite the opposite. But a lot of people seem to think it's cursed."

I wasn't yet ready to take a close look at the victim. Both because he was dead and what all . . . and because there was something decidedly wrong with the body.

Even from a distance, I could sense that there was something *different* about Malachi Zazi.

I took a moment to look around the apartment, side-stepping the emergency personnel, who were dusting for prints and photographing possible evidence. Besides occasional staccato camera flashes, the only light in the room was a dim amber glow from hand-blown sconces. The apartment reeked of cigar smoke and carried the slight aroma of last night's dinner. Tall windows were covered by heavy gold-tasseled red velvet drapes that blocked the afternoon sun; muted Oriental rugs covered generous sections of the dark wood floor; vivid oil paintings lined the paneled walls; and plush leather armchairs invited weary visitors to linger by the massive carved fireplace. There were vases of lilies as well as bright orange marigolds—both were flowers of death: the lilies in many Western cultures, the marigolds in Mexico for Day of the Dead. The whole apartment looked like a stage set for a Victorian play—for some convoluted murder mystery, to be precise.

"Officially, we're on the fourteenth floor," Romero mentioned as he trailed after me. "Not the thirteenth."

"Only because otherwise rational men and women pretend there's no thirteenth floor when they build buildings. It's such a holdover from another time. . . . It's almost charming."

"Charming or not, a man was in here with all these bad luck signs, and now he's dead. Stabbed in the heart. Look, Lily," the inspector continued with a half-embarrassed, half-weary look on his face. "You know it pains me to ask for your help, but I thought you might be able to offer certain . . . insights into this case. Can you tell me anything?"

I thought for a moment.

"You already know about the bad luck signs. But those are mostly superstitions—except for the mirror, and the ladder. Oh, and the poor bird. But even if they were potent, they wouldn't lead to murder. Bad luck omens are more subtle than that, and they tend to work on a bit of a time delay."

"So he was just an eccentric guy who liked signs of bad luck? You don't . . . 'feel' anything?"

I took a deep breath and approached the body. "May I touch him?"

"Go ahead."

I reached out and laid the fingertips of my left hand on Zazi's cold, waxy forehead. He looked only a little older than I, maybe early thirties. Despite the grayish tone of his skin, it was clear he had once been good-looking. Dark hair and delicate wings of eyebrows set off even, romantic features.

Closing my eyes, I concentrated on filtering out the static caused by all the people in the apartment; their nervous energy bounced off the walls and filled the available air. I focused my powers, subsumed my conscious self, and allowed myself to be a conduit.

Nothing.

People—*normal* people—give off sensations, even several hours after death.

Malachi's hands were soft, no calluses or signs of a man who worked with his hands. He wore a ring, a tarnished silver snake that wound around his left finger. Turning his hand palm up, I looked for the faint lines of fingerprints, the markings common to most every normal human on the earth.

The skin was slick, almost shiny. Even the palm showed no lifelines; nothing.

"Could someone roll him for prints?" I asked Carlos.

"What are you looking for?"

"I don't think he'll have any."

"What, you mean like you?"

"Like me."

Our eyes met.

Some of us are born without fingerprints. There is a documented, albeit rare, medical condition associated with the lack of such lines. Still, I sometimes wondered whether there was something metaphysical about it, as though certain folk are meant to go through life without leaving a trace . . . but then I'd decided I was just strange.

Apparently, so was Malachi Zazi.

"Maybe you should check out his DNA," I mentioned.

"What for?"

"Make sure he's human."

Romero glanced around at the crowd, took me gently by the upper arm, and hustled me into the bedroom. Our sudden entrance startled the cat, which ran under the bed.

His hand still on the door, as though holding it closed

by force, Romero blew out a frustrated breath and fixed me with his skeptical cop gaze.

"What are you insinuating?"

"I just think it would be helpful to know for sure what we're dealing with."

"If he's not human, then . . ." He swore under his breath and rubbed the back of his neck. "What would he be? *Please* tell me we're not talking about . . . a demon?"

I flinched. In my world, people don't go around casually invoking the names of demons.

"Of course not," I said. The inspector visibly relaxed. Until I added: "I mean, I doubt it. Could be anything, really."

"Such as . . . ?"

"A doppelganger, a changeling . . . or maybe just odd, like me."

Avoiding Romero's eyes, I started poking around the bedroom. It was a masculine room, full of polished antiques like the rest of the apartment. My interest was immediately caught by an ornate cherry armoire, its doors open to reveal a bonanza of silks and satins— ladies' gowns and gentlemen's suits from another era. The late 1800s, I would say offhand. The clothes were gorgeous, and incredibly rare in such good condition.

"What's all this?" I asked.

"I don't know, and I don't particularly care, if it doesn't have to do with the vic's murder."

I reached into the closet, hugged several of the items to my chest, and concentrated on the garments.

Clothes were usually an easy read for me. They hummed, alive with the energy and whispered traces of the people they had adorned. But not these. These clothes were as soulless as the dead man on the table.

I recoiled, as disturbed as a normal person would have been to suddenly feel vibrations coming from their T-shirt and cargo pants.

"What's wrong?" Romero asked.

I just shook my head. I didn't know what to make of it all. "Could I . . . would it be possible for me to have these?"

Carlos gave me an incredulous look.

"We can't just help ourselves to stuff at a murder scene, Lily. They belong to this poor bastard's estate."

"Oh, of course," I said, feeling my cheeks burn. Some people say witches can't blush. Not true. I can't cry, and I can't sink in water. But I sure as heck blush when I've got cause. And I too often have cause.

"Okay, this guy was supposedly founder of something called the Serpentarian Society—thirteen members all had dinner here last night," Carlos said. "What can you tell me about that?"

"I don't know anything about a society."

"Do you know what Serpentarian refers to? Serpents, like snakes?"

"Sort of. Serpentarius is the thirteenth sign of the zodiac."

"I thought there were twelve signs, one for each month."

"There used to be thirteen, back when there were thirteen months in a year."

"No way."

"Way. Each with twenty-eight days, like February. The old English calendar was called 'thirteen and a day.'" At his still dubious expression, I continued: "Think about it: Thirteen times twenty-eight is three hundred and sixty-four."

Romero's mouth kicked up in a reluctant smile. "You do that equation in your head?"

"Not hardly." I returned his smile. "Math and I don't exactly get along. Anyway, I'm no expert, but if I remember correctly, Serpentarius is the constellation in between Scorpio and Sagittarius."

"Okay . . . how is this Serpentarius guy significant to my homicide?"

"I have no idea. The only thing I remember about Serpentarius offhand is that, unlike the other horoscope signs, he was based on a real man. A medical man. And his sign is a couple of intertwined snakes—hence the name. I'll find out more about him if you like, and let you know."

The little sparrow rose up from wherever it was hiding and started fluttering about the room. The cat took note. I crossed over to the window and pulled back the heavy velvet curtains. Behind them was a pair of sheers, and then a heavy-duty blackout shade. Finally I wrestled with a casement window that probably hadn't been opened since the Nixon administration.

When the window finally swung open, I jumped back, startled by a looming, grinning gray face on the other side of the pane. I caught myself—it was merely the stony countenance of a gargoyle, protruding from overhanging eaves.

"Feeling a little jumpy?" asked Carlos.

"Fixin' to leap out of my skin," I agreed. "This is only my second homicide scene."

"You get used to it after a while . . . unfortunately."

I stepped away from the window, hoping the little bird would take note of the light and the air and leave this unnatural place.

Instead it landed on my shoulder. The cat leapt onto the regal four-poster, its green-eyed gaze fixed on the sparrow, as though ready to pounce on its prey—and on me.

"Go on now, sugar," I turned my head and said to the bird. "Get on out of here."

The sparrow hopped twice, looked at me once more with one bright shiny eye, then flew out the window to freedom. The cat bounded behind it, leaping up to the window ledge and looking out, yearning, after its quarry.

"Did you just talk to that bird?" Carlos asked, giving me a quizzical look.

I nodded.

"You talk to animals now?"

I smiled. "A lot of people talk to animals, but that doesn't mean they understand. Watch: Come on down from there, cat," I said to the feline preening on the window ledge.

The cat remained where it was.

"See, the cat didn't obey," I said.

"Cats never obey."

"True enough."

"The way the windows are covered up, maybe Zazi was afraid of the light. Like a . . . vampire."

"Don't be ridiculous," I scoffed. "There's no such thing as vampires."

"But changelings and ghosts and doppel-whatzits, no problem."

"It's not the same thing at all," I protested.

Still, I saw his point. How does one tease out superstition and folktales from reality? I knew from my training that all sorts of supposedly imaginary creatures are, in fact, real: unicorns and pretty much all the woods folk, elves and brownies and faeries. But others were simply inventions of the creative human mind. Unfortunately, I had never finished my education in the Craft, so I was still unclear on a lot of the details.

Looked like I was going to have to check in with a higher authority: Aidan Rhodes, powerful male witch and unofficial godfather to the West Coast mystical contingent. Speaking of whom . . .

I glanced down at my vintage Tinkerbell watch. I was late for a lesson with Rhodes, who had agreed to help me complete my witchcraft training. I didn't trust him as far as I could throw him, but I surely did need him. Among other things, I imagined he might shed some light on the identity of the late Malachi Zazi, if not on Zazi's murderer.

"I've got to get going. I'll ask around, see what I can find out," I said. "I'm sorry I wasn't more helpful. I can't feel anything—and that worries me. Normally I'd be feeling too much in a situation like this."

"Okaaaay," Carlos said in a cynical tone. He had asked me here himself, but he was still dealing with having invited my opinion on his homicide scene, just as I was still reeling at having been asked. It's not every day that a vintage clothing dealer gets called in to consult with the SFPD. To be fair, the police department had less interest in my expertise in antique Belgian lace than in my talents as a witch. But for that matter, it's not every day that a witch gets called in to advise on a murder case.

I had moved to San Francisco only a few months ago and opened my vintage clothing store in the former hippie haven of Haight Street, near Ashbury. Though I had hoped to keep my witchcraft under wraps, Fate had other plans for me, as she so often does. Already I had been involved in more supernatural mayhem than I would have imagined existed in such a welcoming, friendly city.

Carlos Romero stopped me as I headed for the door. "You want this?"

He held the black cat out to me; the animal hung limp and boneless in Carlos's hands, gazing at me with huge yellowish green headlamp eyes.

"I can't take it. I'm allergic," I said.

"I thought your type loved cats."

"Even among witches I'm a bit of a freak."

The cat stared at me and meowed. Sort of. It was more like a raspy little squeak than a proper meow.

"Don't *you* need a pet?" I said. "I think it likes you."

Carlos gave me a look. "Listen, it's a black cat, and you're a witch. Allergic or not, you two go together like rice and beans. Why not take it home with you; it'll keep your pet pig company."

"I am *not* taking a cat."

"All right," he said and sighed.

"What'll you do with it?" I couldn't help but ask.

"We'll call animal control. They'll take it to the pound."

"And the pound will find it a home?"

He shrugged. "They'll try, but they usually have too many cats as it is."

"Then . . ."

"They may have to euthanize it."

Our eyes held again. "You are an evil man, Inspector."

He smiled.

I took the dang cat.

Chapter 2

"What in the heck is *that*?" Oscar demanded as I placed the feline in the cargo area of my work van. I slid the heavy door shut with a *whoosh* and a *thunk*.

The purple van was parked right outside Zazi's apartment building, but Oscar hadn't bothered to assume his potbellied pig form since no one could see into the back. In his natural state, my shape-shifting familiar was a cross between an imp and a gnome . . . or maybe a goblin. Whatever he was, Oscar was garrulous, perpetually hungry, and opinionated. He had large batlike ears, a face that resembled a grimacing monkey's, claws on his hind feet, oversized hands . . . and all of it was covered in greenish gray scales.

He was so ugly he went clear round the bend into adorable.

The little guy had burst into my life not long ago thanks to Aidan Rhodes, male witch. Before I knew quite what was happening, Oscar was stuck to me like white on grits.

Trust a misfit witch like me to wind up with a drama queen for a familiar.

At the moment said drama queen, Oscar, was flattened against the glove compartment, one clawed hand shielding his face, glowering at the back of the van.

"It's a *cat*," I told him as I climbed behind the wheel. The "duh" was implied. "It's not radioactive."

"Yeah, but . . . *hey*, a witch don't need more than one familiar." Oscar turned to me, huge luminous eyes the color of green bottle glass. "You already got me, so's you can't have *that*."

"The cat's not a familiar, Oscar." I sneezed.

"Gesundheit."

"Thanks," I said with a sniff. "Poor little thing didn't have anywhere to go. I sort of volunteered to find a home for it. I couldn't just leave it there."

"Don't see why not," he muttered.

I sneezed again. Twice.

"Gesundheit, gesundheit."

"I'm much obliged, but you don't have to say gesundheit each time," I said as I reached for a Kleenex from the half-crumpled box in the passenger-side footwell.

"Yes, I do."

"You do?"

He nodded enthusiastically.

"Why?"

His only reply was a shrug. This was the tenor of many a frustrating conversation I had with my ersatz familiar. I love him, but he's downright mysterious.

"Anyway," I said, "the cat isn't up for discussion. And really, it's a sweet thing." I'm more of a dog person, but homeless creatures of all kinds tug at my heart. I know what it means to be abandoned.

"It's not sleeping on my purple silk pillow," Oscar

said, his voice petulant. "Bronwyn got that for *me*. It's *mine*. It's *monogrammed*."

"I know. Relax. It's a temporary situation."

"That's what they always say. Just don't feed it."

"That'll be your job," I said, ignoring his outraged expression. "*And* you can keep it entertained while I'm at my lesson with Aidan."

"But I don't want . . . I mean I . . . okay."

Wait a minute. Did Oscar just agree to do as I said?

"Oscar, listen to me: You will be kind and caring to this cat. It will *not* go missing, or . . ." I wasn't actually sure what a creature like Oscar might be capable of, now that I thought about it. "Or sprout horns, or a second tail, or anything else out of the ordinary. Understand me, young man?"

"Ungeoiudmfh," said Oscar.

"Pardon me?" I said, lifting an eyebrow in what I flattered myself was an imperious gesture. Oscar wasn't the most obedient of familiars. I blamed Aidan. "Did you have something you wanted to say?"

"Nothing, Mistress," he said with a sigh, crossing his skinny arms over his scaly chest and feigning a sudden interest in a wrinkled old map on the floor. He kicked at it, grumbling to himself in a low growl: "*First* I have to wait in the van, and then I have to take care of a stupid *cat*."

"I can still hear you," I said, though I gave him a grudging smile and an affectionate squeeze.

When we'd first arrived at Malachi Zazi's building, Oscar tried to talk me into letting him come up to the apartment. Because apparently I wasn't odd enough all by myself, and Oscar saw no reason why anyone would think bringing one's potbellied pig to a murder scene would be considered out of the ordinary.

"But I can help you," he'd whined, claiming he might be able to tell if there were ghosts or other spirits present. *"Besides, there are gargoyles on this building. I love gargoyles! They're practically family."*

Not long ago Oscar actually had been able to assist me when I was investigating a haunted art school. Still, with the regular old police involved it had seemed like a faux pas—at best—to bring along one's pet pig. But now . . . after my lack of sensing any vibrations up in Malachi's apartment, I was thinking it might not be such a bad idea after all. Could I somehow sneak Oscar up to check out the apartment once the official personnel had completed their crime scene investigation?

I sat in the driver's seat without starting the engine, studying the exterior of Malachi Zazi's apartment building. Based on the architectural details, I was guessing it had been built in the 1910s or 1920s, a symphony of red brick and cream-colored cement. Cornices and handcrafted details swooped out from the façade in a bold blend of Art Deco and Art Nouveau styles. The top of the building was asymmetrical, with terraces and spires and Gothic-inspired gargoyles protruding from all sides. It was decidedly odd. Unique. Gorgeous.

Like all aged structures, it retained traces of the human lives that had passed through and dwelt within its walls over the years, but I sensed nothing untoward in its halls and stairwells. Of course, I had not felt much beyond the norm in Malachi Zazi's apartment, either, though my eyes told me otherwise. It was odd. Exceedingly odd.

This must be how regular people feel, I thought. They move through life without tuning in to each vibration, every wisp or echo of those who had come and gone.

Must be peaceful. Too bad I couldn't just relax and enjoy.

I did feel one strange sensation—as though I were being watched. I glanced around.

A young blond woman pushed a stroller toward the double doors; the uniformed doorman, graying and portly, hurried to help her out, exchanging pleasantries. An elderly fellow strolled into the building, a newspaper tucked under his arm and a black beret perched on his bald head. The driver of a FedEx van pulled up, double-parked, jumped down with two large packages, and handed them over to the doorman. Two uniformed cops came out of the elevator, passed through the lobby, and headed down the street.

Other than the presence of the police, nothing seemed out of the ordinary.

Behind me, the cat mewed, a raspy squeak that made me think of a cartoon character with a pack-a-day habit. I turned to find it staring at me. The guileless look in its huge headlamp eyes reminded me of the way Oscar tended to gaze at me . . . especially in the air of confident expectation, certain that I would take care of whatever and whoever needed to be taken care of.

My stomach fluttered. It was tough, living up to that kind of belief. It made a witch more afraid than ever to fail, to let everyone down. Since I'd become more open about my witchcraft, and had helped resolve a couple of local demonic situations, I'd been feeling the pressure. Not long ago I would have blown town at the first sign of trouble. But now that I was making my home in San Francisco, flight was no longer an option.

"You are special, m'hija," I remembered my grandmother Graciela telling me.

I flashed back to a sunny afternoon, sitting at her kitchen table back in Jarod, Texas, sipping a frosty glass of her special ginger-spiked sweet tea.

"I say this with a heavy heart because such power is bound to be misunderstood. And with great power comes great responsibility. Me entiendes, *Lily? Understand? You must be very careful. Learn all you can about your power, about the other world. But use it rarely, and only when you are certain—certain,* alma mia, *absolutely certain that it is necessary. What have I taught you? The one thing above all?"*

"All things must be in balance," I said.

"All things must be in balance," she repeated solemnly. "You must never forget that, Lilita. No te olvides. *If you do, the consequences will be terrible."*

I nodded and finished my tea. "Could we go try to turn the yellow daisies purple now?"

"Seguro que si," *Graciela replied with an indulgent smile. "But of course."*

I was only now beginning to understand what my grandmother meant, to grasp just how powerful a witch I was. There weren't all that many of us. I had spent much of my life hiding from that fact, avoiding other people and the responsibility their ordinary human selves engendered in supernatural folks like me. Unfortunately, I still didn't feel in control of my talents.

Which was why I was now headed to the San Franciscan tourist mecca of Fisherman's Wharf. It was time for school. For better or worse, I had entrusted the furthering of my witchy education to Aidan Rhodes.

I started driving, weaving through a traffic snarl at the intersection of Van Ness and Lombard. Perhaps Aidan would have some insights into the death of Malachi Za—

"Stop looking at me!" whined Oscar, wrenching me from my thoughts. He was huddling against the front passenger-side door, an appalled look on his already grimacing face. The cat, sitting on the vinyl seat in between us, just stared.

"The cat's not hurting you, Oscar. Get a grip."

"Mistress, make it stop *looking* at me!"

I pulled up to a stoplight and assessed my posse.

"*Cat*, stop it. Oscar doesn't want to be your friend." At the sound of my voice the feline shifted its gaze to me.

"There," I said to Oscar. "All better."

Keeping its eyes on me, the cat moved with stealthy determination, climbing onto Oscar's lap.

"Mistress!"

"Stop it, both of y'all," I said as the light changed.

I spoke in the severest voice I could manage, but it was pretty hard not to laugh. As someone who has been allergic to felines all her life, I knew one absolute truth: Cats had an unerring ability to detect the one person in the room—or van—who least desired their attention. And then they showered that person with affection.

Or with dander. Sneezing again, I drove around until I spotted a parking spot in a residential neighborhood off Bay Street, not wanting to worry about feeding parking meters, or using my powers to find a parking spot and cast a spell over a meter. Lately I was trying to focus all my power and strength on the important stuff.

Easy parking, according to Aidan, did not qualify.

I grabbed my leather satchel from the back of the van, and since the fog was likely to roll in off the bay by the time I left Aidan's office, I also carried my vintage cocoa brown wool coat over my arm. But at the moment it was a gorgeous Northern California spring day, breezy and sunny. As I walked I reveled in the fragrance of pink jasmine and fruit-laden lemon trees . . . trailed by a pot-bellied pig and a cat.

Together we formed quite the parade. Heads swiveled as we passed, but I held my chin up and nodded serenely, trying my best to channel a dark-haired Grace Kelly. I probably more closely resembled a cross-dressing Doctor Dolittle.

One of the best things about being a vintage clothes merchant was having a huge closet to choose from every day, and I had gotten in the habit of advertising by modeling my own merchandise. Today I was wearing an outfit from the late fifties: a wide-skirted, knee-length, yellow-and-red madras plaid sundress topped by a persimmon-colored cardigan. Though I adored the look of vintage shoes, they didn't really suit my active lifestyle—working at the store, investigating murder scenes, running from demons and what all. Instead, I favored Keds. Today's were orangey red, with a hint of sparkle. Looking down, I enjoyed the way the shoes caught the light as I walked the several blocks to Jefferson Street.

San Francisco's Wax Museum is an ever-popular tourist destination, but in my opinion it is creepy on its best day, which no doubt explained why Aidan Rhodes kept an office here. I believe he thinks it's funny. The wax figures, however artistically rendered, made me decidedly uncomfortable; they reminded me too much of poppets, used in many magical systems as stand-ins for humans. As if they were a reserve army of mindless automatons, I feared they could be transfigured, if desired, by someone with enough power.

Like a certain male witch.

There was no denying one fact: I feared Aidan's power . . . but I envied him his mastery. Though my innate talents might rival his, I was nowhere near as in control.

Just as my little entourage approached the museum entrance, a man strode out of the building. He wore heavy-looking black motorcycle boots. Faded jeans. Leather jacket. And a really bad attitude.

A fellow I knew only too well.

A fellow named Sailor.

Chapter 3

Upon spotting me, six feet two inches of muscled man reared back, on guard and wary.

This was the sort of response I'd become inured to as a child in Texas, when my neighbors got the notion I was a witch. But Sailor wasn't unfamiliar with witches; on the contrary, he worked for Aidan—albeit reluctantly— and was himself a powerful psychic. Still and all, he'd been assiduously avoiding me ever since he'd helped me drive a demon out of a building not long ago. Unlike most psychics I've known, who enjoy their abilities to communicate with the beyond, Sailor was not what you'd call at home in his psychic skin. He was also one sorry excuse for a human being. For some reason, I really like him.

"Hello, Sailor," I said as I approached him. "Lookin' for a date?"

"That wasn't funny the first hundred times. What are *you* doing here?" His dark eyes swept over my vintage outfit before shifting to my animal entourage. "And do you think you could cause a bit more of a scene?"

Passersby were starting to take note of the pig.

I gestured to Oscar to go on inside the museum. He herded the cat over to the old-fashioned kiosk that served as a ticket booth. The lethargic young attendant, Clarinda, glared at me, but nodded. Clarinda loathed me—and by extension my pig, presumably now also my cat—but she respected or feared Aidan more. So she cooperated. After a fashion.

"I'd better be going, anyway," Sailor said.

Having been shunned for most of my life, I had developed a fairly thick skin when it came to personal slights. But it still rankled that Sailor was always so anxious to get away from me. After all, we were . . . friends. Sort of. I didn't have all that many, so I figured he counted.

"Wait," I said. "What are you doing here?"

"Asked you first."

"I'm here for a lesson. Aidan's helping me hone some of my skills."

"What?"

"You told me yourself I should get a better handle on my powers. Remember? So I talked to Aidan and—"

He gaped at me, aghast. "You're letting *Aidan* train you? Good *Lord*, woman."

"He's a pretty powerful fellow."

"Uh, *yeah*. That's the freaking understatement of the year. Sure as hell doesn't mean you should trust him to train you."

"Hey, Sailor, know what I've noticed?"

"I have the feeling you're going to tell me."

"You're happy to cast aspersions on Aidan, yet you never explain why. So do you have an actual, you know, *reason* for distrusting him, or are you just still twelve years old?"

Sailor's eyes slewed to the side, looking around us surreptitiously, as though only now realizing we were still standing near the entrance to the Wax Museum. With an agitated quirk of his dark head he strode out into the busy street, looking neither left nor right, assuming the cars would stop for him.

Which they did.

I trotted along behind him. On the opposite sidewalk we were immediately engulfed by hordes of chatty tourists rushing to and from bay cruises, seafood restaurants, and the assorted attractions of Pier 39, the Cannery, and the Ghirardelli Chocolate factory. Their vivacious energy swirled about us, creating a virtual cone of silence.

"Look, if you need training," Sailor said, still surveying the crowd, "which you *do*, why don't you go back to your source? Who started you out?"

"My grandmother, Graciela. But she's back in Texas, where I grew up. She won't come out here—you know how old-school witches are. Attached to the land."

"So move back to Texas. That sounds like a really good idea, the more that I think about it."

"You're saying you wouldn't miss me?" I smiled coquettishly, or at least as close as I could come. I'm not what you'd call a natural-born flirt, and I've never had much chance to practice.

Apparently I still wasn't much good at it. Sailor's mouth pulled even tighter in irritation.

"I'm saying if you're smart you'll get the hell out of Dodge."

"San Francisco is my home now," I said, as much to myself as to him. "I love the Haight, and I have no intention of leaving. Besides, there seems to be a lot of . . . 'activity' in this town lately. I think I'm needed."

I could see the muscles in his jaw working, as though he was biting back words.

Giving him a moment, I inhaled deeply and relished the scenery. The salt off the bay mingled with the aroma of steaming seafood. A child ran past, trailing a bright red balloon. His father followed, laughing, a little girl perched atop his broad shoulders. Two teenage girls in brand-new Alcatraz sweatshirts slouched by, clutching bags of saltwater taffy and loaves of sourdough bread. A small crowd milled around a man whose clothes, skin, and hair were all painted a shiny silver color; when money was dropped into his bag, he performed a jerky, robotic dance.

I love tourists. So normal. So happy. So blissfully unaware that witches and whatnot lurk in their midst.

"I might know someone who could help you," Sailor said finally, bringing my attention back to our conversation.

"Help me how?"

"Train you."

"Rather than Aidan?"

He nodded.

"Sailor, I know Aidan's . . . unpredictable sometimes, but surely he's good at what he does. He's talented, and seems to be in full control of his magick. Other than not liking him personally, is there a reason you're waving me off?"

Sailor finally met my eyes. I knew he couldn't read my mind, a fact for which I was profoundly grateful. But there were times . . . odd moments when I felt as though he really did understand what I was thinking and feeling, even though there was nothing psychic about it. This worried me. Sailor was undeniably intriguing; but when all was said and done he was a bitter, misanthropic shell of a human being. Why should I feel such kinship with him?

"Fine, princess, have it your way." He shrugged. "Just be careful. And don't say I didn't warn you."

He turned on his heel and stalked off toward his motorcycle, parked illegally on the sidewalk. His back was as stiff and as unrelenting as his icy gaze.

Still, I couldn't just write him off. He had helped me not long ago. A witch like me, accustomed to flying solo, didn't forget something like that.

Besides, every once in a while a glimpse of something else shone through Sailor's bitterness: a searching, yearning loneliness that reminded me, too much, of my own.

That topic bore further scrutiny, I supposed. But right now I had an appointment with the male witch Sailor had just warned me about.

I gathered my animals from the sullen Clarinda, thanked her with all the warmth I could muster, then led my entourage up the floating central stairs to the second floor. We passed wax replicas of the Mona Lisa and Elvis—both the young, curled-lip version and the Las Vegas, jumpsuit-wearing edition—walked by the sinister Chamber of Horrors, and proceeded through a small exhibit of European explorers to an arched mahogany door that appeared almost invisible to the throngs of casual visitors who enjoyed the museum.

But to me it beckoned.

Aidan opened the door before I knocked. Though I was prepared for what I would see, the breath still caught in my throat at the sight of him.

Aidan Rhodes, male witch, possessed a kind of soul-melting good looks. Too good. I had witnessed women, and a fair number of men, quite literally stop in their tracks to stare as he walked by. Tall and broad-shouldered, he had golden hair that curled slightly at the nape of his strong neck, while his square jaw held just a hint of manly whiskers. His long-lashed eyes were a captivating periwinkle blue, his crooked smile showed white, even teeth, and his easy laugh was accompanied by a slight duck of the head that gave him an endearing sense of aw-shucks, little-boy vulnerability—an openness that was sheer veneer, of course.

But over and above his physical appearance, Aidan sparkled with power. He gave off twinkly, almost blinding vibrations. Even those who never sensed auras felt his.

And to add to it all, he was capable of using witchcraft to help others attain their desires. Was it any wonder the man had so many admirers? Poor long-suffering Clarinda was charged with screening his potential visitors, he had become so popular.

"Lily, it is always *such* a pleasure," Aidan said, his eyes sweeping over my vintage outfit with a warm gaze just this side of impolite—the kind that left a woman in no doubt as to whether her figure was appreciated. "Don't you look just lovely in that dress? Let me see ... 1960?"

"Round about there, yes."

"You see, I'm learning something new simply by being in your company. One of the many things I adore about you."

He stepped back and gestured to me to enter. Not unlike Malachi Zazi's place, Aidan's office seemed like a holdover from the Victorian era of the old Barbary

Coast, featuring a red-and-gold color scheme, dark wood, velvet, tassels, and wall-to-wall bookcases jammed with magical tools and books. A snowy-white lace doily atop one small table made me think of Zazi's body lying so still upon his dining room table, his life's blood staining the tablecloth. Maybe his death had nothing whatsoever to do with bad luck symbols—broken mirrors and trapped sparrows and black cats. Perhaps it was a simple crime of passion, stemming from jealousy or greed. Weren't most murders, ultimately?

I yanked my thoughts back to the present as Aidan closed the heavy door behind us. Oscar dropped his pot-bellied pig façade, but as usual around Aidan, he remained uncharacteristically silent.

Upon spying the black cat, Aidan's white long-haired familiar leapt into his arms. It glared, then hissed, at the orphaned feline, which ran behind the grimacing Oscar.

I sneezed. Repeatedly. With each *achoo* Oscar whispered, "Gesundheit."

"Who's this?" Aidan asked, eyebrows raised.

"I was hoping you might want another cat." I sniffed. "But it looks unlikely."

"I'm afraid my familiar would object," Aidan said, handing me a monogrammed linen handkerchief. "You know how females are. They like to be cherished, to be the only one."

"So, now we're adding sexism to our long list of faults?" I blew my nose into his soft handkerchief. "Seems to me most men have a problem with sharing as well."

He laughed. "So, have you been doing your reading?"

"I'm up to 'H'—Hauntings, Healing, Heaven, Hell, Hermetics . . ."

I envied Aidan his control in the long run. But at the moment what I really lusted after was his musty, rarified library. Bound in crumbling leather, these thousands of parchment pages held the secrets of the ages. There were thick volumes concerning ancient and contemporary sacred paths, magickal and alchemical grimoires, manuscripts of paganism and Christendom, and books of the dead. Writings of magi, sorcerers, Gnostics, chaos magic priests, alchemists, scholars, and—of course—witches. Encyclopedias of ritual magick from around the world, obscure as well as celebrated secret societies, power brokers, masters of corruption, and healers. Testaments, charts of symbolism, and the complete roll call of angels and demons. Folklore and the foretold, the divine and the defiled, the creators and those whose hunger will never be satisfied, the lost technologies and manifestations . . . and more.

This was the sort of rarified information that still couldn't be found on the Internet—and I had spent many, many hours looking. It was a tempting, somewhat overwhelming world of arcane but essential knowledge. If I could take it all in, memorize it and learn to work with it, I might be able to control my own powers more efficiently, as well as to overcome my frequent cluelessness when it came to other magical traditions.

In the last week I'd made it through the "F" section: Faeries, Financial conspiracy, and Freemasonry. I then moved on to "G": Ghosts, Glamoury, Gnosticism, Goddesses, Gods, Golden Dawn, Grace, and Grimoires. As I persevered in reading the tomes, my mind had started to feel numb and my eyesight blurred. But I was determined.

Aidan chuckled. "I never suggested you should work through the shelves alphabetically."

"It seemed the most straightforward approach," I said. "And as long as there's no math involved, I'm a fast reader, so it moves along pretty quickly. Especially the healing and botanical writings—though I wrote down a few instances where the books got it wrong."

I handed Aidan my notes. He looked down at them with a quizzical expression.

"You're correcting my sourcebooks now?"

"As you know, botanicals are my strong suit, so as I read I compared the books with the notes and recipes in the Book of Shadows I inherited from Graciela." Aidan kept studying the papers in his hand, making me nervous. "Just a few changes," I hastened to add. "Mostly minor."

He acknowledged me with a little lift of his chin. "All right, I'll have to take your word on all this.

"So." He set his cat on the desk and rubbed his hands together in the way of someone getting down to business. "What's on the agenda today? How about taking another shot at scrying?"

I groaned. Scrying was hard.

"I know you must hate to be separated from me," Aidan continued, "but you're supposed to stay in the cloister until you see something. Last time you lasted all of five minutes."

The "cloister" was a windowless five-sided room off the main office, not much bigger than a closet. It was used for the sole purpose of meditation and scrying—or "seeing" with the mind's eye, as in gazing into crystal balls or black mirrors. The cloister was constructed as a magical portal, with a variety of charged stones, mirrors, and charms set up to create magnetic fields sympathetic to the needs of the supernatural.

"I always feel as though I should be *doing* something instead of just sitting there."

"What you're supposed to be *doing* is opening the portals so that you can communicate directly with your helping spirit. You don't even know who, or what, it is. I've never heard of such a thing. No wonder you aren't in control of the magic you're stirring up."

"My spirit comes to me when I brew, not when I stare at black mirrors."

"And crystal balls . . . ?"

"They're even worse." I thought of the beautiful jewel-encrusted crystal ball I had been given, years ago, by one of Graciela's wealthier colleagues. It gathered dust on my bookshelf at home, exquisite and useless as a pampered, dim beauty queen.

Doubt shone in Aidan's too-blue eyes. I feared I wasn't the stellar student he was hoping I would be. I had a lot of power, but it was locked up strangely.

"My grandmother didn't believe me, either."

"It's not that I don't believe you, Lily. It's . . . unusual for such a powerful witch not to be able to read, that's all. Come on, I'll help guide you."

I followed him into the cloister, though I remained doubtful. I had been trying to unlock the secrets of algebra lately, with my friend Bronwyn's help, and hadn't made much progress. If I couldn't master an eighth-grade skill like solving for the x, how was I going to learn the art of "seeing" what is not shown?

Black mirrors hung on each of the five walls. A multitude of charms dangled from the ceiling—mostly silk bags hanging on braided cords—and symbols were drawn in a red, black, and ochre border at the top of the walls. Shallow shelves were adorned with stones. The room carried a powerful scent of sage.

I'm no claustrophobe, but when Aidan shut the door the walls of the little room, lit only by candles in four sconces—one for each direction—seemed to close in on us. I breathed deeply and tried to allow the evident magnetic forces to flow through me, rather than blocking them.

As we said back in Texas, I was as nervous as a cat in a roomful of rockers. Being here made me realize how much I rely on the calming sanctuary of my home, my cauldron, my mortar and pestle and herbs and roots. Maybe I was like Graciela; I would get to the point where I could never relocate, even if I wanted to.

"Bend your head," Aidan said, reaching out for me.

I pulled back.

"Look, Lily," he said in that oh-so-reasonable voice that indicated he was angry, "I know you don't trust me. But this magus-apprentice relationship will be limited until you start to believe. Now, will you at least let me feel your energy?"

I took another deep breath, and nodded.

He put his hands on either side of my face, then bent his head down to mine. Forehead to forehead. Eyes closed. Bodies close, almost touching.

A long moment passed. I could feel him reaching out to me, but I couldn't bring myself to let my guard down. Still, the sense of him was overwhelming.

When he wasn't trying to force me into something or patronizing me, Aidan could be mesmerizing, and not only as a witch . . . but as a man. From the first moment I met him I had felt a strong attraction to him, as though a wire were stretched too taut between us, humming and alive with the tension. Did he and I share something profound, or was this a mere illusion?

Guarded or no, a connection was made.

Moods shifted. Breath caught. His hands upon my cheeks felt electric, charged.

Aidan lifted his head, looked into my eyes.

"Lily. . . ."

From outside I could hear a cat yowl, and Oscar squeal. One after another, the candles fell. Their pewter sconces melted into misshapen blobs.

Aidan let go, grabbed a flashlight, and doused the still-burning candles.

"What in the Sam Hill just happened?" I asked.

He took a deep breath. I was rather gratified to notice it was shaky. "I knew from the start we had a connection."

"What kind of connection? Did we melt the sconces?"

"To be honest, I'm not entirely sure. I'll need to look into it further. In the meantime . . ." He flashed me a crooked grin. "I'd say you and I fooling around is out of the question."

He was referring to sex magic. It could open portals, which, if controlled, were extremely powerful. When not properly handled, though, such magic could result in a lot of collateral damage. If Aidan touching me could melt pewter, I didn't want to think about what else might happen.

"One more time," Aidan said as he relit the candles and placed them on the shelves alongside the stones. "Concentrate not on me, but on the black mirror. Concentrate without thought, on seeing what cannot be seen. I know you can do it. You just showed me you could."

I faced the mirror. This time I could feel Aidan's energy wrapping around me, helping me to concentrate while separating my mind from rational thought. . . .

At first, nothing but blackness. But then, finally, I saw something that looked like an orange cloud, and then pink, then green. Ephemeral, barely there. As I continued to watch, to disconnect from my waking mind, I started to see a white radiance peeking through the colored mist, like the sun breaking through the clouds. Just a bit at first, then bursting through in a bright flash.

And in the flash was a wobbly, miragelike vision of Malachi Zazi, very much alive, a sparrow flitting about his head. In his arms he carried a huge old-fashioned hourglass, with the sand almost finished falling. He set down the hourglass, wrapped his neck in snakes as though they were scarves, turned his back, and walked away.

Chapter 4

I yanked back. I was freezing cold.

"What is it?" Aidan stood right behind me. His arms wrapped around me and I leaned into them, relishing his heat. "What did you see?"

"A man I know to be dead."

"Dead how long?"

"Only a day or two."

"So he could still be present. Did he speak?"

I shook my head.

"You were staring for several minutes."

"It felt like only a second."

"Time is relative. Einstein wasn't the first to figure that one out."

"I don't want to do it anymore," I said. The vision of Malachi frightened me. I didn't know how to interpret it, what to think. And I couldn't get warm.

"All right," Aidan interrupted my thoughts. "Let's play to your strengths for the moment. Did you bring the supplies to make conjure balls?"

Conjure balls are magical amulets made with wax, herbs, and charms.

I sighed with relief. This was my area of expertise.

On a large worktable under the window I laid out the supplies I had packed this morning: a large assortment of herbs and oils, wax, brimstone, four thieves' vinegar, small charms, and clabber milk. Then I brought out my Book of Shadows. Though I had long ago memorized most of the spells, I still read through the recipe before beginning to cast; it was part of my ritual, part of preparing myself to become a conduit for the forces of the universe and beyond.

It may seem counterintuitive that while I was seeking knowledge through Aidan he was having me make all sorts of talismans, brews, and charms. Part of me wondered if he was trying to learn my secrets, but I didn't really believe in keeping my knowledge to myself. I was discreet with my powers for two reasons: First, I was raised to hide my Craft from those around me out of fear; and second, most people did not have the ability to invoke powers, or worse, to control whatever it was they managed to call up.

In Aidan's case, as a witch fully in control of his abilities, I was happy to share what I knew . . . up to a point.

"I prefer beeswax for malleability, but paraffin or any other candles can be melted and used if you're after particular colors," I explained as I set up a little flame under a beaker. "The best wax I've found actually comes from those individually wrapped cheeses coated in red wax. If you knead it long enough with warm hands it becomes supple and malleable."

Since I didn't have any such cheese wax at hand, I hacked up a red candle and put the pieces in the beaker to melt. I shaved some tin onto a small plate, and arranged my charms: a small metal heart, a promise ring, some gold glitter. I then started stripping herbs—lemongrass, Devil's Shoestring, lavender, Queen Elizabeth root. I crushed and blended them with the ancient mortar and pestle Graciela had given me when I left home—the one that reminded me of the timeless chain of *curanderos*, or Mexican witch-healers, of which I was now a link.

As I prepared my herbs I noticed Zazi's black cat sitting near the doorway, watching my movements. What secrets might be locked in that feline brain? Or was its steady green gaze pondering something distinctly banal, like lunch?

Aidan's white cat, Noctemus, meowed and jumped onto the table. I sneezed.

A quiet "Gesundheit" emanated from under the table.

"Aidan, do you know why cats are associated with witches? And why people are scared of them?"

"You know the way cats will suddenly look in a particular direction as though they see something?" Aidan asked, stroking his beautiful cat and gazing at her with affection. "Even nonfamiliars are able to see things normal humans have no access to. In Europe they came to be feared, but in other parts of the world, most obviously in Egypt, that talent was precisely why felines were revered. Anything powerful evokes both respect and fear, as two sides of the same coin."

I pondered that as I rolled my conjure balls, sprinkling in the prepared herbs and roots. I decided to make love amulets, and started working with the wax, infusing it with my thoughts. Pouring some more hot wax into the palm of my hand, I felt the slight burn, between pain and pleasure.

"In addition," Aidan continued, "felines, just like the night and the moon, are associated with the female."

"Why would that be frightening?"

He grinned. "I suspect you want a measured response to that one, rather than the obvious."

"If you don't mind."

"I imagine it is because females bring forth life amidst blood. As I said, fear and reverence are often two sides to the same coin. Males cannot create life. Some of them will spend their karmic energies trying to control what it is that women accomplish naturally. And if they can't control it, they denigrate it."

"Which translates into . . ."

"Witch burnings, paternalism, sexism . . ." He shrugged. "Basically, men acting like jerks."

I thought about the men I knew. I tried not to tar them all with the same brush, but it was true that my experiences hadn't been particularly positive. My father abandoned me as an infant, the men from my hometown ran me out on a rail, and even the fellow I'd been sort of seeing lately, Max Carmichael, was having a hard time dealing with my special abilities.

"Speaking of bitter men," I said, "what's the deal with Sailor?"

"The 'deal'?"

"Why is he so beholden to you, yet so reluctant to use his powers?"

Aidan shrugged and refilled the beaker with more chunks of red wax. "He's not a natural psychic. Wasn't born with his current abilities, I mean. He's had a hard time adjusting."

"How did he become psychic, then?"

"I helped him out."

"You can do that?"

"Lily, when will you stop underestimating me? Don't you know by now that I can do anything?"

"Somehow I find that a little hard to believe."

He chuckled.

"Anyway," I said. "How does that work, exactly? Could you make *me* psychic?"

"This from the woman who already can barely deal with her natural talents? You want to become *psychic*?"

"When you put it that way, I guess not. I just thought maybe it would help me catch a clue. So you're honestly telling me you *made* Sailor psychic? How? Why?"

"I said no such thing. You inferred."

"Did I infer correctly?"

"Your tin shavings are starting to hum," he pointed out. I looked down to see the tiny metal pieces vibrating madly. "What now?"

"Love balls include love herbs and other talismans, such as a wedding ring, a lock of a loved one's hair, or a scrap of clothing. Luck balls might include dice, magnetic horseshoes, and herbs that attract good fortune, such as Little John and Master of the Woods. Oils of frankincense and rosemary boost the energy as well. I roll them anywhere from the size of a small marble to a big gumball; I usually make it large enough to accommodate the charms without looking all whomperjawed."

"'Whomperjawed'? I take it that's a Texas expression?"

"Sort of lopsided, not fitting properly. Ugly as homemade soap." I smiled. "You might even say cattywhompus."

"What about Goofer Balls?"

I went still. Despite their rather silly-sounding name, Goofer Balls are nothing to fool around with. They're hexes, evil charms made of black wax, and include nail clippings, hair cuttings, pieces of the enemy's clothing, whatever you can get of that person. They often include snake powder made from shed skins. Goofer Balls are typically placed in the yard of the intended victim, or tossed into corners in the house.

I glanced down at my Book of Shadows, splayed atop the large worktable. It lay open to a gruesome illustrated page describing the recipe for, and potential of, Goofer Balls.

Aidan had flipped through it.

Which meant two things: Aidan was overstepping his bounds—*no one* looked through a witch's private journal/spell book/diary—and my Book of Shadows, which was imbued with much more power than a standard tome, had allowed him to do so. It would have hidden the page otherwise.

Unlike the Wiccans I was hanging out with lately—my friend Bronwyn and her good-natured coven—I don't shy away from hexcraft. Just last week Bronwyn had challenged me on this, asking: *Don't you believe in karma, or some sort of final judgment?* Good question. But to tell the truth, I didn't think much about it. I knew my powers were drawn from a continuum of good and evil, and I tried to keep on the positive side of things. But there were times when an enemy needed to be stopped in its tracks, or sent back to nothingness, or banished, or even bound. But any practitioner of the dark arts must share in the damage she or he causes.

"If you want to cast hexes, Aidan, you'll have to figure it out yourself. I'm focusing on a love conjure at the moment. And as you know, there's no place for wandering minds in spell casting."

I started to intone my love charm. I always recite as Graciela had taught me, in a kind of Spanglish with a smattering of Nahuatl, her native language. I didn't speak Spanish particularly well, much less Nahuatl, but the spells were as natural and automatic as breathing to me. They linked me to my ancestors, and to my spirit guide.

Using my *athame*, a special ritual knife, I cut a tiny slit on the palm of my hand, held it palm down, and let a drop of my blood fall upon the wax. I waited. Nothing.

"That's the strangest thing," I said. I glanced at Oscar, huddled against a cherry cabinet, ready for the apparition. He seemed as stunned as I. "Usually when I add my blood, my guiding spirit comes and finalizes things. This time I . . . I'm not even sure the spell worked."

Aidan met my eyes, his too-blue gaze perceptive and full of unsaid things.

"Let's try it at your place."

"*My* place?" I was hesitant to invite Aidan into my apartment. I wasn't sure why, though it was my habit not to invite anyone into my inner sanctum. In my quest to become more open to friendship I had been trying to change that tendency, so recently I'd invited Bronwyn and Maya over a few times. And obviously Oscar was familiar with it. But the only man who had visited was an overnight guest: Max Carmichael. Best not to think about *him* right now.

"Your spirit needs to feel your call directly," Aidan said. "I imagine my energy is mucking up the communications network."

"That makes it sound like some sort of satellite system." As I spoke I realized I had exactly no idea of how this all worked. For all I knew there *was* some sort of strange, supernatural, primordial satellite orbiting about the earth.

"Have you heard from Matt?" Aidan asked out of the blue, making me wonder if he was reading my mind.

"You know perfectly well his name is Max. Max Carmichael."

"Max. Right. That's what I meant," Aidan said with a smile. "How is dear Max?"

"He's still back east. He should be home soon."

"In time for the Art Deco Ball?"

"Maybe."

"My offer still stands. I'm available to escort you. I was planning on coming by your shop soon to put together a costume."

"I can't imagine why you want to go."

He just grinned. "I wouldn't miss it. You have no idea how good I look in the clothes from the era."

"Oh, I'll wager I do." Aidan would manage to look good in the powder blue polyester leisure suit that came into the shop last week. Maya, Bronwyn, and I voted it the Ugliest Item Ever to Cross Our Threshold.

I started working the wax again, thinking perhaps I'd missed a stage. As I rolled, I began thinking about the vision of Malachi, the hourglass, and how he'd wrapped snakes around his neck. The hourglass could be a symbol of time running out, of course, but the snakes? Was it simply a reference to his interest in Serpentarius?

Graciela never liked snakes, so I didn't know that much about their magical potential. But many belief systems revered serpents for their ability to slide between the upper and lower worlds, in constant contact with the earth and the underground. They are primal symbols of fear, knowledge, sexuality. And perhaps most important, they periodically shed their tired skins and appear reborn, fresh and new.

Personally, I had no problem with the creatures. In fact, snakes had once saved my life.

I looked down at the table. Without meaning to, I had rolled several conjure balls into slender wax snakes. They had taken on a life of their own: A dozen red snakes full of herbs and small charms slithered around the marble slab, snapping at one another, blind and confused.

It was a rookie blunder.

One must never allow one's mind to wander while spell casting, m'hija. How often had Graciela told me that?

I mumbled a quick antidote and gathered the small serpents together in my hands, concentrating and chanting until I felt them calming. When they turned back to wax, I blended them together again in one sphere as big as a baseball, forcing myself to ponder the inadvertent conjure, then to undo it.

I looked up to find Aidan staring at me. His familiar was perched on the bookshelf, staring as well. Oscar, and even the black cat, observed me warily from the corner.

"Sorry," I said. "My mind wandered."

"And you accidentally created serpents?" Aidan said in a low, unusually serious voice.

"You don't like snakes?"

"It's not that." He cut himself off, as though he wanted to say more but thought better of it at the last minute.

"Anyway, they're taken care of. But speaking of snakes . . . have you ever heard of the Serpentarian Society?"

Aidan dropped the beaker of melted wax, its red

juice running like blood onto the table, soaking into the cloth.

"The Serpentarian Society . . . as in Malachi Zazi?" He grabbed my wrist, intent. "Was that the dead man you saw? How do you know Zazi?"

"How come you always answer my questions with questions?" I asked, wrenching my hand away. Looking out the window, I noted that a thick layer of fog was rolling in off the bay. "It's aggravatin' to say the least."

"Just tell me your association with Malachi Zazi."

"I don't exactly know him . . ."

Just then Noctemus chased the black cat from under the worktable.

Aidan scooped the feline up and cradled it to his chest.

"This is Malachi's cat." The statement sounded like an accusation. Suddenly the black cat yowled and jumped from his arms, scratching in its haste to be down. A streak of crimson appeared on the back of Aidan's hand.

I moved to help him, but he waved me off.

Noctemus leapt onto Aidan's shoulder and tried to stare me down. Like I would be intimidated by a feline. Still, I did shift my eyes away. That cat put me on edge.

"Well?" Aidan said. "Tell me about Zazi."

"He passed away."

"As in moved on to the next dimension?"

I nodded.

"When was this?"

"Sometime last night, or more specifically, in the very early morning hours of today. I think. That's what the police said."

"And you know this how, exactly?"

"Inspector Carlos Romero—remember him? He worked

on the other cases? He wanted me to see if I could feel anything at the scene."

"Why would he want you to do that?"

"The victim's body was surrounded with bad luck symbols of all kinds. It was . . . odd."

Again with the staring. Feline and masculine eyes were on me, assessing me, trying to read me. I kept my guard up, but they were a powerful double whammy. Normally a witch's familiar might step in and help her hold her own against an antagonistic white cat, but Oscar was conspicuous by his absence. He used to work for Aidan—and for all I knew, he still did. Though Oscar liked me, I feared his loyalties might be divided.

"Are you telling me," Aidan finally spoke, his voice even more hushed, "that officials with the SFPD are asking witches to weigh in on murder scenes now?"

"I don't think it's become a matter of departmental policy, if that's what you mean. But in this case, yes, the inspector was asking my opinion."

I started packing up my supplies, carefully placing the lavender, rosemary, and rue back in their tiny labeled jars, and the loose chunks of wax in a resealable Baggie. Then, trying my best to ignore Aidan and Noctemus, I carefully pulled on my coat, buttoning it and turning up the faux fur collar against the afternoon chill blowing in off the waters of the bay.

"And I'd appreciate you either telling me why you're having conniption fits or dropping the whole subject. This bullying act isn't going very far with me."

I'm a witch, dag nab it, I thought. I don't cave that easily, powerful spook or no.

Apparently my anger was casting about, uncontrolled. The wax ball disintegrated, once again becoming a pile of small serpents.

"Oh, for heaven's sake," I grumbled, gathering them all up and trapping the writhing creatures in the Baggie with the rest of the wax.

I stared malevolently at Aidan's malevolently staring familiar.

"And I *don't. Like. Cats.*"

As if on cue, I sneezed again. The cat jumped from his shoulder and Aidan dropped whatever supernatural intimidation scheme he was trying to lay on me.

Instead, he shifted to his regular old patronizing ways.

"Stay away from Malachi Zazi, Lily. Walk away."

"Gee, seems like I've heard that before."

"Just do it."

"Tell me why."

"I'm not in the habit of having to explain myself," Aidan said, his voice rising.

"Nor am I," I snapped.

Aidan bristled. *"Do as I say in this."*

I ignored him.

"Let's go, Oscar. Bring the cat." I flung the door open and stormed out of Aidan's office.

In the corridor, a dozen museum visitors stood frozen in midstep.

The walls, floors, ceiling prickled and popped with hostile energy. Power whooshed along my skin, raising the hair on my arms. I felt the sensation of an army of ants running up and down my spine.

"Move," I said to Oscar and the black cat as I hustled my brood past the Chamber of Horrors exhibit.

As we passed by, the Texas Chainsaw killer and Lizzie Borden started breathing. Shifting. Reaching out toward us.

"Mistress . . . ," Oscar whispered, rearing back.

"Keep walking," I commanded. Aidan had done this to me once before—but then he had been teasing. This was different. This was angry. The sensation of wax characters coming to life—and coming toward us—was sinister, even for a witch.

I stroked my medicine bag, kept my head down, mumbled a protective incantation, and hurried toward the stairs, holding tight to the banister lest a blast of energy from Aidan send me headfirst down the steps. I kept Oscar and the cat on the other side of me, shielding them from Aidan's direct gaze . . . for what that was worth.

I was only too aware that if Aidan really wanted to stop me, he could do so. There was a reason the entire West Coast contingent of witches both respected and feared Aidan Rhodes. With his easy manner and flirtatious ways, it was too easy to forget.

As I was only too aware, I was more a stay-at-home-and-brew kind of witch. This mano a mano kind of fighting magic had never been my strong suit.

When we reached the bottom of the stairs I glanced up to see Aidan looking down over the ledge, Noctemus perched on his shoulder, the air around him still crackling and glittering with power.

He let me go.

But he was pissed. It gave a witch pause.

Chapter 5

Ah. Rosemary and rue.

I took a deep cleansing breath as I stepped across the threshold of Aunt Cora's Closet. The shop carried the fresh aroma of clean laundry, and yesterday I had created new herbal sachets that would lend their welcoming aroma to the air for weeks. The racks were crowded with everything from Depression-era cotton slips to 1970s polyester leisure suits, from Victorian silk petticoats to early '80s padded-shoulder jackets. In addition, there were shelves and cases full of shoes, hats, gloves, purses, silk stockings, and jewelry. I even had one "costume" corner that was expanding rapidly, full of things like boas, tuxedoes, uniforms, and cowboy accoutrements. In a city like San Francisco, the costume pieces were particularly appreciated.

My store was located on the corner of Haight and Ashbury, right in the heart of the neighborhood made famous during the Summer of Love, 1968. The original flower children now sported thin gray ponytails, carried AARP cards in their wallets, and gulped down glucosamine for joint health. Still, their legacy lived on through plentiful head shops, an overabundance of street kids looking for the meaning of life, and most important, a kind of generalized bohemian style still prevalent among the neighborhood merchants and residents alike.

In fact, there were so many bizarre iconoclasts and odd misfits roaming these crowded streets that, most of the time, a witch with a stubborn Texas accent could feel downright normal. I loved the openness of this community, the live-and-let-live attitude that was slowly but surely helping me to admit who—and *what*—I was. After growing up amid censure and loathing in my hometown, and then searching the globe for a safe place to land, it still amazed me that I now had acquaintances who actually seemed *pleased* to have a witch for a friend.

The shop had closed just a half an hour before, so it still carried a happy leftover hum from customers and my friends who ran the place when I was gone.

Still, I was surprised to find Aunt Cora's Closet empty. Bronwyn and I had made plans to have dinner and then to tackle a high pile of laundry. Now that Aunt Cora's Closet was open on Mondays due to high customer demand, it was harder than ever to deal with the bane of the vintage clothing dealer: Silks and satins, much less crinolines and wools, can't simply be popped into our jumbo-sized washer and dryer.

Once my initial relief at being home waned, I felt a tingle. . . . Something was off.

For all her flighty ways, Bronwyn always kept her word. And she was never late.

I glanced over at the answering machine. The little red light was flashing, indicating new voice mail.

"I'm so sorry, Lily, but I won't be in today, and per-

haps tomorrow," Bronwyn said on the recording. Her voice sounded stuffy, as though she'd been crying. *"Maya agreed to cover for me. I . . . I'll explain it all to you in person when I can. For now . . . peace, and Blessed Be."*

I dialed her home number; no answer.

I watched the black cat meander around the shop floor while I pondered. Outside of my grandmother Graciela, Bronwyn was my first true friend. As such, I was unclear on the myriad unwritten rules of such a relationship.

It sounded like she wanted to be left alone. Should I honor that?

Oscar was already snoring on the monogrammed purple silk pillow Bronwyn had bought him. It was situated right beside her little herbal stand, which was decorated with floral garlands and cheerful Wiccan-inspired sayings. Bronwyn was one of the most giving, loyal, dependable people I had ever had the privilege to know. I was lucky to have her in my life.

The cat skulked over to Oscar and stealthily curled up beside his sleeping form.

Rules, schmulz. It seemed to me that when one's pal was in trouble, it was time to get pushy.

Bronwyn lived just a few blocks away, in an old brightly painted wooden Victorian typical of the Haight-Ashbury neighborhood. I let myself in the main door to the broad foyer, which today was aromatic of fresh cinnamon rolls. The two men who lived downstairs were always baking something decadent and delicious, filling the air with mouthwatering scents, yet they both remained excruciatingly slim. One of life's many mysteries.

Worn wooden treads squeaked in protest as I climbed

the steep stairs, but I loved this building. It gave off a vibrant, distinct hum. Bronwyn told me it had once been inhabited by Janice Joplin and other musicians during the sixties heyday of the hippie movement, and it was easy to believe. It carried the resonance of creativity and music in its tall wainscoting and multipaned windows of wavy glass. Harmony emanated from its bones.

Bronwyn had painted a border of cheerful daisies right above the wainscoting, leading all the way up to her bright purple door at the top of the stairs. A hemp doormat read: *Welcome, all ye who enter here.* And a hand-painted, flower-bedecked sign on the door held a line from the amiable creed of her Wiccan faith: *An it harm none, do what ye will.*

Bronwyn was a wide-open, smiling, rosewater- and patchouli-scented soul, the type who would as soon hug you as look at you. Normally. But not today.

In response to my loud knock, she opened the door just a crack. It didn't take supernatural sensitivity to know she wasn't particularly happy to see me.

"Bronwyn? What's wrong?" I stuck my foot in the door, just in case.

"I . . . this isn't the best time, Lily." She looked behind her, whispered something, then turned back to me. "I don't suppose you'll go away, let me call you later?"

I shook my head.

"Lily . . ."

"Bronwyn, you know how stubborn I can be."

"Really, I'll call you—"

I started humming and looking at my fingernails. I did not remove my foot from the door.

Bronwyn sighed, stepped back, and swung the door wide.

She wore a typical Bronwyn-style dress: purple gauze over a tie-dyed slip. Her brown hair was as fuzzy as ever, but lacked the floral decorations with which she usually adorned herself. Her feet were bare, her shoulders uncharacteristically slumped.

Bronwyn's apartment, like mine, was filled with herbal sachets, crystals, and charm bags hanging above windows and doors. Mirrors were set up opposite the front door and several windows to deflect bad energy. But unlike me, Bronwyn felt no reason to hide her wannabe witchy ways: On the walls hung numerous rainbow-hued goddess paintings, and every horizontal space was graced with stones, herbs, candles, books on Wicca, a crystal ball, a pentacle.

And today, two young children were sitting at a low coffee table in the living room amid scattered markers and recycled paper scraps.

"Lily!" the girl said as she jumped up and ran to give me a hug.

Eight-year-old Imogen reminded me of her grandmother Bronwyn. She had soft brown eyes and unruly hair, an open heart, and an innate sense of joy. I hugged her back, savoring her pure, straightforward vibrations.

Her fair-haired brother James, a studious six-year-old, looked up, mumbled a shy "Hi, Lily," and went back to his coloring book.

A three-legged calico cat ran up to greet me right after Imogen, rubbing against my legs. I sneezed.

"I don't suppose you'd like another cat? I have a very sweet one looking for a home. It even has all its limbs," I teased. Bronwyn took in the rejects from the pound—the ones slated for death.

"Oh, I can't, Lily. My landlord would kill me. He

barely agreed to the last two, and that was only after I cast a spell of cooperation on him. I know I shouldn't have, but it was for the sake of the animals."

"I want a cat!" said Imogen. *"Mom!* Could we take Lily's cat?"

"No. Cats are dirty," came the voice of Bronwyn's grown daughter, Rebecca, from the direction of the kitchen.

Imogen smiled up at Bronwyn and rolled her eyes at her grandma, while Bronwyn beamed at her and winked.

I took a minute to admire the children's artwork; Imogen's drawing depicted a woman with a tall hat and a veil up in a castle tower, like a princess of yore. James was fond of cars and monsters, and thus was designing a series of monster-cars.

"Go on back to your coloring now," I said. "Grown-ups need to talk."

Intoning a charm under my breath, I kissed my thumb and touched each child's forehead in turn, casting a co-cooning spell over them. No need for them to hear what we were talking about. I remembered learning too many things I shouldn't have by listening in when the adults thought I was otherwise occupied.

"Come on into the kitchen," said Bronwyn. Her anklet of bells jangled as she led the way.

I had only ever seen Rebecca in her usual guise: sleekly put together; highlighted chestnut hair worn in a smooth, styled coif; makeup perfect; clothes spotless, neutral, and expensive. So I barely recognized the woman sitting at the brightly painted kitchen table: Her cheeks were tearstained, her big amber eyes rimmed in red.

Bronwyn had been only nineteen when she gave birth to the daughter she originally dubbed Rainbow, raising her in an urban commune right here in the Haight. Rainbow left for college a year early, changed her name to Rebecca, married an ambitious young scientist, and moved into a posh condo on upper Broadway, where she was now a stay-at-home mom with live-in help. As far as I could tell, she seemed to visit her mother, Bronwyn, only when she needed emergency child care.

"Hello, Rebecca," I said.

"Hi," she said with a loud sniff, and little warmth. She turned to Bronwyn. "For the love of *God*, mother, could you refrain from the witchcraft crap, just for the day? You know I don't allow that sort of thing in front of the children."

Bronwyn hummed under her breath, ignoring Rebecca's remark. She busied herself at the stove, heating a kettle of water and preparing a pot with homemade herbal tea pouches.

Ironically, Rebecca needn't have worried about any potential powers from her mother embarrassing her. Any change of heart the landlord experienced had been due to simple ethics rather than any enchantment Bronwyn had managed. My friend was many things, but her true gift—her magic, so to speak—was in her wide-open heart and the unconditional friendship she offered her friends. When it came right down to it, Bronwyn couldn't enchant a squaddie onto a swayback.

But still, Bronwyn was a devoted Wiccan and she lived by the Wicca Rede: She harmed no one. She enjoyed practicing certain pagan rituals, observing the solstices and making simple offerings—usually wine and cake—to the ancient lord and lady, to the gods and goddesses of nature. There certainly was no harm to it, and it was a durn sight kinder than a whole lot of organized religions I could mention. Not for the first time, I wondered whether Rebecca would be as disdainful of her mother for being Episcopalian, or Jewish, or any other religion considered more acceptable by the greater society.

"Tell Lily what's going on, Rebecca," said Bronwyn as she poured water from the steaming copper kettle into a porcelain teapot decorated with a daisy chain. "She might be able to help."

"Somehow I doubt that," Rebecca said, her gaze running over my vintage outfit and her nostrils flaring slightly, apparently displeased. She had a discomfiting way of looking down her nose at those around her, reminding me of the children I grew up with. It amazed me that she and Bronwyn were of the same blood.

"I can't guarantee I can help," I said, taking a deep breath and concentrating on emanating understanding. "But I'll do what I can."

She blew on her tea, looked around the kitchen, and finally spoke.

"It's my husband, Gregory . . ." Her voice trailed off, and she sipped her drink. "He was accused in . . . a murder."

I tried to keep the expression on my face neutral. I knew from a few vague comments from Bronwyn that Rebecca's marriage had been on the rocks lately, so I had expected Rebecca to mention a separation, perhaps a divorce. Nothing like this. I was doubly glad I had created a cocoon of silence for the children.

"Of whom?" I asked. "He's been arrested?"

"Not exactly," Bronwyn said, handing me a cup of fragrant tea in a chipped earthenware mug. I smelled rose hips and chamomile along with orange peel and . . . was it cardamom? Bronwyn was forever experimenting in search of the perfect cup of tea. "He was named as a 'person of interest,' that's all. It could be nothing."

"Or everything," Rebecca said glumly. I put my hand over hers, casting a quick comforting spell. In reaction, she took a deep breath and steadied herself slightly. I sensed the dank smell of shame, overriding fear, and dread. I had the distinct sense that the public humiliation was weighing on her more than the fear that her husband might have perpetrated a crime.

"Do you have any reason to think he might have done it?" I asked.

Rebecca's eyes flew to mine, sparking. "Of course not! What kind of man—why would you—he would never do such a thing!" she sputtered. I could practically see orange-red bristles of aural anger coming off of her.

"I'm sure you're right," I said. "I just . . . I've never met Gregory."

"He's a good man," Rebecca said, eyes once again welling with tears. "He's . . . we've been having trouble lately. He's had some problems at work—some of his experiments were compromised. And he's started drinking. A little. But then a couple of weeks ago he was stopped and charged with a DUI."

"Was that the first time?"

She nodded. "But it's been one thing after the other. And now . . . I can't believe this! It's like we're cursed. I'm almost ready to believe mom's right—maybe we've got bad juju or something."

"Who was the murder victim? Someone Gregory knew?"

"His name is—was—Malachi Zazi. He and Gregory went to high school together, and Gregory attends dinner parties at his house every month."

Coincidences in my life did not bode well. They usually added up to something fishy, something that a witch had to get involved in, whether she wanted to or not.

Did SFPD inspector Carlos Romero know about my connection, through Bronwyn, to Gregory? Was that why he asked me to look at the crime scene? I felt my own spikes of orangey-red anger and disappointment rolling off of me. Carlos was smart. It was hard to believe he would overlook something like that. So what was he doing, involving me? Did he think that since Bronwyn was a member of a coven, and I was a witch, and we could be linked to the man accused of killing Zazi . . . then what?

I let out a deep breath of consternation. I didn't know what to make of it.

"What can you tell me about Malachi Zazi?" I asked.

Rebecca shrugged, blew on her tea, took a sip, put the mug back down. There was a faint damp ring on the tabletop where it had been before; I watched as Rebecca set the mug in exactly the same place, tweaking it until it was precisely where it had been. Her graceful hands were tipped by a perfect French manicure; a thick gold wedding band and a huge diamond and emerald ring glittered on her finger.

"Rebecca?" I urged.

"Do you know there used to be a thirteenth sign of the zodiac? Malachi put together these dinner parties and called his little association the Serpentarian Society, after that sign."

"What was the purpose of the society?"

"The idea was to debunk superstitions, to prove that

the world is ruled by rational science, rather than magical traditions and old wives' tales." She glanced over at her mother, and then at me. She shrugged. "No offense."

"None taken."

I wondered how much Bronwyn had told Rebecca about me. We had only met a few times, at the shop, and since she was so clearly not a believer—and so invested in her own lifestyle—I had immediately put her in the category of people around whom to maintain a nonmagical façade. But Bronwyn wasn't known for her discretion. Her openness, so appealing under normal circumstances, could also be something of a drawback.

I made a mental note to talk to her about that. Yes, I was opening up more about my abilities, hiding less, but even in this day and age—even in a place as accepting as the Bay Area—one didn't bandy about the notion of being a witch. At least I didn't. Lessons learned early ran deep.

"So Gregory joined these dinners?"

"Every month, on the thirteenth, always at midnight. I found it to be rather ridiculous, but like Gregory said, the dinner invitations were basically a who's who of San Francisco movers and shakers."

"More like the children of the movers and shakers," said Bronwyn.

"Some of them are doing things in their own right. Like Gregory," Rebecca said. "It's just . . . people don't understand what it is to be raised in that kind of privilege. It can be its own burden."

Bronwyn snorted and rolled her eyes in an exasperated gesture so un-Bronwyn-like that it took me aback.

Our eyes met, and she explained: "All I know is that any one of those kids could be out changing the world with their resources, and instead they party and play around with things they don't understand."

"Okay, let's back up just a second," I said. "Are we talking about children or adults here?"

"Adults who *act* like children," said Bronwyn. "They're in their thirties, but they grew up with everything, in complete privilege, and they can't seem to get past it. They go to all the right society events to be photographed: the Black and White Ball, the openings of the symphony and the ballet. Then they snort coke and stay out all night getting into trouble."

For someone as typically nonjudgmental as Bronwyn, this was saying a lot.

Rebecca shrugged. "They're overshadowed by their parents—that much is true. It can't be easy growing up as the child of a U.S. senator, for instance. Or even Gregory—his parents were never there for him. He had money, but he practically had to raise himself. They're just all getting their footing, that's all."

"Were you ever invited to these dinners?" I asked.

She shook her head. "It wasn't a 'date' kind of evening. There were only thirteen slots—twelve, actually, since Malachi was always there. It was considered quite prestigious to be invited. I thought maybe it was like a modern version of playing golf, a chance to get to know the next generation of San Francisco's leaders." She fiddled with her teacup. "Besides, they aren't all slackers. The head of Perkins Laboratories was there."

"Mike Perkins?" Bronwyn asked. "Isn't he Gregory's boss?"

Rebecca nodded.

"Who's Michael Perkins?" I wasn't exactly familiar with San Francisco movers and shakers.

Rebecca looked at me, eyebrows raised in surprise, as though I'd asked her to name the current president of the United States.

"Seriously? Mike—not Michael—Perkins, head of the huge pharmaceutical company? He's one of the richest men in America. They've got that antiaging serum? He and his wife are forever giving charity balls, taking part in public events. They're in the *Chronicle* society section *every* week."

"Lily's been out of the country," Bronwyn came to my rescue. "She's not exactly up on such things."

"It's true. I'm about dumber than dirt when it comes to this sort of thing. So, Perkins and his wife went to these Serpentarian dinners?"

"Just Mike. There were no married couples." She took a sip of her tea, then added with an edge of bitterness, "Or at least that's what Gregory told me. I don't know *what* to believe anymore."

"Who else came to the dinners? Do you know?"

She sighed. "A lot of them knew each other from way back. They went to the best schools. Oliver Huffman, the senator's son, for instance, was an old high school friend of Gregory's and Malachi's; Oliver's a venture capitalist, but lately . . . it looks like he has a drug problem. Another dinner participant with a string of bad luck. His sister used to come to the dinners as well."

"So there were a number of women there."

"Oh, yes, always. Half and half. I think that was part of the problem, it was harder to find women interested in attending. But on top of everything else, they dressed for dinner."

"As in tuxes and tails?"

"In vintage clothing. Stuff from the era, Gregory said. I guess that would be right up your alley, right?"

"Any idea where they got the clothes?"

"Zazi provided them. He took care of everything."

I thought about the silks I had seen in Zazi's armoire. I'd like to get back into that apartment and take some more time with those clothes, or bring them back to my place so I could perform a proper spell, see what they could tell me. With everything else so perplexing, they might be able to give me a sense of what was going on.

"Will you help us, Lily?" Bronwyn was asking. "Do you think you could ask around, try to figure out what's going on?"

When I first arrived in San Francisco, still somewhat shell-shocked from my wandering life, afraid of myself and my own powers, Bronwyn had greeted me with bear hugs and unconditional love. She introduced me to her friends in the Haight, invited me to join her Wiccan coven, and showed me that I could develop friendships, even admit that I was a witch, without putting myself at irredeemable risk.

How could I say no?

Besides, Carlos Romero had already asked me to weigh in on the crime, so I was even sort of legitimate in making inquiries. Tomorrow I should go talk to him, and to Gregory, and see what I could figure out. True, I was no psychic—I couldn't read people's minds—but I was a powerful witch. I had skills.

And maybe I could make sense of that vision of Malachi, which I couldn't seem to get out of my head.

Chapter 6

The next morning I awoke to the upside-down face of a goblin.

Perched on the brass headboard of my bed, Oscar hung over so his face was almost touching mine.

The first few times he had awakened me thus I had jumped with fright, which often resulted in books flying across the room, and once, a broken windowpane. But by now I was getting used to it.

I groaned, squeezed my eyes shut, and hoped he'd go away. After a long moment, I could still feel his breathing. It smelled vaguely—disturbingly—of fish. I opened one eye. He hadn't moved.

"I take it you need something, Oscar?"

"That *cat* touched my tuna."

That would explain the fish breath. The coziness of the bedcovers beckoned. I rolled over and snuggled deeper. "Uh-huh, well, open another can."

"That's *my* tuna fish! The *feline* touched it with its nose! Now it's contaminated!"

This from the creature who regularly rooted through the garbage for scraps.

"Did you offer the cat some?"

"No."

"Oscar, think about this for a moment. Have you ever known me to fix myself something to eat without offering something to you?"

He scrunched up his face, as though pondering.

"The answer is no," I prompted. "I have never eaten in front of you without sharing. Where I'm from, that just isn't done. The cat is our guest. It's hungry. Share your tuna with him." How can you tell gender with cats? "Or her. I think it might be a her."

Oscar leapt off the headboard, trampolined off the bed, and galumphed out of the room in high dudgeon, muttering something under his breath about the multiple ways of skinning a cat.

"Be *nice*, Oscar. That's an order."

The warmth of my cozy bed was seductive, but once I'm up . . . I'm up. I had to push aside the books I had been reading late into the night when I couldn't sleep, including a heavy tome on Roman gods that contained a detailed section on Serpentarius.

In *The Sigils and Seals of Solomon*, I had read:

The image of Serpentarius is a man holding the head of a snake in his right hand and the tail in his left: it is in the sign of Scorpio and is a Northern constellation of the nature of Saturn and Mars; its power is that if this image is carved in a stone that protects against poison, it protects against death from poisonous animals, and also protects against poison if you drink liquid that the image has been washed in.

Serpentarius was said to have been a gifted medical man who revived the near dead and recently dead with the blood and venom of snakes. According to the story, Hades, god of death, worried that Serpentarius would eventually keep anyone from dying. Hades begged Zeus to kill Serpentarius, which he did, but then Zeus honored the talented human by setting him in the sky as a constellation and giving him the Greek name Ophiuchus, which means "the Serpent Bearer." The Romans called him Serpentarius.

Serpentarius is now considered the patron of physicians. The American Medical Association, even today, uses a staff wrapped with serpents as its symbol in his memory.

All of this was fascinating, but it didn't tell me anything about why Malachi Zazi would be organizing dinners in the man's honor. Did Zazi simply enjoy the idea that Serpentarius was the thirteenth sign of the zodiac, and through the association with the number thirteen that it was thought to bring bad luck? Or was this somehow related to medicine and healing, a subject near and dear to my heart? Or could it involve the association with snakes?

Unfortunately, though I riffled through all the books at my disposal last night, I found few answers relevant to this case. Much less the one I really wanted: What was it about my involvement with Malachi Zazi that had made Aidan so furious?

The brass headstand of my bed glinted in the rare early-morning sunshine that streamed in through my bedroom's multipaned window. It was well past time to start the day. I liked to get downstairs to cleanse Aunt Cora's Closet and light a candle of protection before opening for business.

First things first, though. Time to negotiate with the animals.

I walked into the kitchen—my favorite room in the apartment—which I had painted in shades of bright pink, canary yellow, and chalky turquoise, inspired by the cheery colors I saw during my sojourn in Jamaica. Bundles of herbs hung from overhead beams, and a motley assortment of jars contained everything from cooking spices to freeze-dried bats. The lunar calendar hung near the sink, a pot of live basil attracted good luck, and my iron cauldron sat at the ready.

At the moment, a black cat also adorned the tile countertop. Upon seeing me it let out a raspy squeak. Unless I managed to find a home for the cat soon, I would need to buy some actual cat food. In the interim I opened a can of sardines and poured a saucer of the raw milk I kept on hand for spells. Other than the leftovers from a gumbo dinner I had made on Saturday, my refrigerator contained more ingredients for spell casting than for cooking: raw milk, fresh spring water, fresh herbs and roots of all kinds. Still, I kept a lot of canned foods and frozen items on hand, for what Graciela used to call "pantry cooking." She always seemed ready for the apocalypse with all her canned and dried foods—and for all I knew, that's exactly what she was waiting for.

The cat purred so loudly while eating, it made me wonder how often it had been fed. Its sleek black coat was soft as velvet. Allergies be damned, I spent a few minutes doting on her . . . or him. It lifted its head and bumped its wet little nose against mine.

I sneezed and washed my hands thoroughly.

"Gesundheit," Oscar said as he glowered at the cat.

"If you're really gonna keep that . . . *animal* here, you should at least cast a spell against your allergies."

"I'm afraid it's not that easy."

"But, Mistress, couldn't you just brew . . . ?"

"To change an inborn trait requires strong, continuous magic. It's costly."

"But you wouldn't charge yourself, would ya? It's free to you."

"I didn't mean that kind of cost. I meant it would be exhausting, and it would sap my energy for more important things." No, by far the best idea would be to find her a loving home with people who don't have an exaggerated immune response to her very presence.

"You've got lots of magic, though, Mistress. Like what happened with the wax figures with Aidan."

"The wax figures?"

He looked suddenly guilty, as though perhaps he'd said something out of turn.

"I just meant, the way when your magics mingle, all hell breaks loose."

"You're saying when my magic mingles with Aidan's?"

He nodded. "I guess you'd be hard to stop, you and Aidan as a pair."

Is that what happened with the candle sconces? Could that be why Aidan was helping me—did he have some sort of "use" for me or my power?

I couldn't think about this right now. I needed to open up shop, then go talk to Gregory and see what I could figure out about Malachi's murder. I only hoped Gregory wasn't guilty.

Most mornings I walked a couple of blocks to a local café called Coffee to the People for caffeine and breakfast. But since I was already tending to the animals, I brewed coffee and ate a leftover biscuit with a slice of cheese.

"We should at least name the poor little thing," I told Oscar, looking at the cat while I prepared a peanut butter and jam sandwich with the last of my homemade wheat bread and apricot preserves.

"We don't even know if it's a boy or a girl."

"True. How about this: You pick a name for it."

"Me?" Huge shiny eyes stared at me. "How could *I* pick a name?"

"Why not?"

"But that's . . . it's like adopting it if I name it. Like when you named me Oscar." His gnarled face screwed up in a smile. "That was a good day."

"Just think of it as a friendly gesture. For all we know, it already has a name. Maybe it will find a way to let us know, but we need to call it something in the meantime."

"Let's call it LTN, for 'Less Than Nothing.'"

"Very funny."

"How 'bout 'Thing that crawled out from under a rock'?"

"Oscar . . . ," I warned.

"Or Beowulf."

"Beowulf?"

"It's from history."

"I know where it's from. I just think it's an interesting choice."

"Is it a bad choice?"

"No," I said, laughing. "It's not a bad choice at all. It's a great choice."

"I'll keep thinking. Maybe that's not right."

"Does it look like a Beowulf to you?"

"Not sure. How about Napoleon? Or Genghis Khan? Reginald?"

"So you think it's a male cat?"

"Dunno. Pandora, maybe?"

"Tell you what, Oscar. You think on it a while," I said, patting his scaly shoulder. "No need to rush into anything."

I left him staring at the feline. I found it interesting that the cat didn't appear to notice any difference between Oscar the pig and Oscar the goblin/gnome/gargoyle. It was a good thing—I could only imagine trying to coax a frightened cat to come out from under the bed and visit with a creature like Oscar.

After showering, I put my long dark hair up in a loose knot, swiped a quick bit of mascara on my eyes, and dressed in a green tweed two-piece with a wide skirt and bolero jacket with pointed tips, which I pulled on over a crisp white blouse. Studying myself in the antique standing mirror, I decided I looked downright businesslike. I hoped it would give me courage in my new role as detective.

When I emerged from my bedroom, Oscar was still staring at the cat, reciting a whole stream of names. Now that Oscar was interested in it, the pet acted completely oblivious to him. It walked away, leaving Oscar to trail behind it like a confused, rejected little monster.

Dastardly felines.

I went downstairs and out the front door to deliver the sandwich and a travel mug of sweetened coffee to Conrad, a neighborhood fixture who spent much of each day sitting on the curb outside my shop.

"Anything new on the street lately?" I asked.

"Duuude," said Conrad. It was a sort of all-purpose

response that sometimes led to a longer discussion, and sometimes was a sentence in itself.

I waited a beat. Apparently, today that was all there was to say.

Soon after I opened Aunt Cora's Closet, Conrad—or "the Con," as he called himself—and I sort of adopted one another. He was one of the hundreds of young people who flocked to the Haight each year in search of freedom. What they usually found, instead, was a sort of homeless, in-between existence. They called themselves gutter punks, and were generally reviled by the merchants and permanent residents of the neighborhood. Part of me understood why—their panhandling and general lack of hygiene left a whole lot to be desired. But they tugged at my heart, not unlike a recently orphaned black cat I could mention. In my estimation people, and animals, should never be treated as throwaways.

Though Conrad wasn't ready yet for my help in fighting his obvious chemical addictions, he watched over my store and did small tasks for me, while I made sure he had breakfast most days, and I welcomed his friendly, mellow presence outside my shop.

"Enjoy your sandwich."

"Duuude," Conrad repeated, this time by way of "thank you."

I retrieved the *San Francisco Chronicle* from the concrete stoop and went back inside.

Perching on a high stool, I spread the paper out on the glass counter and searched the pages to see if Zazi's death had rated a story. I was just about to give up when I found a brief article, relegated to page nine. According to the story a man had been found dead in his apartment, an apparent homicide. There was no mention of bad luck symbols, but it did refer to Malachi Zazi as founder of the famous—or notorious—Serpentarian Society dinners. There was even a picture, a black-and-white image of several men and women in period attire. I counted: There were thirteen members, including Malachi Zazi himself.

Then I noticed the byline on the story: Nigel Thorne. Nigel was a senior journalist who had spoken to me a while back about a series of missing children in the Hunters Point neighborhood. Why would he write this short, nothing article about a homicide? Could he be working on a bigger story? Nigel had become the unofficial go-to guy for strange things—paranormal things—for the *San Francisco Chronicle*.

I checked my watch: It was still early, before nine. I made a mental note to call him a little later. And as soon as Maya and Bronwyn got here, I would go talk to Gregory and try to figure out what was going on. And to Inspector Carlos Romero. Had he known I was connected to Gregory when he asked me to weigh in?

But in the meantime there was plenty of work to do. Witch or no witch, I still had to fill out paperwork and payroll and health benefits and sales tax. Running a retail shop of any kind, I was learning, was no easy thing. Good thing I loved it so much.

The little bell on the door tinkled when Maya arrived a little before ten, a chai latte in hand.

"Good morning, Lily. Hey, who's this?" Maya asked, picking up the black cat and cradling it in her slender arms. I could hear its raspy purring from where I stood.

"I sort of agreed to find a home for it. Looks like you two are hitting it off—would you like to keep it?"

"I wish I could. I live in a no-pet building. It's adorable, though. You should keep it here as a shop cat!"

"Black hairs on the merchandise? I don't think so."

"I guess you're right," she said with a smile. "Too bad it's not a bookstore."

As though to prove my point, Maya put down the cat and brushed a few stray black hairs off her saffron-colored sweater. She went to the back room to wash her hands; clean hands are an occupational necessity in the vintage clothing business.

Mondays at Aunt Cora's Closet were typically mellow. Within half an hour of opening a half dozen women were perusing the merchandise, and a couple of college students were trying on skirts in the communal dressing room, which was cordoned off from the rest of the store by heavy velvet curtains. Most of the customers were dressed in the uniform common to local students and artists: old jeans or long skirts—or both—topped by tatty T-shirts, faded hoodies, and worn backpacks slung over their slim shoulders.

I felt a surge of satisfaction. Aunt Cora's Closet was my first attempt at making a normal living, and so far we were in high cotton, as we'd say back home. The shop was developing a loyal following, and I was becoming a true scavenger: From auctions to garage sales to personal reference, I was Johnny-on-the-spot when it came to acquiring great old clothes.

"Hey! Guess who came into the shop yesterday," Maya said over the gurgle of the steam machine. She started meticulously smoothing out a Jackie O–style ivory linen shift with a matching jacket trimmed in faux ermine. I found the chic outfit balled up in a dresser drawer at a white elephant sale last month at the Oak-

land museum. I bought it for five dollars; the buttons
were missing and there were a few small tears in the
fine linen, but Maya's mother, Lucille, was a gifted
seamstress. After a thorough laundering, Lucille mended
the holes, and then unearthed four antique buttons
made of carved bone to replace the missing originals.
Perfect.

"Who?"

"That chick from that movie . . . what's her name?"

I laughed. "You're going to have to give me a few
more clues. I don't read minds, remember?"

Maya smiled, teeth flashing very white against the
smooth mocha of her skin. "Blond, sort of elfin-looking . . .
she was in that movie a few years ago, the big blockbuster
about vampires? Spells her name funny . . ."

"Sorry," I said as I moved behind the counter to start
organizing the weekend's receipts. "As you know, I'm
about the last person in the world you want to ask about
movies or TV shows."

"Was it Nichol Reiss?" asked a petite dark-haired
woman. She returned a beaded top to its crowded rack
before joining Maya and me at the counter. I recognized
her as a client who had recently purchased a vintage
1920s flapper dress for the upcoming Art Deco Ball in
Oakland. While she was here, she had also asked Bronwyn and me to mix a love charm for her.

"That's it!" Maya said. "Nichol Reiss. Sounds like 'Nicole,' but spelled with a 'ch' and no 'e.' Anyway, she
didn't buy anything but she spent a while looking. I
guess she's from San Francisco, so it's not all that surprising, but still."

"You're Claudia, right?" I said to the woman who
had spoken. "How nice to see you."

"I wasn't sure you'd recognize me," she said. "You must get gobs of women in here asking for your help."

"Of course I remember you," I said with a smile.

One of the benefits of my powers was an excellent memory, but I would never have forgotten Claudia, even with terrible recall. She had dark olive skin, long near-black hair, and the kind of exotic features that indicated a mixed ancestry. She also happened to be the first person who had actually come into Aunt Cora's Closet looking not only for vintage clothes but specifically asking for a magical spell . . . and I had mixed a charm bag for her. To someone like me, who had spent the first thirty-plus years of her life trying to keep her witchiness under wraps, it had been a milestone worthy of note.

I dropped my voice a tad. "How did the love charm work out?"

She grinned. "He called and asked if he could escort me to the Art Deco Ball. Maybe it would have happened anyway, but that charm didn't hurt. I'm still using it."

"That's good." Most spells were not a onetime thing; rather, the continuing steady influence of intention brought them to fruition.

Truly powerful love spells could result in zombielike, mindless obsession. I kept away from such things. Any witchcraft that forced others to act in ways not natural to them was dangerous to all concerned. In contrast, the mellow "love charm" I had prepared for Claudia would open the gates a bit, simply ease the natural progression of things. People tended to get caught up in outside forces—what other people thought, worries about their careers, insecurities, and extraneous life goals. The charm I had prepared for Claudia helped her to clarify her own desires, and to clear the way for the object of her desire to respond.

"Hey, not for nothing," Claudia said, "it's great that you're getting discovered by celebrities, but . . ."

"What?"

"Nichol Reiss has a little bit of a problem."

"Oh, the shoplifting thing?" Maya asked.

Claudia nodded.

"I didn't even think of that," Maya said. "You're right, though. That's why she sort of dropped off the radar after that movie. It was such a big hit, too."

"What shoplifting thing?" I asked.

"She was caught red-handed shoplifting at some high-profile store on Rodeo Drive."

"This is a movie star we're talking about?" I asked. "Why would a big star need to shoplift?"

"I don't think it was a matter of need per se," Maya said. "It can be a compulsion, a cry for attention, that sort of thing."

"Oh, of course," I said, feeling insensitive. But as a shop owner, I was also concerned. Theft was a serious problem for any retailer, but it was a particular issue along Haight Street. When I first opened the shop I had created an antitheft charm and hung it over the door—a red leather bag filled with charged caraway seeds and old keys. Plus, I cast a spell of protection over the store every morning. Still, those simple enchantments wouldn't chase off every ne'er-do-well. The most determined could still manage to overcome such hindrances. The human spirit was a powerful thing.

I had considered casting a stronger guardian spell, but a complete lockdown tamped down other forms of creativity as well. It was a conundrum. There is always, *always* a cost to the use of power.

"Anyway, I don't think she could have taken anything," Maya said, a slight frown marring her otherwise smooth forehead. As usual she wore a shiny collection of silver cuffs on her delicate ears, but today her black locks were decorated with fresh wildflowers, making me think that Bronwyn's nature-loving ways must be rubbing off on her. "She was the only customer in here at the time, and she knew I recognized her, so it would have been tough."

"And just think," said Claudia. "If Aunt Cora's Closet starts getting known among celebrities, you'll be all the rage."

"I've always wanted to be all the rage," said Maya.

"Me too," I said with a smile. "So, Claudia, are you looking for anything special today?"

"Just picking up my dress for the ball, but of course I couldn't resist browsing while I was here."

"Mom finished the alterations on Claudia's gown," Maya explained. "I gave her a call to come pick it up."

"Oh, great! Would you mind trying it on before you go?"

"You think it might not fit?" asked Claudia.

"Oh, I'm sure it will. Lucille is an amazing seamstress. Mostly I want to see you in it one more time."

When Claudia first came into Aunt Cora's Closet in search of a dress for the Art Deco Ball, she had her mind set on a different-style outfit altogether. But I have a gift for sensing what fashions suit my customers. Sometimes I have to practically bully people into trying on a particular dress or ensemble, but I'm almost always right. It gave me great satisfaction that at least in this one, admittedly limited area, I was very much a master of my craft.

When Claudia emerged from the communal dressing room a few minutes later, she had her long dark hair piled loosely on her head and a huge grin on her face. She practically glowed.

"It looks even better than I remembered," said Claudia.

The 1920s gold lamé flapper dress managed to appear at once quaint and exotic. The chemise-style gown had an underbodice that fit snug to the body, while the gold drape gathered in a bow at the left hip. The outer fabric featured a delicate woven border pattern of Egyptian stylized lotus blossoms—a sign of the sun and rebirth. The vibrations from the gown, which I had picked up at an estate sale in Bernal Heights, were dancing, alive, almost giddy. It was ideal for Claudia at this point in her life.

"I tell you what: Between that dress and your smile," Maya said, "your sweetie is toast, love charm or no."

A trio of customers came over to admire Claudia, commenting on the fabric and the fit. Oscar, never one to miss out on a party—especially one consisting entirely of women—snorted and wound through our legs, making everyone laugh. The feeling of the place immediately became festive, and I basked in the warm sensations. I could scarce believe how Aunt Cora's Closet, quite without explicit intent, had become a natural, jovial meeting place. Whenever there were several women trying on clothes in the communal dressing room, giggling and sharing—almost like children playing dress-up— the store felt like the setting of a spontaneous girls' night out.

As a young woman, even as a child, I had never been part of the easy, cheerful way of women when they're alone and unobserved. Indeed, until I met Maya and Bronwyn I had never had friends at all.

Claudia's fashion success inspired several other young women to try on gowns from the era. They streamed in and out of the communal dressing room. But when they started chatting about the upcoming Art Deco Ball, I felt the first whiff of worry and disappointment come off of Claudia. Since everything was all set with her dream date, I wondered what was on her mind. Still, I hesitated to ask in front of everyone and risk changing the tenor of the moment.

I carefully packed Claudia's altered dress and wrote out care instructions as Maya ran her credit card through.

"Hey, what are these?" Claudia asked, pointing at some new carved talismans in the display case. "I think I may need a good luck charm."

"The love charm wasn't enough?"

"So far that part is great, but ... this is going to sound weird, but I went to this dinner last month and I feel like I've had bad luck ever since. And now I'm helping set up the Art Deco Ball and our toastmaster was"—her voice dropped—"he was found *murdered* yesterday."

Maya gasped. "Murdered? That's terrible. What happened? Who was it?"

I'm no mind reader, but I already knew. San Francisco was a marvelous environment for coincidences, at least when it came to me and mine.

"Malachi Zazi."

Chapter 7

"They found him in his apartment," said Claudia. "I don't know any details—I only know that much because I live in his building. Sort of. I'm just apartment and pet sitting—I could never afford that area normally. But anyway, that's how I got involved with the Art Deco Society; Malachi told me about it."

"I thought you wrote the newsletter," I said.

"I do. In fact, that's how I found your store, from a newspaper article your friend Wendy sent us. But Malachi's the one who got me the newsletter gig in the first place."

"Zazi's part of the Art Deco Society?"

"Oh, yes. He had a love of historical things—his apartment's like a museum. His stuff's earlier than Art Deco. That's for sure. More like Victoriana, but I guess he enjoyed a lot of different things."

"Sounds like you knew him pretty well."

"I wouldn't go that far; I attended one of his dinners last month, but that was enough for me. It kind of weirded me out."

"In what way?"

"I thought it was just a kind of historical reenactment or something—we all wore clothing from the era, and the dinner was quite ornate. But here's where it gets weird: I guess Malachi was trying to poke fun about bad luck symbols or something. There was a broken mirror, and an open umbrella, a ladder to walk under . . . I never really thought of myself as superstitious before, but it really started to bother me."

"And you feel like you've had bad luck since then?"

"It's probably my imagination, right? But I always figure, why tempt fate?"

Why indeed?

"Could you tell me anything else about him? Was he the kind of guy with a lot of enemies, anything like that?"

Claudia smiled. "Now you sound like a cop. They already came by and asked me a million questions yesterday. Besides the Art Deco stuff and the dinner stuff, he pretty much kept to himself, never went out during the day." She paused. "Why are you asking? Did you know him?"

"Not exactly." Carlos Romero hadn't sworn me to silence, but I didn't suppose he'd want me to broadcast that he'd brought in a civilian to give him witchcraft advice on a crime scene. "He was sort of an associate of a friend of mine."

"Oh, I'm sorry."

The bell over the main door rang as several new people wandered into the store. A young couple headed straight for the lingerie section. A man with a goatee entered with two women, one a redhead, the other with an overabundance of curly blond hair. They already looked as though they were in costume, and indeed, they made a beeline for the costume corner.

I liked to let people wander the aisles without being bothered, so after a friendly nod of welcome I continued my conversation with Claudia.

"I'm on the board of the animal shelter, and a while back Malachi asked me to keep an eye out for a black cat. He adopted one not long ago. And now this. How sad is that?"

"Did he go down to the shelter to pick out his cat?"

"No, to tell you the truth, I went against regulations . . . I've never done so before. But I happened to know we had a black cat, which was his only stipulation. He didn't care about age or gender. We have so many cats, and they all need homes . . . anyway, I brought the cat to him. He reimbursed me for all the fees."

"Weren't you at all concerned about the cat's welfare?" I knew shelters had to be especially careful with black cats around Halloween. There were crazy folk who took the poor felines to be used in dark ceremonies and the like.

"I know it was against regulations, but . . . Malachi seemed so . . . gallant? I guess that's the word. Sort of courtly and old-fashioned. I just felt sure he wouldn't harm the cat . . . he was such a sweet soul."

"Despite his penchant for bad luck charms."

"Yeah, I guess that was sort of odd."

"I don't suppose you could take the cat back to the shelter?" I said, looking around for the feline.

"The cat? Malachi's cat? I didn't think to ask what happened to it. Do the police have it?"

"Actually, *I* do."

"You mean *Zazi's* black cat? How did you get it?"

"It's a long story. It's around here somewhere. Would you be willing to take it back?"

"Of course, we can take it back at the shelter. I can't take it myself because I'm apartment sitting and they already have two dogs."

"If the cat goes back to the shelter . . . ?"

"We're a no-kill facility," Claudia hastened to say. "But I can't guarantee we'll find it a home. It's a little older than most people like. And as strange as it is to say, there's a prejudice against black animals among adopters. I guess they're associated with bad luck, still, in a lot of people's minds. Black dogs are even worse, interestingly enough. Something about them being devil's creatures. . . . It never ceases to amaze me how mean people can be."

"Never mind," I said. "I'll try to find it a home."

Claudia thanked us again for our help with her dress for the ball and left. The bell over the door tinkled when she let herself out, and I watched her walk down the street until she was out of sight.

Claudia was apartment sitting in Malachi Zazi's building. She came into the store for her dress and love potion last week, long before I had ever been called in to consult on a crime scene, or heard of anyone named Zazi. Could it truly be a coincidence, or was there some sort of link? Could Malachi have known about me— had he been some sort of supernatural practitioner himself? That would help explain the strange lack of vibrations from his garment collection, as well as the whole apartment seemingly wiped down for psychic prints.

On the other hand, Claudia mentioned seeing the write-up of Aunt Cora's Closet in the Art Deco newsletter. So maybe it was just that simple. Unfortunately, there wasn't a whole lot of "simple" in my life.

"Poor Claudia," said Maya as she changed the paper roll on the register. "You're still planning on going to the dance, though, right? Even if Max isn't back?"

Talk about a lack of "simple." Flying solo was not a new concept for me. But not long ago I'd met a journalist, Max Carmichael, and I was intrigued at the idea of actually having an escort to the Art Deco Ball. Unfortunately he was back east on assignment . . . and while he was there, he was trying to figure out how he felt about me. As I said to Aidan earlier: I wasn't willing to explain myself. Max had a hard time with my powers, and I wasn't about to deny them or hide them for his comfort.

But all my bravado aside, I was hoping he'd find the strength to deal with what was, for him, a whole new magical world.

"Have you heard anything from him?" Maya continued.

"He's called a couple of times."

That was almost an exaggeration. Max had called once on the store phone, but I wasn't alone and our conversation unfolded like one of distant friends: *How are you? How's Oscar? How's business?* He also called and left a message on my home machine, marginally better: *I've been thinking of you.* I was embarrassed to admit I kept the message and had already replayed it twice. Still, I hadn't heard from him again, and there had been plenty of opportunity. Every night before bed I thought maybe he'd call, *hoped* he'd call. But he hadn't. I was tempted to cast a spell to force his hand, but I stopped myself. I might have a certain moral flexibility when it came to using my powers, but I was above forcing a man into wanting me.

Obviously, as a twenty-first-century woman, *I* could call *him*; but he was three hours ahead, and under the circumstances of our parting ... it felt like I should let Max come to me when he was ready, rather than push him.

In the old days—the burning times—men who loved witches were considered pawns of the devil's handmaidens, and were often condemned to death by hanging, drowning, or burning, just as were their mothers, wives, daughters. Thousands, maybe millions had died alongside their womenfolk.

These days the immediate consequences for being close to someone like me weren't nearly so dramatic or so gruesome, but there was still a cost. No matter that I was finding a supportive community; I wasn't the kind of woman an ordinary man would be proud to bring home to meet the parents.

I was still weird, still frightening. Still Other.

So I was hurt. But I understood. It wasn't easy to love a witch.

A tingle of awareness yanked my attention from my thoughts.

Time slowed, elongated.

One of the recently arrived customers walked toward me with a hips-first, runway-model stride, her kinky dishwater blond hair falling in a mass around her face and down her back. She was backed up by her two companions: a petite but chubby woman who cut her auburn hair short, like a pixie, with green eyes and freckles; and an older man, goateed, with hair dyed a sooty, fake-looking black.

The blonde was not nearly as young as her hair, bright makeup, and gauzy costume might imply; I would guess in her early fifties. She was tall and thin, more striking than pretty. Her bright blue-green eyes were abnormally shiny, fixated upon me.

"I'm Doura," she said in a quiet, high-pitched, almost baby-doll voice.

I looked around, but I could feel myself moving as though in slow motion, or underwater. The other customers, and Maya, were still moving and talking, but time had slowed. They appeared not to hear us.

Doura held something in her hand. Was it a power stick of some sort? No, a plain old pen. *My* pen, the one I had left on the counter. The one I had been holding only seconds ago. The one I had absentmindedly put to my mouth as I wrote out Claudia's care instructions for her new ball gown.

"Leave this matter alone," Doura said. "Walk away."

"What are you talking about? Who are you?" My voice sounded deep and distorted, as though it were in slow motion as well. It was a nightmarish sensation.

"Walk away. Malachi is no concern of yours. Consider this your warning."

She gave me a wicked, sickly smile as she deliberately set the pen back down on the counter.

I stroked the medicine bag hanging on the braided belt around my waist, closed my eyes, and mumbled a protective spell.

"Speaking of the Art Deco Ball," said Maya, bringing me back to reality. Time seemed to normalize. "Mom says she'll have the alterations on your dress done by tomorrow, but she wants to do one more fitting with you."

"Great. Thanks," I said, looking around for the woman. She and her companions had disappeared. "Maya, did you see . . . did you notice the blonde who was in here? She was with another woman and a man with a goatee . . . ?"

"Not really. Is something wrong?"

"I . . . no, everything's fine." Except it wasn't so fine. Unless I was very much mistaken, I had just been visited by some sort of witch. A powerful witch.

Could Aidan have sent her? Would he have stooped so low? Doura didn't scare me much with her witchy parlor tricks, but she certainly got my attention. Anyone who could muck with time, like weather, garnered a lot of respect in my book. Besides, to be perfectly honest, I felt a little twinge of . . . something. Aidan and I might not see eye to eye, and it was true that we were on the outs at the moment, but I still thought we had a special sort of connection. As though I was his only female witch.

Now that I thought about it, I realized that despite his reputation for running the local witchy contingent, I had never seen him with other witches before . . . much less another woman.

I left the shop in Maya's capable hands, and went off in search of answers.

Chapter 8

Only heaven knew what kind of trouble Oscar might get into today with the new cat, so I put a couple of blankets, a few snacks, and a jug of water in the back of my purple work van and packed up both animals.

Then I headed for the offices of the *San Francisco Chronicle*, at the corner of Fifth and Mission.

I'm probably the last soul under the age of eighty without a cell phone. As an outcast, I rely on my assessments of people to survive; as a witch, I could feel their vibrations, note their eyes, their hands, their twitches. So rather than call ahead, I just stopped by in the hopes that I might find a disinterested source. Nigel Thorne was at the top of that list.

As I rode the elevator up from the parking garage, I couldn't help but think about the last time I was here. Max Carmichael had challenged me, belittled me, then wound up following me on a visit to a voodoo priest. And asking me out on a date.

The good old days.

The offices were essentially one big room of cubicles,

ringed by glassed-in offices. Under the fluorescent lights the writers and staff looked, to a person, gray-faced and hassled. Nigel fit right in. Today he wore khaki pants, a light blue button-up shirt, and a brown tweed jacket. He had a coffee stain on his shirt, right where his paunch strained at the buttons. His graying brown hair frizzed out from the side of his head, and his eyebrows were hawklike and overgrown, giving him a demanding air that was betrayed by the gentleness in his voice.

Nigel Thorne's vibrations were warm, with an edge of cynicism I wasn't surprised to find in a man who spent much of his time investigating and reporting on crime and criminals.

"Good to see you, Lily."

"You, too, Nigel. How's your family?" His messy cubicle was personalized with multiple framed photos of his wife and daughters.

"Everyone's great, thanks. My youngest'll be finishing up college this spring. You believe it?"

"You can't possibly be old enough to have grown children."

"Yeah, right," he snorted. "Nice try. You're no good at lying, ya know that?"

I smiled. "Do you have a quick minute?"

"Sure," he said. His desk chair squeaked as he leaned back and clasped his hands behind his head. "Waiting on a bunch of callbacks, anyway. Mondays. What's up?"

"I noticed that you wrote a short piece in today's paper on the death of Malachi Zazi."

"You know him?" he asked.

I shook my head. "Did you?"

He cocked his head in a gesture that was neither a nod nor a shake. "I interviewed him once about his club."

"The Serpentarian Society?"

"Yep. You know it?"

"I've heard of it, but only in relation to him. Could you tell me about it?"

He sat up, put his elbows on his knees, and leaned toward me. "It was based on an old group called the Thirteen Club, which operated in the late 1800s in New York City. Spiritualism of all sorts was huge back then, and a group of wealthy men set out to debunk the notions by addressing bad luck symbols, that sort of thing. They met at eight thirteen on the thirteenth day of the month, with thirteen people around the table."

"A whole club based on unlucky thirteen?"

"Pretty much. Problem is, one of them died."

"How?"

"Pneumonia, something like that. But the superstition was that someone would die within the year, and that's what happened."

"A club like that makes some sense for that era, but doesn't it seem odd in today's world?"

"You would think, right? But triskaidekaphobia—" He smiled. "That's the fear of thirteen. Took me a *month* to learn to pronounce that one—anyway, it's pretty widespread, and not just here. In Scotland there are no gates thirteen in airports; some airplanes skip the row thirteen; and you know as well as I do that buildings often skip the thirteenth floor. Some streets skip over the address as well. There were thirteen people at the Last Supper; Loki was the thirteenth fellow invited to a disastrous dinner at Valhalla; on Friday the thirteenth the Knights of the Templar were arrested and destroyed."

"There's also a strong association of thirteen with paganism," I said.

"That's right, because of the thirteen lunar months."

When organized religion took over in Europe, denigrating thirteen was one of its accomplishments. The Druids and Celts had twelve signs of their mundane zodiac, and a secret thirteenth called "the weaver," or the cosmic spider in the center of life. There were also thirteen covens of Logres in Britain. The number was prominent on the female side of occult work.

"Anyhoo, the members of the original Thirteen Club in New York were besieged by bad luck, every last one of them."

"What kind of bad luck?"

"Deaths in the family, business failures, injuries ... just about anything you can think of. The group finally disbanded when they seemed to be proving anything but what they'd set out to do."

"That's interesting," I said. Had they truly called havoc down upon their own heads?

He pushed a manila folder over to me. Inside were photographs: sepia, slightly fuzzy pictures of people dressed in gowns and suits.

"Are these original photos?" I asked. They appeared much newer, or photography was better back in the late 1800s than I would have guessed.

"Oh, no, these are from Malachi Zazi's group."

"All dressed up."

"Uh-huh. Apparently Zazi bought the stash of clothes at auction. Those outfits are supposedly from the original Thirteen Club."

"Do you know who they are?"

He pointed at faces as he listed them off. "That's Malachi Zazi there, Ellen Chambers, and Gregory Petrovic, Nichol Huffman, and that must be her brother, Oliver, though he's turned away from the camera—they're children of Senator Huffman—and this is Mike Perkins, of course."

"I understand Perkins is a pharmaceutical giant."

"That's an understatement. Haven't heard of him having any bad luck, but Petrovic's not doing all that well, and the Huffmans are all screwed up. Ellen Chambers is in the hospital following a car accident, and a lot of the other dinner guests have had a string of bad luck: accidents, problems at work, broken bones, divorce."

"And it's all being attributed to playing with bad luck symbols?"

He nodded.

"How did you get hold of these photos?"

"The dinners themselves were private, but in actuality the club was all about the publicity. They were promoted to the public, photographed, and even filmed. The point, after all, was to prove that the superstitions were false; that's why Zazi set the place up like that."

"And now the bad luck host is dead. What do you make of all this?"

He shrugged. "If you're asking whether I think Zazi died of bad luck, I say it's a bunch of baloney. Zazi inherited money—that's a more likely source of murder than a broken mirror."

"His parents were wealthy?"

"His mother had money. But his *father*"—Nigel rolled his eyes exaggeratedly—"*whew!* Talk about your freak shows. He wasn't society, though. In fact, before he became the devil guy he played the Wurlitzer over at the Lost Weekend Lounge."

"The 'devil guy'?"

"Malachi's father—calls himself Prince High Zazi."

"He's royalty of some sort?"

"Not exactly. You're not from here, so you probably never heard of the 'black abode' on California?"

I shook my head.

"Back in the sixties and seventies, things were in upheaval. Lots of strange stuff going on locally—the Symbionese Liberation Army kidnapped and brainwashed Patty Hearst, there were cults on the rise, then the tragedy of Jonestown."

"I've heard of those."

"So this guy buys a house, a typical Victorian job on California out in the Richmond District, paints the whole thing black. The whole damned thing, walls inside and out, trim. Everything. Surrounds the place with a security fence. Then he installs these cameras, like video cameras, on the outside so he can see who's coming. Back then it was a big deal—no one had cameras like that except maybe the embassies, the White House."

"What was he up to?"

"That was the house Malachi Zazi grew up in. Prince High claimed he was all about the devil. I'm not sure how far he took the whole thing, but he wrote several books on the subject. Made lots of money by saying scandalous things against established religions and espousing a sort of materialistic philosophy when most of the world was exploring cooperation."

"You think he really believed in it, or was it a stunt of some kind?"

He shrugged. "I'm a journalist. I don't dismiss anything until I've had a chance to research it. Then again, I don't believe anything until I delve into it, either. Anyway, by the eighties the whole furor had died down. Prince High keeps to himself these days."

"Where did you say the black abode was? Out in the Richmond?"

"You're not planning on going over there, are you?"

"Just thought I'd do a roll-by, get a visual."

"Don't underestimate the guy. I don't buy the devil garbage, but I know for a fact someone like that's gotta be a whack job. Anyway, as I understand it, Malachi and his father have been on the outs for some time. Malachi inherited plenty of money from his mother, and he kind of took on the whole society thing, most likely in opposition to his father."

"I have to say, I'm surprised to learn that there's a 'society thing' in San Francisco. The town seems so laid-back and West Coast, I hadn't realized."

"Oh, sure. Doesn't hold a candle to New York, nothing like that, but it's there. Malachi went to the college prep with all the other rich kids. Too much money, too much time on their hands. They're always into something. These dinner parties he has, the whole bad luck thing seems to me like a challenge to his father's world. It's become chic to attend. But whether it's his father's shenanigans or his bad luck dinners, the whole thing still makes me nervous."

"About what?"

Nigel shrugged and scratched his head. "I don't buy into this whole supernatural deal, but it bugs me when people fool around with it. You never know when they'll slide on over into animal sacrifice, that sort of thing. Scares the hell out of me."

I nodded. Best not to follow that one up. Nigel was open-minded, but witchcraft was a bit much to ask most anyone to swallow outside of the Haight.

"Do you think the dinner participants talked themselves into the bad luck somehow?"

"Could be. I—"

His eyes shifted over my shoulder.

I whirled around to see what, or who, he was looking at. My heart pounded, thinking it might be Max.

It wasn't.

It was a woman I'd seen with Max once before. Lovely. Sleek. Wearing a very expensive chic outfit. Very put together in a career-woman-on-the-go sort of way. Her eyes settled on me briefly before skipping past me to land on Nigel.

"How's that piece on city hall coming?" she asked him.

"Just waiting on a callback with a final confirmation. I'll send it over shortly."

"And the SoMa article?"

"I'm on it."

She nodded, seemingly unconvinced. Her pretty eyes settled on me once more.

"I know you."

"Yes." I stood and held out my hand to her. "Lily Ivory," I said. "We haven't officially met, but I was with Max Carmichael one time—"

"Oh, right. That's it." She ignored my hand, turned away. Over her shoulder as she left she said to Nigel, "No time like the present, right?"

Nigel didn't respond, other than to lean back farther, hands linked over his belly. His desk chair protested the move. When I sat back down and met his eyes, one side of his mouth hitched up in a half smile.

"She's fond of Max Carmichael."

"So am I."

"That's the problem." He smiled and shrugged one chubby shoulder. "She's a hard-ass, but she puts out a good product. Speaking of Max, have you seen him since he got back?"

"Max is in town?"

"Uh . . . yep." There was something like a blush on his cheeks. "I guess he hasn't had a chance to call."

"I guess."

Nigel leaned forward and shoved the manila envelope toward me. "Take this, if you like. Some of the names are on the back of the photos. You might want to check out some of the participants, see if any of them are willing to talk to you."

"I won't be stepping on your toes, then? Mucking up your investigation?"

"I've been pulled off of it," he said, telegraphing his anger and frustration. "They're keeping me busy on other things, and lately I'm not in a position to rock the journalistic boat. This story needs telling, though."

"Do you think someone's trying to stifle the story?"

"Hard to say. I don't have any proof of anything, just my journalistic intuition. There are a lot of powerful people on that list; or more to the point, these are the children of powerful people." He tapped the envelope. "There are probably a whole lot of folks who'd rather keep this whole story under wraps—such as one Mike Perkins. Not to mention Senator Huffman." He wrote something on the back of his business card and handed it to me. "Here's my cell number. Feel free to call if I can help fill in any details. It's probably best if you call, though, rather than stopping by."

I thanked him, stood, and shook his hand.

"Lily—be careful. These folks may be wing nuts, but some of them are wing nuts with powerful connections."

"I will be," I said. "Oh, you wouldn't like to adopt a cat by any chance?"

"A cat?"

"It seems perfectly healthy. Sweet-natured, pretty, all black."

He shook his head. "I'm a dog person. Got two golden retrievers at home, that's more than we need already."

"Thought I'd give it a shot," I said with a shrug. "Thanks again for your help."

"Anytime," he said. His eyes shifted over to the glassed-in office again. "Next time give me a call, and I'll meet you somewhere. Not here."

I nodded. "Will do."

Despite our talk of bad luck and "black abodes," as I made my way onto the elevator and down to the parking garage, one thought kept echoing through my head, and my heart: *Max is back. But he hasn't called me.*

That could only mean one thing . . . couldn't it? He'd decided he couldn't deal with my witchy ways.

I felt a surge of anger. Car alarms began to blare as I walked past.

Max was a coward. A *cowardly cowan*, just as Oscar liked to call him. How was it possible that a gargoylelike goblin like Oscar would be smarter than I at romance?

As I walked across the parking lot, I rooted around in my satchel for my keys. Finally I looked up to see a man leaning against my car.

Max?

Chapter 9

My heart leapt.

Like Max, the man beside my car was tall and dark-haired. But he was leaner . . . and I would wager he was a durn sight meaner.

"What in the Sam Hill are *you* doing here?" I said.

"Hello to you too, Ms. Grumpy-pants," Sailor said.

"I . . . wasn't expecting anyone." I unlocked the van and threw in my bag, trying to cover my thoughts of Max by acting surprised. Normally Sailor couldn't read my mind, but at the moment I was so focused on Max I'd be surprised if my grandmother wasn't feeling my hurt and yearning all fifteen hundred miles away in Jarod, Texas. I took a deep breath and turned back to Sailor. "What do you want?"

"You're saying I have to have a reason for visiting my favorite witch?" His voice was smoky, his eyes heavy-lidded and seductive. A bit of mysterious sadness showed through his gruff exterior. Though I had seen him act this way to others, he had never turned his dubious charms on me.

"You don't like witches," I pointed out, immediately suspicious.

"I don't like Aidan. Nothing against witches per se."

"Uh-huh. So what are you doing here?"

He laughed. I had never heard the sound. It was deep, and surprisingly pleasant.

"I felt bad about yesterday. I tend toward the churlish, I know, especially after spending time with Aidan. Anyway, I'm turning over a new leaf. The truth is . . ." As his voice trailed off, he shrugged and avoided my eyes. "I don't have all that many friends. It may be time for me to reach out."

I doubted him. Seriously. I imagined he really was working for Aidan, I just couldn't figure out exactly why. But upon reflection, I decided I could use some company at the moment. I didn't relish the thought of traipsing around after murder suspects on my own. Usually I was a solo act, since normal humans couldn't protect themselves as well as I could. But Sailor was different. Whether he liked it or not, he was strong. And it might be useful having him around. I had barely started asking questions about Malachi's murder, but already there seemed to be much more to this than a simple crime of passion, or the result of bad luck symbols, for that matter. Maybe Sailor could read some minds, some vibrations, and help clue me in on what was going on.

"All right," I said as I climbed into the driver's seat. "Jump in."

"Great," he said in his more familiar sardonic tone, as he saw Oscar and the cat in the back of the van. "Me and the menagerie. Maybe we can pick up a stray dog, or maybe a raccoon, and make it a party."

By the time I pulled out onto Harrison the cat had

moved to sit in Sailor's lap. Sailor reared back, looking as appalled as Oscar had in the same situation.

"Not a cat person, I take it?" I asked.

He didn't deign to answer. Instead, a strange look came over the strong planes of his face. He laid his broad hands upon the feline, ducked his head, and fell silent.

"This is not your cat," he said after a long moment.

"No," I responded, though it wasn't a question.

Sailor met my eyes.

"Can it tell you something?" I asked, suddenly excited. Could Sailor find out from the cat what happened in Malachi's apartment that night? "It may have been witness to a murder. Can you read its mind?"

But he was shaking his head.

"They don't process like we do. They're mostly about visuals, pictures, sensations."

"Yes, but . . . Did it see what happened?"

"No. But there was something there . . . something evil."

I sat back, disappointed. "A fat lot of help you are, Mr. Psychic. I think I figured that much out as soon as I saw the man sprawled on the table with a piece of broken mirror stuck in his chest."

"What are you talking about?" Sailor asked, and I realized he knew nothing of Malachi Zazi's untimely death. I gave him the abridged version.

"So I thought maybe you could tell me something, from the cat."

"Hey, it's not my fault," Sailor said. "I do what I can. Have *you* ever wandered through the recesses of a cat's thoughts? It's mostly about smoked ham and dust motes."

Oscar snorted loudly from the back of the van.

I pulled over and consulted a San Francisco road map, checking the street signs against it, and the address Rebecca had given me.

Sailor watched me for a moment. "Where are you trying to get to?"

I told him the address.

"That's in the Tenderloin."

"Is it?"

"It's about three blocks from the newspaper offices."

"It is?"

"Next time I'm driving. Take a left."

San Francisco is a small town, geographically speaking. Thus, one can pass from a prosperous, well-tended area to a run-down, poverty-stricken neighborhood within the space of a city block or two. Though the Tenderloin sits cheek by jowl with the theater district, the denizens here could scarce afford a movie, never mind an off-Broadway show.

We passed a soup kitchen with a long line of scruffy people waiting, defeated and patient. Several men crowded the corners, holding signs declaring they were available for work. The women, many wearing garish makeup and clothing far too skimpy for San Francisco's changeable weather, looked as though they did whatever they had to in order to survive.

"At least there's plenty of parking," I said as I pulled to a spot at the curb in front of a dingy white four-story building. An old half-lit neon sign flickered near the double doors: HOTEL WHARTON—VACANCY.

"There might not be much left of this van by the time we get back."

"Sounds like a good reason for you to stay here, keep things safe." Though it was nice knowing that Sailor was nearby, I didn't feel any need to have him accompany me to interview Bronwyn's son-in-law, Gregory. Besides, I wouldn't know how to explain him to Rebecca. I'd rather save him for bigger fish, presuming I could track any down.

I climbed out of the vehicle. Sailor did the same.

"You're not coming with me for this," I told Sailor as we both slammed our doors. "I'd rather talk to this fella alone."

"Who is it?"

"None of your business. It's personal. Stay here with the animals."

Just then a building alarm rang out. A series of muffled pops sounded suspiciously like gunshots. A small group laughed and smoked on the corner, selling a questionable collection of stained clothing that hung on the Cyclone fence behind them.

Sailor snorted. "Yeah, I can just imagine explaining this one to your friends at Aunt Cora's Closet. *'Guess I shouldn't have let her go into the worst dive in the city alone. So sorry about that knife in her back.'* Peace-loving Wiccans or not, they'd put a pox on me."

"Really, I don't need a bodyguard, Sailor. I've got talismans that are a darned sight better protection than you are."

He shrugged and came over to stand beside me. "You're a witch, not an immortal."

A man reeled toward us on unsteady feet. He wore jeans and an old pin-striped vest that barely hid his sweaty, hairy beer belly; as he neared I noted the stench of alcohol and body odor. The man's rheumy eyes fixed on me and he gave me a moist leer.

I leaned into Sailor.

My self-appointed bodyguard looked down at me, amused. "How quickly the mighty change their tune," he said in a low voice. Still, he draped his arm around my shoulders and glowered at the drunken man. Then he urged me toward the hotel doors. "Let's go, tiger."

Black leather jacket and permanent scowl or no, Sailor was a psychic, not invincible. Save for premonition, testosterone, bravado, and his fists, he had no actual way of keeping himself safe. I fished around in my Filipino woven backpack until my hand wrapped around a talisman I had carved and charged during the last full moon. I put it around his head, laid my hands flat on his chest, and chanted a quick charm of protection.

When I stepped back, his eyes were dark and searching, though as always hard to read. Full of questions, that much was clear. And something else, something unusual, unexpected. Vulnerability?

The moment passed.

I cast a quick spell of protection over the van and its inhabitants before setting off to find Rebecca's errant husband.

"This is just lovely," grumbled Sailor as we stepped into the dingy lobby. The eye-watering chemical aroma of Pine-Sol wasn't sufficient to hide the underlying scent of unwashed humanity.

"Your place isn't a whole sight better," I pointed out.

"Give me a break. My apartment building may be run-down, but it's nothing like this."

He was right. Not all poverty is the same: In many instances, it leads to a neighborly interdependence, strong family bonds, hard work, and determination. Often, the more people have to rely upon one another, the more they retain their cultural integrity and remain loyal to their family and friends. But here, in this section of the Tenderloin at least, the grinding poverty was part and parcel of degradation, addiction, and hopelessness.

The Hotel Wharton was the kind of place that rented rooms by the hour. As a domicile its chief advantage, as far as I could imagine, was the price, and the fact that no one would ask questions. About anything. Their recent spate of bad luck notwithstanding, surely the Petrovics had the resources for Gregory to stay someplace decent upon being expelled from the family home. I would imagine Rebecca's husband feeling most comfortable at a Marriott extended-stay hotel, someplace corporate and shiny and new.

There was only one obvious explanation: Gregory Petrovic was punishing himself.

No one stopped Sailor and me or asked who we were looking for as we made our way down a first-floor hallway. The indoor-outdoor gray carpeting was threadbare and stained, and the cracked stucco walls vibrated with despair. Sounds of televisions and loud conversations seeped through the series of thin doors.

I knocked on the door of room 112.

The man who answered was of average height, pale, with thinning light brown hair. His eyes were surprisingly pretty, large and long-lashed in the way of Maybelline models. Heavy-lidded, they might have been very romantic if they hadn't been rimmed in red from lack of sleep, or drink. He was lean and fit, with that signature Bay Area upwardly mobile professional look of a man who mountain bikes and windsurfs in his downtime, making it a point of pride to maintain a flat belly after the age of thirty. It was easy enough to imagine that with a change of clothes, he and Rebecca would make a polished-looking affluent couple.

Everything about him looked out of place in this hotel, except for the defeated look in his eyes and a grimy bandage on the ring finger and pinky of his left hand.

"Gregory? I'm Lily Ivory. I work with Bronwyn, your mother-in-law?" I said. His expression remained flat, vacant. "Rebecca sent me. Could we talk?"

"Who's that?" he asked, glancing behind me.

"An associate of mine. Sailor."

Gregory shrugged, stepped back, and let us in. The room was standard flophouse: a twelve-by-twelve space with a single window looking out over an alley, a sagging double bed, a scarred bureau with one drawer missing, and a tattered love seat near the window. I had stayed in worse in my time, but always in much more exotic surroundings—Morocco, Thailand, Amsterdam. There it seemed rather romantic. Here, plain miserable.

The bed was neatly made, but clothes were strewn about, and papers spilled out of an open briefcase at the foot of the bed. An empty grease-stained Kentucky Fried Chicken bucket sat on the floor, and a bottle of expensive bourbon stood on the nightstand.

"Is Rebecca ready to see me?" Gregory asked.

"I'm sorry. I don't actually know. I came to speak to you about Malachi Zazi."

"Oh." He drooped like a deflated balloon, sinking down onto the side of the bed and cradling his head in his hands. He let off a defeated thrum, like a funeral dirge. "When Rebecca called and said you'd be coming by, I thought maybe it had to do with us. Her and me, I mean. She told me she'd think about letting me visit with the kids. . . ."

After a moment he looked back up, as though surprised to see we were still there.

"Oh, sorry. Have a seat."

I perched on the room's single wooden chair.

Sailor remained silent, standing at the door. He crossed his arms over his broad chest, leaned back against the wall, and glowered. My own personal Secret Service detail.

"The police haven't pressed charges against you, have they?" I asked. "Do you expect them to?"

"I have no idea. The way my life's spinning out of control lately, probably."

"Tell me what's been going on."

"I wish I knew. Everything . . . first my research experiments were tampered with. The results were forged, and it looked like I did it, but I didn't. I swear. I spent less time at home, trying to make up for what was spinning out of control at work. But then we got an audit notice from the IRS, and we owe a bunch of back taxes. I got into a fender bender. And then I started . . . drinking. I managed to get a DUI. I even smashed my hand in the car door," he said, holding up his bandage with an almost petulant sort of "Why me?" look on his face. "And now this. I'm accused of *murder*."

Outside a siren blared, grew unbearably loud, then passed. Someone shouted the name "Carrie" repeatedly. Drunken laughter. Smells of marijuana smoke, fried foods, and car exhaust wafted in through the open window. Sailor and I shared a look. Despite my earlier bravado, I was very glad to have him standing guard.

"What kind of research do you do?"

"Antiaging, mostly. The secret to longevity."

"Have you found it?"

"The secret?" He gave a bitter laugh. "Not quite. I'm afraid there's no magic potion. We're investigating regimens of hormones and vitamins, different sorts of medications."

"You work at Michael Perkins's company, Perkins Laboratories?"

"Mike Perkins. Yeah."

The eternal search for youth. I thought about the botanicals I knew that helped people stay younger longer: angelica and cinnamon oil, to name just a couple. But they were mostly about maintaining vitality and health, not just surface beauty. I imagined anyone who came near to inventing such a product would make a fortune.

"Do you think this 'curse' you appear to be under has to do with Malachi's dinners?"

"Six months ago I would have laughed at the very idea. But I'm beginning to wonder whether you can really tempt fate like that and not pay for it eventually."

"So you believe? In the bad luck symbols?"

"I'm a scientist. I believe in things that are proven, and provable. But contrary to popular belief, that doesn't mean I'm closed to the idea of something . . . well . . . things that we don't know about yet."

It made sense. Scientists deal with outlandish ideas all the time—just look at the inspired lunacy of Galileo. They were among the more open-minded people I'd ever met when it came to magical systems. All they asked for was proof.

"For instance, say Joe from down the hall comes to me and tells me aliens have just landed down at the corner," Gregory continued. "He wants to bet me a hundred dollars. I wouldn't take the bet, but I'd sure go down and check out the corner, just in case."

"Tell me what happened with Malachi, why the police would be suspicious of you."

"It was right before dinner Saturday night. I arrived early to speak with Malachi. Oliver came in and overheard us arguing. I guess he told the police." He shook his head. "Oliver Huffman. Of all people."

"Why do you say that?"

"We've known each other for years, since high school. I just can't believe he'd accuse me."

"He told the police you killed Malachi?"

"Not in so many words. He said he overheard me arguing with Malachi. Said I threatened to kill him."

"And did you?"

"I may have. I don't really remember . . . I was upset." His jaw set tight, the muscles in his neck drew taut, as though he remained seated through sheer force of will. He clenched his fists. "I just wanted him to stop it."

"Stop what?"

"All of it. To lift the curse."

"You really think Malachi cursed you?"

To me, that was a serious accusation. As my grandmother Graciela would say, *Words have power, m'hija, las palabras son poderosas.* I would never curse a person without cause. But then, I knew what my power could do, and I was careful with it. Could Malachi have been a beginner, or worse, someone who used magical powers for his whims?

"He must have cursed me. Why else would all of this be happening?"

"Even if that's true . . . Why? What motivation would Malachi have to do such a thing? Were you and he enemies?"

"No, no, not really. We've known each other forever,

since school. But we were both angry that night, and I may have lost it. I guess maybe I did threaten him. And Oliver heard me, and he told the police, and now they think I'm the killer."

"Gregory, talking to you about an argument is not the same as pressing charges. I think you should try to relax and not assume the worst will happen."

He just sighed.

"Think carefully. Was there anything different about that last night at Malachi's place? With the dinner, or how any of the guests were acting?"

He shook his head, ran his hand through his thin hair. "I can't think of anything. Except . . ." He shrugged.

"Anything at all."

"There was a different guest there. Since Ellen was hospitalized, we needed a new woman."

"Who was it?"

"Lots of hair . . . Dora? No, Doura. And she insisted we play a bunch of ridiculous parlor games. Like the Ouija board, that sort of thing."

"And you all did that on Saturday night? What did you ask the board?"

"It's just a stupid game. You probably played it when you were a girl, at slumber parties."

I was never invited to slumber parties when I was a girl, and even if I had been, I sure as heck wouldn't have "played" with a Ouija board. Those things scare me.

"Tell me, though. What did you ask the board . . . and what did it reply?"

"Someone must have been pushing the pointer. It spelled out "d-e-a-t-h." Everybody seemed pretty shaken up, but you know the whole point was not to believe in such nonsense."

"And yet I'm getting the distinct impression that you do believe."

"I never used to. But now . . . that's not all. Want to hear the really weird thing?"

"Sure." I took a deep breath.

"I . . ." He swallowed and looked around. I smelled the acrid scent of fear. "I thought I saw him."

"Him who?"

"Malachi."

"When?"

"Today. This morning."

"Is this the part where you bet me a hundred bucks?"

"I know it sounds crazy, and it probably is. But I haven't had a drink for a week."

Unbidden, my eyes slewed to the bottle on the night-stand. Gregory reached over, grabbed it, and handed it to me.

"Check out the seal. Unbroken."

I nodded.

"I think Malachi's coming after me. From the grave."

Chapter 10

This was one scientist who was a whole lot more than open-minded. As my mama would say: He'd done gone round the bend and lost his way.

"Why would you think Malachi's coming after you?"

"I saw him—I thought I saw him. All wrapped up in scarves, wearing a hat and sunglasses like he always did when he was outside."

"So it could have been anyone, right? Did you see his face?"

"No. But Doura said . . . over that stupid Ouija game she said that death was coming for Malachi, but that he would escape it."

"What else did she say? How did she act?"

"She and Malachi went way back, she said, though he didn't really seem all that happy to see her, to tell you the truth."

"Can you remember anything else she might have said? Anything out of the ordinary?"

He shook his head.

"Did she arrive alone, or was she with somebody?"

"Actually, she came with Mike Perkins. I guess she knew him, but that goes for just about everybody in San Francisco. I've seen her at Perkins Laboratories a couple of times."

"Did you tell the police that she was at the dinner?"

"I don't think I remembered to mention it."

I brought out the manila envelope Nigel had given me and extracted the photos. "Do you see her in any of the photos?"

"Where'd you get those?" Gregory looked up at me, surprise in his pretty hazel eyes. But then he shook his head. "I don't think she was in the official group photo, though ... I can't really be sure. I think I drank too much, I can't really remember what happened after we played with the Ouija board. But I got home before two—Rebecca vouched for me."

"What about the other members? Who were they?"

He listed a few names I already knew: Ellen Chambers, Mike Perkins, Oliver Huffman, his sister Nichol. I noted them on the back of the picture.

"Did you notice Oliver's face is turned away in the photo?" I asked. "Do you think there's any significance to that? Did he not want to be associated with the dinners?"

Gregory shook his head. "He's always been in them before. Everyone knows we're all friends with Malachi." His voice dropped. "Or were friends with Malachi. I swear I don't know what's happening to me. Even my hair's falling out."

I took a moment to examine him. He was pale, his eyes red. I wouldn't be surprised if he were losing weight, unable to sleep. Common symptoms of anxiety and misery.

I don't usually offer help that hasn't been asked of me. But in this case, the despondent, ill-looking man in front of me was Bronwyn's son-in-law, and Imogen's daddy. He wasn't destined to be one of my favorite people, but he was important to Bronwyn's daughter, and even more so to her grandchildren.

"Gregory, if I mix you a tonic, would you take it?"

"Like a gin and tonic? I'm trying to cut back."

"No—this is the kind of tonic you'll have to trust me on. A brew made of botanicals."

He looked me up and down, really seeing me for the first time since I'd arrived. There was a dawning realization in his lovely eyes. They narrowed, marred now with doubt and a sort of disgusted loathing, as though he had just discovered something slick and rancid on the bottom of his shoe.

"Wait a minute—you said you work with my mother-in-law?"

I nodded.

"Oh . . . Okay. Now I get it. Look, lady, no offense, but *please*. I don't truck with that stuff."

"And yet you believe you're suffering under a curse?"

"All I need is to get back to work, get my family back, and get everything back to normal. You know, my own parents were never there for me. I respect Rebecca's wishes for the interim, but I want to be there for my kids, one way or the other, no matter what."

The thrumming was back, dank and funereal.

I reached out and grabbed his hands, holding them lightly in mine. I had to ask.

"Gregory," I said, fixing him with a steady gaze. "Did you kill Malachi Zazi? Accidentally, maybe? Or in a rage, maybe it wasn't your fault?"

"No. I swear I didn't."

"And the only reason the police were questioning you is because of the testimony of your friend Oliver, who overheard the argument?"

He nodded.

I wished I could believe him one hundred percent, but my witchy lie detector abilities weren't all that accurate. I had been fooled before, and probably would be again. Still, Gregory gave off waves of fear and anxiety, but I sensed no deep, soul-wrenching guilt.

I glanced over at Sailor, who gave me a quick shake of his head.

I sighed. "Okay, let's go."

"Go where?"

"I need you to take me to see this Oliver person. Your old school buddy. Your accuser."

"I don't see why we're doing this," whined Gregory as we drove across town toward Oliver Huffman's house, which, according to Gregory, was part of a "family compound" out by the Legion of Honor. "Why are you even involved in this?"

"I just am."

"But—"

Sailor kicked at the back of Gregory's seat. "Accept what's being offered with good grace, pal."

I smiled at Sailor's reflection in the rearview mirror.

"Oliver won't even talk to us, probably," Gregory continued, seemingly on the edge of tears. His whipped-victim act was making me much more annoyed than sympathetic.

Clearly he was not at his best, I thought, attempting to be charitable. Still, I didn't have a lot of patience for folks who go through life with a sense of entitlement, as though the world owes them something, and then fall apart at the first sign of difficulty.

"That's why we didn't call ahead," I said. "We'll stand a better chance face-to-face. Why don't you tell me about him as we drive."

"We were good friends in high school. A bunch of us were. His father's a politician. A U.S. senator, a very big name. But lately he hasn't been doing all that well, either. I'm telling you, we've all felt the aftereffects of those dinners."

I glanced in the rearview mirror again. Sailor was slumped in the backseat, scowling. Oscar was cowed by Sailor's mere presence, but the cat kept trying to win him over. I smiled as I watched the animal nudge Sailor's elbow with staunch feline persistence.

At Gregory's instruction, I turned off the main drag and into a pristine maze of neat, manicured, Mediterranean-style homes. Between the houses I caught fleeting glimpses of the Pacific. I imagined the residents had enviable, multimillion-dollar views of the sea.

Finally we pulled up to an elaborate gate with a security kiosk. The elegant white stucco, tile-roofed home looked like something straight out of the heyday of Hollywood. I half expected Cary Grant to come strolling out the ornately carved front door and down the driveway.

The security guard approached the passenger-side window and asked who we were. Gregory hesitated.

I leaned over him: "We're here to see Oliver Huffman?"

"Your name?"

"It's Gregory Petrovic and friends."

"One moment." The man consulted a clipboard, went

into his little kiosk, made a phone call, nodded, then opened the gate and waved us through.

Gravel popped and crunched as I pulled ahead into the elegant circular driveway, with the main house ahead of us and several cottages and outbuildings on each side. A well-tended lawn, a fountain, and clipped menagerie hedges made up the front yard. This would be quite a spread anywhere, but in a town like San Francisco I imagined it was almost unheard of. Stuck as it is on a thumb of land surrounded by water on three sides, the City by the Bay has no room to grow, and land is at a premium.

If this was the sort of privilege Oliver, Gregory, and Malachi had been raised in, they clearly were the movers and shakers—or at least the children of the movers and shakers—of this town.

"I'll stay with the . . . livestock," Sailor said, jerking his thumb toward the animals in the back.

"Fine, thanks," I said, handing him the keys, just in case. "We shouldn't be too long."

As Gregory and I got out of the car we were greeted by a muscular young man with an earpiece and a shaved head. He wore a pink polo shirt and white pants, adding to the Hollywood vibe of the place. His dark skin gleamed in the afternoon sun.

"Follow me," said the man.

Our footsteps crunched on the crushed granite driveway as we trailed him to one of the charming stucco cottages on the grounds, right past a tiny, lush, perfectly green lawn ringed with roses, lavender, and paperwhites.

Inside, the place was decorated in a chic but impersonal style, rather like a posh hotel. Over the mantel was a huge family portrait that had been taken on the beach with the Golden Gate in the background; to a person they were blond and affluent-looking, wearing spotless white tennis outfits.

A dozen or so people, with name tags affixed to their chests, stood and sat in the small living room. Everyone seemed to be arranged around, and looking expectantly at, one man on the couch.

Could this be Oliver Huffman, the "venture capitalist," as Rebecca had referred to him? Blond and good-looking, he was nervous, twitching. I recognized the signs from Conrad and a lot of the other street kids in the Haight: Oliver Huffman had been too long on too many drugs. Even young, otherwise healthy bodies fight back. The vibrations of an addict are of a very specific sort—they ricochet, out of control, mostly out of reach. The energy called up by the drug quickly disperses, leaving a void, a nothingness. Nature abhors a vacuum, so negative forces rush in, take up residence. The only immediate relief is more narcotics. It must be horrific.

"Come in, come in. I'm Senator Jonathan Huffman. You're welcome here," said a man in his late sixties, with a booming, commanding voice.

He was hale and hearty, a ruddy glow under an expensive haircut. Dressed in a navy blue jacket over khaki pants, he wore an honest-to-gosh ascot at his throat. He exuded wealth and privilege, innate confidence. And an overanxious need to be liked. He had one arm wrapped around a woman similar in age, who was fragile and birdlike, almost lost in her Nancy Reagan–style bright red ensemble. She nodded at us and smiled.

"You're friends of Oliver's, I presume?" asked the senator.

"Oh, hey, Gregory," said Oliver with a lift of his chin, his voice quavering slightly. "Dad, you remember. These are some friends from high school. Gregory Petrovic, and . . ." His voice trailed off as he realized he didn't recognize me.

All eyes focused on me. Suddenly I wished Sailor were here.

"I'm Lily Ivory," I said. "I'm sorry. Are we intruding?"

"Aren't you here for the intervention?"

"Intervention?"

"I think they may have stumbled into this accidentally, Dad," said a well-groomed man as he stood to talk with us. He looked like a less good-looking, slightly older version of Oliver. Though his comments were directed to us, he met Oliver's eyes as he spoke. "I'm Oliver's brother, Atticus. Oliver has a substance-abuse problem, and we're gathered here today to let him know that his friends and family, while we love and support him, are no longer willing to support him in his habits."

"Right, right you are, son," the senator said. "We don't want to see anything happen to Oliver here."

I searched the room for a therapist running things. There were no likely candidates, no one speaking up. Most of the attendees seemed enthralled with their watches, or their hems, or the view from the large multi-paned windows that looked out over the lush seaside garden. There was another blond woman who bore a striking resemblance to Oliver, a couple of men his age, a few teenagers, and several aging women who might be relatives. None of them wanted to be here, all of them sending out waves of embarrassment and discomfiture.

"Sorry you got caught in the middle of all of this," said Atticus.

"No, we're the ones who should be apologizing," said

Gregory. "We certainly didn't mean to interrupt. We'll just leave you to it—"

He turned toward the door.

"Don't leave," said Oliver. His eyes were rimmed in red, and despite his natural handsomeness he looked dissolute, the type whose looks soon would be ravaged by too much abuse. "Dude, I feel really bad about the cops going after you like that. I didn't mean for that to happen. I was just . . . like I just told them what I heard and they came to their own conclusions."

"I know," Gregory said. He stopped his nervous shifting, met Oliver's eyes, and spoke in a surprisingly warm, calm voice. "No worries."

"Glad you're not behind bars, anyway," said Oliver.

"Behind bars?" Oliver's father asked. "What are you talking about?"

"I haven't even told you this part," Oliver said. "There was a murder."

"A *murder*? And you were involved?"

"Just barely. It's the bad luck," Oliver mumbled. "Everything in my life has turned to sh—"

"*Oliver,*" snapped his father. "There are ladies present."

"Sorry," Oliver said, eyes flickering over to his mother.

"This totally blows," said one of the younger participants, a fair-haired teenager who looked as though he might be a cousin. All in all, the Huffman family resemblance was startling. "I'm *so* gonna bounce. I'm outta here."

He got up off a muted gray couch and went out the front door, trailed by two other teenage girls. Like an anthill that had been disturbed, the others began to shift in their seats, looking for their own excuses to leave.

"A murder." The senator shook his head, his ruddy complexion turning even redder. "Are you kidding me? Just when were you going to mention this?"

"Maybe once you chilled over this thing," said Oliver. "*Damn*, I woke up to all of you, all of this—"

"It's one o'clock in the afternoon!"

"I was out late," Oliver said.

"I'll just bet you were. Out late and involved in a *murder*?"

"He wasn't involved," said Gregory, stepping in to stand up for his friend—the same friend who had fingered him to the police. "It happened night before last. And Oliver was just a dinner guest, like I was. Later that night, after we'd all left, our host was killed. It has nothing to do with any of us."

"Yeah," Oliver said. "Nichol and I came back early. The police already checked the kiosk security log."

"And who was this host?" asked the senator.

"Malachi Zazi."

He threw up his hands. "I thought I told you to stay away from that lunatic!"

"He wasn't a lunatic, Dad," said the lovely young blond woman in a soft, sweet voice.

The senator ignored the interruption. "Do you have any idea what Malachi Zazi's father is capable of? Are you kidding me?" The senator made a disgusted sound, whirled around, and went to stare out the window, hands on his hips.

"So you were there that night also?" Atticus asked of us.

"Just me," said Gregory. "And Oliver, and Nichol was there as well."

"And your friend . . . ?"

Again, all eyes rested on me. I was clearly the odd one out.

"I wasn't there, but the police asked me to look into the crime," I said. My phrasing made it sound more official than it was. I cringed inwardly that I hadn't thought to come up with some logical description of who I was, and why I was asking questions.

"You're a police officer?" asked Atticus, clearly doubtful.

"No, I—"

"Don't say another word," bellowed Senator Huffman to everyone still gathered in the room. He stuck his arm out, hand held up, as though stopping traffic. "None of you. I'm calling my lawyer."

"Oh, dear," said the mother, the first peep out of her.

"It's not that kind of thing," I said. "I'm not a police officer; nothing I hear could be used against you in a court of law." It sounded like a rather twisted version of the Miranda rights.

"I'd still feel better if you left, young lady," the senator said, his cell phone already held up to his ear. "This is a private family matter."

"I understand," I said. "I apologize that we broke in on your meeting. I'll go."

"I'll see you out," said brother Atticus.

"I'll join you," said the blond woman who spoke earlier. Her name tag read "Nichol."

As we stepped outside into the cool air, I asked, "Nichol Reiss?"

She laughed, a tinkling, lovely sound. "That's my screen name, yes. Thank you for recognizing me."

Atticus came up behind his sister and put his hand on her elbow.

"I thought we'd never escape. The whole intervention thing's a good idea, but Dad insisted on doing it himself, without a real therapist, and . . . Sorry. This isn't your problem. But I appreciate your coming along and giving us an excuse to break up the sad little party."

"I take it you both know about what happened to Malachi Zazi?" I asked.

The siblings exchanged a significant glance.

"I'm not a cop, or a reporter. I give you my word," I said. "I'm just looking into this, in part to help Gregory. Maybe we could sit for a minute, talk about a few things?"

After another shared look, Atticus shrugged. "I guess it couldn't hurt."

We all took seats at a glass café table situated under a low-hanging Canary palm. The air was heavy with the scent of honeysuckle and the brine of the ocean. Birds twittered, splashing in a nearby carved birdbath. Sad to think a person could grow up in a place as bucolic and graceful as this and still turn out to be a miserable, drug-addled adult.

"You'll have to excuse our dad," Atticus said. "He's a politician, always has been. The habits run deep. But we all really care, as a family, about what happens to Oliver."

"I can see that," I said. "So you both knew about Zazi's murder?"

"Yes," said Nichol, her beautiful eyes filling with tears. "Dad's been out of town 'til today, so I guess he didn't hear. But the police came by and talked with us. We all knew Malachi, since way back in high school. He was a friend. And I was at that last dinner, too."

"Look, Oliver has a drug dependence—that much is

clear. And we're going to get him into treatment, one way or the other." Atticus shook his head. "But even when he's high, he could never do anything violent to anyone. That's just not his way."

In my experience people could do things under the influence of drugs they would never imagine. It snatches a bit of one's soul—that was precisely the problem.

"Did you witness the argument between Gregory and Malachi as well?" I asked Nichol.

She shook her head. "But you know, it's embarrassing to say—it always took me so long to get the damned dress on that I was always late. We all were, all the women."

A little brown sparrow swooped onto a low branch near the table. It made jerky, robotic movements with its head, reminding me of the bird flitting through Malachi Zazi's apartment, signifying death. Funny how something so innocuous in one setting could be so threatening in another.

"What was Malachi like?" I asked Nichol.

"He wasn't like they say. He wasn't crazy." Her eyes shone with tears. She was truly lovely, almost otherworldly. "He set those bad luck symbols out to disprove their power, in the pursuit of rationalism."

"I hear his father was . . . odd. Were the symbols—"

Nichol jumped up, hurried across a patch of lawn, and disappeared into the cottage next door to Oliver's.

"Nichol and Malachi had a . . . relationship," Atticus explained in a low voice. "She's been very upset over his demise."

"Oh. I'm sorry to hear that," I said. "Is that why your father was so upset to hear Malachi Zazi's name?"

"Like I said, Dad's a politician. I guess none of us

turned out quite the way he'd like. We're far from perfect offspring." Giving a self-deprecating smile, Atticus tucked his head and looked for all the world like a child at that moment.

Atticus said, "You've probably heard of Nicky's famous Hollywood meltdown, and now Oliver...." He let out a breath and shook his head, then leaned forward and put his elbows on his knees. "We've been trying of keep him out of the news for the last couple of years. He's an addict. It's a disease, plain and simple. But you know how these things play out in the public eye. It becomes fodder for every tabloid TV show on slow news days. Dad's up for reelection this year. It would be a public relations disaster."

"I can imagine. Sounds like your father wasn't wild about y'all having any kind of relationship to Malachi."

"You can say that again."

We all fell silent for a moment. I thought I could hear the sound of the ocean, the mighty Pacific pounding against the rocks at the bottom of the cliff. I wouldn't mind a nice cleansing walk on the beach at this point.

"So your whole family lives here together?"

"Oliver and Nichol still live here with my folks, but I haven't spent more than a night under my parents' roof since I went off to Princeton. They're good people, and they were loving parents. But I had my fill of political dinners and cocktail parties by the time I was in middle school. It's not really my style. I couldn't wait to get out of this life."

"Atticus is the one escapee from chez Huffman," said Nichol, returning to the table with a small bundle in her hands and a beaming smile on her face, suitable for an *Entertainment Tonight* photo shoot. A delicate pink

blush around her eyes was the only sign she'd been crying. She had refreshed her makeup and lipstick, and
looked radiant and beautiful.

I thought about her coming into Aunt Cora's Closet
yesterday. This seemed like one too many coincidences,
but I couldn't figure out how they would all fit together
as part of some plan.

"Atticus lives out in the Marina, with a great wife, two
beautiful kids, the perfect dog, and he even has a real
job. Dad must wonder why he couldn't have just made
three of us in his mold."

"Are you kidding me?" Atticus said, mimicking the
deep voice of his father. "What would Dad do without
his little princess? He adores you."

Nichol reached out and fluffed Atticus's hair. It must
be nice to have a sibling, I thought, to have that kind of
ease with someone. And they were both clearly commit-
ted to helping their brother Oliver as well. The Huffman
parents must have done something right, to instill such
closeness in their children.

Nichol set the package on the table—it was an old-
fashioned stack of letters sealed with red wax and tied
with a baby blue satin ribbon. I thought they might be
antique, but the envelopes showed none of the yellow-
ing that comes with age.

"Malachi sent me these," she said, reverence in her
voice.

"What are they?"

"Love letters. Poems." She undid the bow slowly; the
blue satin gleamed in the sun. She extracted the top letter and handed it to me.

"I didn't think anyone wrote real letters anymore," I
said. "Sealed with wax, no less." The wax had been

pressed by a ring with a snake design, a symbol of Serpentarius.

"I know, right? Malachi was so gentlemanly, old-fashioned," Nichol said. "It was as though he'd been pulled out of another century."

I glanced over at the silent Atticus.

"Don't look at me," he said with a duck of his head. "I haven't exchanged more than a dozen words with the guy since high school. I was never invited to his exclusive dinner club."

Nichol elbowed him good-naturedly. "Don't act like you were missing out. I could have gotten you an invitation if you'd really wanted."

"People sitting around in costumes, looking at bad luck signs?" He smiled and shook his head. "Not what I'd call my thing."

"Oliver mentioned that he'd had a lot of bad luck lately," I said. "Gregory feels that way, too. Have you experienced anything like that, Nichol?"

"My whole life's been bad luck."

Atticus gave her a wry look.

"Okay, it's true that I've had a hand in that myself. No, any bad luck I've had is my own fault." She looked at Atticus and smiled. He nodded as though proud of her.

I bowed my head and concentrated on the letter from Malachi, trying to sense any emotions coming from it. I felt sadness, a deep kind of soul in darkness, as in depression. But the sensations were vague, muted partly because I couldn't concentrate properly with all these people around, and partly because I wasn't as sensitive to other objects as I was to clothes. Which reminded me . . .

"Did you happen to take your gown home, Nichol?"

"The gown we wore to the Serpentarius dinners? Actually, I have several of the women's gowns here. We'd meet here first and help each other button up, that sort of thing. Those dresses are a real pain."

"Do you think I could take them with me when I go, check them out?"

"Check them out how?" asked Gregory.

Only then did I realize it sounded like an odd request. What possible normal reason could there be for wanting to look at the dresses?

"I wanted to compare them to some of the old pictures of the original Thirteen Club, the one that the Serpentarius Society was based on," I said. Not that it made any sense.

"Oh, okay," said Nichol with a shrug. "Sure. They just make me sad now, anyway. Go ahead, read the letter."

I opened the envelope. A slanted, elegant hand had written a long, emotional ode to Nichol's beauty, grace, and smile. It was an eloquent treatise on love and devotion, and it ended: *One day it will all be as it should be, and you and I shall walk arm in arm, facing the world as a couple, walking as two should walk, never again alone.*

A wave of sadness washed over me as I remembered the man in my vision, huge hourglass in his hands . . . his time running out.

"Can you believe that?" Nichol asked, staring at me, tears once again welling in her eyes. "You really think the son of a devil could write something like that?"

Chapter 11

"The 'son of a devil'?"

"That's what everyone called him."

"Back in school," Atticus explained. "I was a couple of years older, but everyone heard the rumors. We all knew his house. Poor kid tried to be normal, but with a dad like that . . ."

"Did you know his father?" I asked.

"Only by reputation."

"The 'Prince'?" Gregory spoke up. "I've caught sight of him once or twice. But we all knew what he was about. And I guess we knew a little about what Malachi went through in that house. It couldn't have been easy to be raised that way."

"Do you know why his father called himself a prince?" I asked.

"Not exactly . . . I always figured he was what you'd call self-proclaimed royalty."

"In what sense?"

"In the sense that he pretty much made himself king, or prince anyway, of his little world."

"As in . . . Prince of Darkness?"

"Something like that."

"Wow. No wonder his son was a little . . ."

"Screwed up? True. But he wasn't a bad person."

"So it was Malachi, Gregory, Nichol, and Oliver at that last dinner. Who else?"

"Mike Perkins," said Nichol.

"I can't believe Mike would get mixed up in that sort of thing," said Atticus with a shake of his head. "Mike's many things, but I wouldn't imagine he'd be interested in the occult in any way."

"How do you know him?" I asked.

"I used to work at Perkins Laboratories, but that was a few years ago. The money was great, but I was happy to move on. My dad was an investor in his company years ago, and Mike donated to Dad's campaigns. I thought it might be perceived as a political problem that I worked for him, too many connections."

"So you and Gregory both worked for Perkins? And your father was connected to him politically?"

"Sort of. Oliver worked for him for a while as well. It's not as odd as it might sound—the man owns an important corporation, and employs people he's known and trusted for years."

"I think I was the first connection there," Gregory said. "Mike recruited me as a researcher straight out of grad school. Then I got Oliver the job, though he didn't last long. But half this city's had dealings with Mike Perkins; even Malachi's father, Prince High, was an investor in Perkins Laboratories."

"I guess everyone's looking to diversify," said Atticus. "Even the devil himself."

"Atticus, Nichol, do either of you know a woman named Doura?"

"There was a woman by that name at the dinner on Saturday night," said Nichol.

"Did she say anything about herself? Do you have any idea how I could get in touch with her?"

Nichol shook her head. "She looked lovely, though. She wore a red brocade that really set off her coloring."

I glanced at Atticus.

"I don't know her," he said, shaking his head.

There didn't seem to be much more to discuss. Nichol and Atticus retrieved several plastic-shrouded antique gowns from Nichol's cottage, and together we carried them to the van.

This perfect, precious little world seemed marred by the presence of my dusty purple van in the drive. In this glittering picture of privilege it should have been a shining Jaguar or Lexus, like in the car commercials. It was sad that despite all the outer trappings of beauty, the Huffman family was marked by difficulty, substance abuse, shoplifting. . . . Only Atticus appeared relatively unscathed, but I knew how that went: He was the perfect one, the one keeping it together because he had to hold up everyone's end. I wondered whether, if Nichol and Oliver ever managed to pull themselves together, he would fall apart.

I thought about what Rebecca had said, that it couldn't be easy to grow up as a senator's child. Or like Gregory, with his wealthy but absent parents. Or certainly as the son of a man who considered himself a devilish prince.

On the other hand, Oliver and Atticus and Nichol had one another, as well as parents—however challenging—who loved them, which was a lot more than many of us could claim.

When I first encountered Malachi's corpse on the table mere days ago, I thought he must have been orchestrating something evil, something wrong. But now, reading his letters, talking to his friends, it was hard to know what to think. They painted a different picture of the man entirely. As though he were yet another victim. Could he really have been simply trying to disprove the tenets of his father's life, reacting to the superstitious chaos he had grown up in?

"Thank you for helping to figure things out, for finding out what happened," Nichol said, a little hiccup in her throat. She hugged me.

I was never sure what to do in these circumstances. I'm not really a hugger. Feeling awkward, I patted her on the back. Nichol's vibrations were young. Younger than her years. I was getting the distinct impression that most of these Serpentarians were immature and silly, rather than sinister.

I noted a bracelet on Nichol's arm that had been covered by her sleeve earlier. It was distinctive, made of lace and worked silver links.

Last time I saw that bracelet, it was in my shop, near the display shelf of silk scarves.

"Nichol, how did you come to pass by Aunt Cora's Closet yesterday?"

"What kind of closet?"

"It's a vintage clothing store on Haight Street."

"Oh! I did go by there. How did you know?"

"I own that store. My assistant mentioned that she saw you. She recognized you. She's a fan," I added, covering up the suspicions of shoplifting.

"When I get stressed out I shop. I know what you're thinking," she said to her brother. "But it's not like that anymore . . . I just . . . the last time I was at Malachi's apartment I saw this newsletter for the Art Deco Society and it mentioned that store had a lot of pieces from the era. That was back when I thought Malachi and I were going to go to the dance together. Before . . ."

Her voice trailed off; she looked out toward the main house, her gaze far away.

"Why is a shopkeeper looking into a murder?" Atticus asked, a quizzical expression on his face.

"It's a little hard to explain . . . but believe me when I tell you I'm trying to help."

Atticus took a deep breath and let it out in a slow, thoughtful sigh. Then he nodded. "We'd appreciate your keeping our family's name out of any of this, to the extent that you can."

"Of course," I said. "I can't speak for the police, of course, but if Oliver wasn't even there after the dinner, there's no reason his name should be mentioned in conjunction with the case."

"Tell Oliver good-bye from me," Gregory said to Atticus. "Tell him to give me a call when things are a little calmer."

"I'll let him know."

We said our good-byes. Gregory and I climbed into the van and pulled down the driveway. My mind was racing, thinking of my next stop.

It was high time I went by the "black abode." Not that I believed Malachi was the son of any sort of devil, but I wanted to have a little chat with Daddy Zazi.

*   *   *

We dropped Gregory back at his temporary dwelling, the Hotel Wharton, and watched him slump in through the front door.

"About time we got rid of that sad sack," Sailor said. "What a *drag*."

"So says Mr. Happy-go-lucky."

"Hey, compared to him I'm a ray of sunshine."

"Gregory's got call to be sad. He thinks he's losing his family."

"With an attitude like that, they're better off without him. Anyway," he said, clapping his hands together loudly enough to make our animal companions both jump and pay attention, "is it just me, or is it well past lunchtime? I thought the least those rich folks could have done was to offer us snacks."

Oscar snorted his approval.

"I guess I'm a might peckish as well," I conceded. Glancing down at my watch, I saw it was after two o'clock.

"I know a great taco truck not too far from here," said Sailor. "Best carnitas in town. Take a left on Fourteenth."

Oscar, who had turned back into his natural form, harrumphed in the backseat. Given that he spent half his time lately as a potbellied pig, he had become sensitive on the subject of pork. I never ate it anymore myself. Or bacon . . . and I used to *adore* bacon. My mouth watered just thinking of it.

I followed Sailor's directions to a truck that had set up business in the parking lot of an abandoned-looking drugstore. I ordered vegetarian options for me and Oscar, and chicken for the cat. Sailor, refusing to be cowed by what he called a gremlin, ordered beef and pork.

While Sailor waited for the food, I took advantage of a rare public telephone to check in at Aunt Cora's Closet. Maya told me all was well, Bronwyn had arrived, sales were good, and then added, "Max called."

"He did? What did he say?"

"He's in town, I guess. He's looking for you."

Terrible timing. This whole Malachi Zazi thing seemed custom-tailored as the sort of supernaturally charged mess Max would not want to be mixed up in. But still . . . I was glad he called. And Maya didn't really know what I was up to, so—

"I didn't talk to him, Bronwyn did. They had quite a long talk. She told him all about what was going on at home, poor thing."

"She told him everything?"

"She said you were helping out, talking to some folks. That you started by talking to that other reporter over at the paper. Hey, I've got a line forming. I'd better go."

I kept my hand on the phone receiver for a moment, thinking. *Great.* Max had finally called, and now I reckoned he knew exactly what I was up to. Bronwyn told him all the details, no doubt. Would he try to talk me out of what I was doing, or mind his own business, or go after—

"Food," Sailor said, interrupting my thoughts. He gestured at me with hands full of overstuffed tacos.

We sat on a low cinder-block wall to enjoy. I put the animals' food on the cracked concrete sidewalk in front of us.

"So when you read Gregory's mind, did it tell you anything?" I asked, biting into a scrumptious cheese and guacamole taco. It was so good I sighed and let out a little moan.

Sailor looked amused. "Hungry?"

I smiled. "I hadn't realized 'til right this minute."

He took a huge bite of taco and shook his head. "I didn't read Gregory's mind."

"You didn't? Back in the hotel room?"

He shook his head again, finishing off one of his *carne de res* tacos.

"But you gave me a little signal when I looked over at you, a little flick of your head."

"That had nothing to do with reading his mind. It meant he was a jerk."

"So we don't know for sure that he's innocent?"

"I think it's pretty clear. I doubt a man like that is capable of murder."

"And you know this how? Why didn't you read his mind?"

"I don't just go around reading minds on a whim, you know. It takes work. It takes energy. And it's kind of . . . creepy."

"'Creepy'?"

"Makes me feel like a stalker." Sailor seemed almost embarrassed. "There are privacy issues, for crissakes."

I blew out a frustrated breath. Super. A reluctant psychic with an overdeveloped sense of ethics.

Two sets of eyes were riveted on us. Oscar and the cat had inhaled their snacks and were now attempting porcine and feline mind control, respectively, trying through sheer force of will to compel Sailor and me to drop our food.

"We're not far from the Richmond District, are we?" I asked.

"What do you need in the Richmond?"

"I'm going to the Devil's House. The black abode. Whatever it's called."

"You can't just go over there."

"Why not? Do you know the 'prince'?"

"No, of course I don't know him. No one in their right mind would associate with a man like that."

"Do you even believe in that sort of thing? That devil stuff?"

"No, but . . . I believe that he believes. In a way it's worse. At least when you're dealing with an actual demon there are clearly established rules of the game."

"I guess you're right at that. Anyway, that's where I'm headed. Suppose Aidan will mind?"

Sailor looked at me, startled, guilt in his dark eyes.

"Come on, Sailor, we both know that Aidan sent you."

"He did not."

"Did too. I don't have to be a psychic to figure out that much. What does he want?"

He shrugged.

"Did you really expect me to buy the idea that you just wanted to 'hang out' with someone like me?"

"You're not that bad."

"From you, I'll take that as high praise. So what did Aidan tell you to do? What are you looking for?"

"Dunno exactly. I'm supposed to keep tabs on you."

"Keep 'tabs' on me?"

"That's what the man said."

"What does that consist of, exactly?"

"I'm sort of playing this by the seat of my pants here," Sailor said with a shrug. "With most folks, I can track them from afar. Since I can't read your mind, that wasn't an option. So here I am. Like a very poorly paid private eye following an unfaithful spouse."

"And then what? You tell Aidan where I've been?"

"Something like that. It appears that his other sources haven't been all that reliable."

He shot a glance toward Oscar, who snorted, ducked down, and became suddenly fascinated by the cat.

"Well, I'm headed to the black abode," I said as I stood and started to gather our trash. "Want me to drop you off somewhere on the way?"

Sailor let out a long-suffering sigh. "No, I'll go with you."

My reluctant stalker.

Chapter 12

The Devil's House was pretty easy to spot.

A run-down Victorian on a busy street, it was painted a solid black that might once have been shocking, but which now had faded to a matte dark gray. A chain-link fence topped with barbed wire surrounded the front yard: a patch of tall dry grass strewn with papers, plastic bags, a couple of smashed wooden chairs, a bureau missing half its drawers, and a soiled mattress. In the driveway sat a generic-looking silver Honda Civic, its everyday blandness making the stark house seem even stranger.

Glancing at the perfectly normal Victorians on either side, prettily painted in shades of white, gold, and yellow, I couldn't help but wonder what the neighbors must think.

"Looks like the Addams family home the day after a frat party," Sailor said as I pulled into a parking space at the curb not far from the house. "I don't suppose I can talk you out of this?"

"I just want to talk with him."

"I can't go in there with you. There are reasons. . . ." His voice trailed off, and then he just said, "Aidan wouldn't allow it."

"Stay here with the animals, then. That's best anyway."

He held my eyes for a long moment.

"Screw Aidan. If you need me, I'll come with you."

"No, Sailor, really. I'm more likely to learn something useful if I speak to him one-on-one, in any case."

"If you need me, shout. Loudly."

"Literally, or psychically?"

He smiled. "Psychically should do it. Just let me know you need me, put some of your considerable power behind it, and I'll come."

"Thanks."

As I walked to the gate, I told myself that however underwhelming the black abode might seem at first glance, it was best to take it seriously. Evil can lurk behind the most mundane façades: the quaint tile-roofed adobes that dotted the town of my youth; a bucolic thatched-roof hut in Botswana where I barely escaped a pointed finger and a whispered accusation of "witch"; the fairy-tale houses of a remote Bavarian town where I finally tracked my father, and found so much more than I'd bargained for, so many years ago.

Anyone who would name his home after the devil, whether it was just a ploy to make money or a sincere belief, was to be treated carefully.

I was reaching out for the gate when a man's voice came from behind me.

"Lily."

It was a voice I knew well. Max Carmichael.

"*Max*, what in the world are you doing here?"

I glanced back at the van, hoping Sailor had the sense to quite literally lie low. The last time Max spotted Sailor he hauled off and socked him in the eye. Not over me, mind you, but still. Things were feeling a little unpredictable at the moment. The last thing I needed was boys fighting in front of the black abode. Talk about a frat party.

"I called the store. Bronwyn told me you were working on a case involving her son-in-law. Then Nigel told me you were asking about the father of the victim, and the location of his charming house."

"So you figured I'd come here."

He smiled. "Hard to believe you'd talk to this guy alone, but then again . . . it made a certain kind of sense, in Lily-land."

I noted a coffee stain on his white T-shirt and a few crumbs on his jeans. He appeared haggard, his gray eyes weary. And yet, somehow, he looked great.

"You mean you sat in your car, just waiting for me? How long?"

He shrugged. "I had lunch. Good a place as any."

"You still haven't told me why you're here."

"I thought I might need to rescue you."

"Rescue *me*?"

"After a fashion."

"From?"

"That man's a nutcase."

"I have no need of being rescued. Much less a desire to be rescued. If there's any rescuing to be done I'll do it myself, thank you very much."

Out of the corner of my eye I saw a flutter of drapes. Someone was looking down at us from a second-story window. I raised a hand in greeting. A buzzer sounded, and I unlatched the gate.

Max stayed close on my heels. Apparently I had swapped one bodyguard for another.

The gate clanged shut behind us.

The cement walkway was cracked and studded with weeds; the wooden porch steps were rotting, the boards sagging and creaking under today's pink Keds–clad feet. An improvised beam of wood lying atop two ladders seemed to be holding up the roof of the front portico. I was getting the distinct sense that business wasn't great these days.

A moment later I heard voices coming from behind the door. Again, like the house itself, they seemed less frightening than mundane, everyday voices squabbling over who should answer the door. Two female, one male.

Finally, the door swung inward. Creaking. Just like a haunted house. I rolled my eyes. But I was brought up short, the laughter dying in my throat at the woman standing in front of me.

It was the woman I had seen in the store. The time-bender, Doura. She smiled, one bloodred-tipped hand clutching the edge of the door as though ready to slam it shut. A mass of blond curls hung down to her ample breasts, much of which were on display above a sweetheart neckline. Her eyes were outlined with heavy black liner, accented by bright blue eye shadow.

"I wondered when you would show up," she said with her jarringly baby-doll voice, malevolence in her blue-green heavy-lidded eyes.

"How nice to see you again," I lied, hoping—but not expecting—to win her over with exaggerated good manners, as my mama would do.

"Who's *this*?" she asked, giving Max a blatant once-over and a sexy smile.

"I'm her bodyguard," Max said. "Pretend I'm not even here."

"Easier said than done, handsome," Doura said.

"I was hoping to find Prince High Zazi at home?" I interrupted.

"Prince High? Oh, Prince High!" she called over her shoulder, still studying me, smiling.

Descending the shadowy stairs was the goateed man who had accompanied Doura when first I saw her. He moved slowly, one gaunt hand gripping the banister, the other holding a cane for support. He was a lanky man, and must have been taller, I thought, before the ravages of age. His hair and goatee were dyed that sooty black. His eyebrows formed dramatic, upside-down vees over his eyes.

"Prince High?" I asked.

Doura laughed again.

"It's the *High* Prince!" said the man. His voice betrayed none of the frailty of his physical form—it was deep, mellow. I thought of what Nigel said, that this man had once been a magnetic, charismatic leader. "How many times do I have to tell you people? *High Prince of Hell.* Not Prince High. It's as though people mangle it on purpose."

Demons refer to themselves as "high princes." I might be unsure about a lot of things lately, but this much was clear: The old man before me was no demon.

"My name's Lily Ivory," I said. "We sort of met the other day . . . I was hoping I could ask you a few questions about your son."

"My son." He leaned back, appearing more thoughtful than sad. "My son has passed."

"I know that, sir. I'm sorry for your loss—"

"And who's the stiff?"

"Max Carmichael," said Max. I noticed that neither man put his hand out to shake. Once again Doura's heated gaze raked over him, and she quite literally licked her lips.

"You're with the paper," said the Prince. "You enjoy exposing frauds, if I'm not mistaken."

"Among other things," Max said and nodded.

"I'm no fraud."

"Then there's no problem."

"Do you think we could sit, talk perhaps?" I interjected. I didn't want this discussion to be taken over by allegations of fraud. I had my own questions.

"She's a witch," Doura said to the Prince. "Don't you remember? The one from the thrift store."

"A witch?" he asked.

I nodded.

"You don't look much like a witch."

"You don't look much like a prince of darkness."

He smiled. "What kind of witchcraft do you practice?"

I took a deep breath. I still wasn't accustomed to just coming out and talking about things that were such deep, dark secrets not long ago. And I was acutely aware of Max's presence right behind me. "Root work, botanicals, mostly."

"Do you believe in sacrifice? Blood sacrifice?"

"When necessary."

His face split into a grin. An unsettling grin.

"Excellent. Most excellent. Shall we retire to the living room, where we can be more comfortable?"

"Surely, thank you," I said as I trailed his limping form through the dim foyer, into a living room dominated by a huge orange velour sectional sofa. Book-shelves and artwork covered just about every inch of wall space.

As we walked, he gestured behind him with one hand. "I believe you've met my high consort, Doura. And this," he said as the short-haired redhead joined us, "is another priestess, Tracy."

The Prince sank into the middle of his huge sectional, and the women sat on either side, sandwiching him.

"Nice to meet you both, officially," I said. Too nervous to join them on the sofa, I looked around at the objects in the room. Max leaned up against one wall, arms crossed over his chest, much as Sailor had earlier.

I noticed a large carved chair—almost a throne—with a small brass plaque identifying it as having once belonged to Rasputin. A vintage Tyrone Power *Nightmare Alley* movie poster adorned one wall, and a bright red cape with devil horns was draped across the shoulders of a mannequin, like an ornate grown-up Halloween costume. Human skulls, a shrunken head, and a Venus flytrap sat on one high shelf. Beside a vintage gramophone sat a small bed of nails.

A stuffed and mounted wolf guarded one corner, and as I walked toward it I smelled the unmistakable scent of reptiles. On the shelf behind the wolf were a number of aquariums, a fat snake in each. And near them, close enough for all of them to smell one another, a small brown sparrow trapped in an elaborate gilt cage.

"What's with the bird?" I asked, hoping it wasn't lunch.

"Don't you like pets?"

"It just seems . . . it's so close to the snakes, I would imagine it's frightened."

"Life is a frightening endeavor. Wouldn't you agree?"

I wasn't about to get into a philosophical discussion with this poser. "Still, would y'all mind if I moved it?"

Zazi poked Doura in the ribs. She, in turn, gave Tracy a look. Tracy rolled her eyes but came over and helped me move the cage about ten feet to one side of the snakes. I imagined they would move it back the second I left.

I gritted my teeth and reminded myself that my mission didn't have to do with animal cruelty, but with ascertaining what Prince High had to do with his son's death.

On a nearby bookshelf were several tomes attributed to the High Prince Zazi: *Devilish Rituals*, *The Devil's Bible*, *The Devil's Workshop*, *The Devil's Business*.

"*New York Times* bestsellers, almost every one of them," he told me proudly. "You know, others tried to establish their own, similar churches, but none came close to my success. I am the high priest and magister, the Magus of the Devil's Church. I even went on the *Phil Donahue Show*—there's a signed picture with him, right over there near the fireplace."

I took a look. Indeed, there was a much younger— but still goateed—Prince High, sitting onstage with the gray-haired Phil Donahue. There were several other photos of Prince High in the grouping; one of Aidan Rhodes and a woman I recognized as a local voodoo priestess, my friend Hervé's mentor, who had passed away several years ago. Aidan looked exactly the same in that photo as he did when I last saw him, two days ago.

"I have a theory as to why I rose so high above my competitors. Would you like to hear it?"

"Of course."

"America admires business savvy, rewards it. Simple belief isn't enough. The more successful, the richer I became, the more popular I was. I based my church on the writings of the great Ayn Rand, Friedrich Nietzsche, Jack London. They stood for individualism, the religion of materialism. *That's* what I admire. You are your own God."

"You are, or the devil is?"

"What is the devil?"

"I thought you might know, since you're the one who wrote the books."

He laughed. "Do you know Satanism is now a recognized religion in the U.S. military?"

"I didn't know that, no," I said. "But I had heard that Wicca is now recognized."

He made a disparaging sound and waved the idea away.

"You don't care for Wiccans?" I asked.

"All that hippie nonsense? No, not at all. You're not *that* kind of witch, are you?"

"No, I'm not Wicca," I said. My eyes alighted on a rich oil painting of a richly attired boy, à la the *Blue Boy*. Except that this one had fangs: It was a vampire child.

"Malachi posed for that when he was ten," Prince High said, pride in his voice.

"Why?" I asked. "I mean, why portray him as a vampire?"

He laughed. "Why not? Vampires are immortal, you know."

"And that very immortality is their curse, isn't it? Their damnation?"

"I suppose some think so. Personally, I wouldn't mind giving it a shot."

"Speaking of not aging, I understand you're an investor in Mike Perkins's antiaging business?"

"I am, yes."

"Is that just a run-of-the-mill investment, or do you have a particular interest in his research?"

"Look at these two." He smiled and gestured to both of his companions, who remained mute. "Aren't they beautiful? You'd never guess their ages. Go on, try."

"Oh, I'm no good at that game."

"Give it a whirl."

"Um . . ." I shaved a hunk of years off what I thought. "Thirty?"

"Ha! You see? Both of them are over forty. You'd never guess, would you?"

I smiled, trying and failing not to feel awkward with talking about the two women as though they weren't right here in the room with us. "They're lovely. But I never quite understood the motivation of trying to stay young. I mean, doesn't age bring with it knowledge, experience, all that? Why try to be something you're not?"

"It's the American dream, to remain young forever."

"Doura, I understand you were at Malachi's dinner on Saturday night?"

Without skipping a beat, she said, "No, I wasn't. I was right here."

"Are you sure?" I asked.

"She's quite sure," answered Prince Zazi.

"Is it true that you know Mike Perkins?"

"That part is true," the Prince interrupted. "Doura looks after my interests at Perkins Laboratories."

"What do you do there?" I asked her directly.

She just smiled, but remained mute.

Tracy could pass for someone's minion, remaining silent and allowing others to speak for her. But Doura was another matter. I had the distinct impression that if she wasn't talking, it was because she'd decided not to. Unless I was sorely mistaken, she was very much in charge of the situation.

"Were you close with your son, Malachi?"

"What kind of question is that?"

"I just wondered. He was found surrounded by bad luck symbols. Do you have any idea why?"

"I guess his luck ran out. You can't play with such things, you know. I'm sure you understand that much. These things have to be respected."

Max snorted. I'd wondered how long he would be able to maintain his composure while listening to this discussion.

"In any case," the Prince went on, "Malachi's thesis was faulty. In fact, if you check into his guests, they did have bad luck."

"I've heard that. And you think it's because they tempted fate?"

"Of course," he said, absentmindedly rubbing the handle of his cane. "I don't know where I went wrong with that boy. I taught him everything I knew, but by high school he gave in to peer pressure. I never should have allowed him to go to that prep school. He met the wrong sort of people. But his mother insisted. Then he spent his whole life trying to prove me false. Can you believe he set out to do that to his own father?"

Zazi spoke with the special disappointment fathers show to their children, a tone that another parent might use if Malachi had been involved with drugs or a criminal lifestyle. I wondered what my own father thought of me, a woman who now stood against everything he believed in as well.

"Those kids he invited to the dinners, *they're* the problem. I imagine one of them killed Malachi's earthly form."

"I believe the police are speaking with all of them."

"They're bad news. They're only interested in what they can get."

"But I don't understand—isn't that precisely the kind of materialism you espouse in your religion?"

He shook his head. "When it has no spiritual framework, no philosophical underpinnings, there is only selfishness and shallowness."

I didn't really "get" materialism as a life philosophy. In my mind, it had always been a condemnation, a bad thing. The belief that ephemeral, earthbound rewards were more important than nature, or love, or our very humanity. Perhaps I was naïve, but I couldn't bear to live in a world where material goods and comfort ranked higher than the sound of a child's laugh, or a lover's glance, or a friend's smile.

"If I've satisfied your curiosity, I'd like to get back to my bedchamber," said Prince High. He rose from the sofa with difficulty, leaning heavily on his cane. "It's time for my nap."

"Of course," I said, moving toward the foyer. "I like your house. How long have you lived here?"

"Since 1965. My son was born some years later, as I established my house of worship. You know, I believe my son will rise again. I even founded my church June 6, 1966. 666, a very powerful number. The devil's number."

"Actually, wouldn't June 6, 1966, make it 6666?"

He looked rather discomfited. "Yes. Of course."

Doura flung the front door wide, and met my eyes. I couldn't repress a shiver. Unlike Zazi, Doura had something . . . special about her. But why would someone with her obvious abilities be willing to act as a lackey to the likes of Prince High Zazi?

"Doura, could you and I get coffee sometime? Have a chat?" I asked, as though we shared an interest in needlepoint.

"Maybe," she said. "I know where to find you."

Chapter 13

"Is it just me, or did that sound like a threat?" Max asked as we exited the metal gate and stood on the sidewalk.

I nodded. "Sounded like a threat to me."

"Why do you want to speak with her?"

"I think she's rather more than Zazi's consort. Do you know anything about her?"

He shook his head. "I've never even met the 'Prince' until just now, though I'm familiar with his reputation."

"He seemed to know you."

"A man like him keeps track of the press," Max said. "He's probably read my articles."

"So, Max," I said, letting out a breath. "When did you get back from your trip?"

He looked uncomfortable. "A couple days ago."

"You didn't call."

"No. I . . . I needed a little time."

"By all means. Take all the time you need," I said, turning toward the van.

"Stop, Lily. We need to talk." Max glanced around, as though searching for inspiration. "Have you eaten?"

"What?"

"There's a Russian neighborhood not too far from here. Amazing pirogis."

"You're asking me if I'm *hungry*? Besides, you just ate. And so did I."

He shrugged, looked uncomfortable. "I thought we might grab a bite, talk."

"We're talking now."

He glanced over at the house, where the pale visages of Doura and Tracy were visible in the front window, until they ducked back behind the curtain. "We're talking outside the devil's black abode."

"Seems rather appropriate to me," I said.

"Lily . . ."

"If you need time, Max, why are you here now?"

"I was worried about you. And I wanted to see you. You look beautiful, by the way."

"Thank you."

Our gaze held for a long moment. Max had gray, light-filled eyes that reminded me of rays of sunlight breaking through a storm at sea. I could feel myself melt a bit, even while stubbornly fostering a hard kernel of anger at my core.

"Answer me one question," I said. "That woman at the *Chronicle*, the city editor?"

"Violet?"

"Are you two . . . do you have a . . . thing?"

My heart sank when he didn't answer right away. As sure as I was that I couldn't be with Max if he refused to accept my magic, I hated the idea of him being with someone else. At least this soon. I let out a breath and made a resolution: no more ordinary humans. Oscar was right. There must be someone else more appropriate for the likes of me. I knew several attractive magical men, a couple right here in San Francisco. Of course, one of them was mad at me and the other didn't like me that much, but still. Couldn't I choose one of them, for Pete's sake?

No sense in putting off the inevitable.

"I take it you've decided you can't love a witch?"

"Lily, I do care for you. But I can't pretend that your . . . 'powers,' or whatever you want to call them—"

"Powers is fine. And don't say it in that tone of voice, if you please. You've had evidence, Max. How much more do you need?"

"That's what I'm saying. I've done nothing but think about this, Lily. Believe me. I've seen what you can do, and what you're like when you're doing your witch thing. It . . . scares the hell out of me."

I rolled my eyes. *Coward. Cowardly cowan,* I thought.

"It's not fair to you if I can't love all of you, including . . ."

"My freakishness?"

"You're not a freak," he said in a very soft, gentle voice.

I snorted. It was all I could manage.

"My brother tells me he's seen you a few times," Max said.

I met Max's brother, Luc, a short time ago, while clearing the School of Fine Arts of a haunting. Luc was handsome and charming. But I felt nothing for him like I did for Max.

"He drops by the shop occasionally," I said.

"I'll just bet he does."

"Jealous?"

"Yes."

"Good," I said, turning away. He grabbed my arm, pulling me back to him.

His mouth came down on mine. Gentle at first, the kiss deepened. And then some.

His strong arms wrapping around me felt as natural as breathing. He smelled wonderful, of soap and a manly, subtle musk scent. A visceral memory washed over me, of the night we shared, how perfect we were together. Despite my fears and distrust and anger I could feel myself let go of my misgivings, sink into him.

The traffic, the sunshine, even the black abode faded to nothingness. I desired, yearned, and at this moment everything I wanted seemed embodied in this man in my arms. I reveled in the feel of his mouth, his body, his . . .

The van horn blared. Startled, we pulled apart.

The hapless countenance of a potbellied pig appeared in the windshield of my purple work van.

Max's arms remained wrapped around my waist. He smiled down at me. "How's the pig?"

"Ooooh," I exhaled, reality slapping me in the face, "same old pig."

"He likes to ride around with you, like a dog?"

"Something like that. There's a cat in there, too. Long story. I don't suppose you're in the market for a new pet?"

"I'm already inheriting my dad's dog," he said with a shake of his head. "And I'm not sure of my plans yet. Whether I'll even be staying put."

Talk about a slap in the face. Not only was he still unsure of me, but he might be moving, in part to get away from me. Lovely. I was more confused than ever. Did he want me or not? Did he even know himself?

"I've got to go."

I stalked back toward the van.

"May I call you?" Max called out after me.

I didn't answer. Instead I climbed into the van, gunned the engine, and zoomed away from the curb.

"Nice," Sailor said as he crawled out from his hiding place in the back and sat in the passenger's seat. "You two want to get a room? I hear they rent by the hour at the Hotel Wharton."

"I don't want to hear about it," I snapped. "If you're going to stalk me you're going to have to deal with whatever you witness. Just think how much fun it will be to tell on me to Aidan. First the black abode, then Max. He ought to be just thrilled."

"I thought you weren't seeing Carmichael anymore."

"What made you think that?"

"That's the scuttlebutt."

I glanced in the rearview mirror, but Oscar was making himself scarce. "Mmm. Best not to believe everything a pig tells you, I guess."

I drove down busy California Street, weaving through pedestrians and trucks double-parked in the right lane. The silence was too good to last.

"He's not worth your time."

"Thanks for your thoughts."

"I'm serious. He's a wounded soul."

"Takes one to know one, huh?"

"He won't be able to give you what you need, Lily, and he sure as hell isn't going to be able to support your witch behaviors."

"It's astounding, Sailor. You hardly speak ten words at a time to me except under duress, yet now it turns out you're a couples' counselor. I had *no* idea you were a therapist." I was spending too much time with Sailor. His sarcasm was rubbing off on me.

"Just saying . . . you might want to watch it, is all." He slumped down in his seat and stared out the window.

Oscar snorted in the back. For some reason he didn't like to transform in front of Sailor, even though I was pretty sure Sailor knew exactly what Oscar was.

I tried to shake off the aftereffects of the kiss, trying desperately not to think of passion. Of sex. That was one thing that could really mess with a witch's energy. Though, now that I thought about it, I was tired of living like a nun. I'd like the chance to get to really understand sex magic, and learn to control it. I reckoned I'd enjoy that homework just slightly more than algebra.

Enough. I forced my thoughts back to the really important matter at hand: Malachi Zazi's murder, and Gregory's involvement . . . or lack thereof. If Oliver's testimony about an overheard argument was all the authorities had against him, then I couldn't imagine they would actually be pressing charges. Still, I needed to check in with Carlos Romero, ask him where things stood. Meanwhile, I sure would like to know more about this Doura creature. Among other things, now that it seemed unlikely Malachi was any kind of supernatural practitioner, someone else must have wiped down the apartment of any vibrations, muting them unnaturally. Doura seemed more than capable of that kind of magic, given her time-bending abilities. And according to Gregory and Nichol she had been at the dinner that last night, so she had opportunity. The fact that Doura herself denied being there only made it seem more likely.

Who *was* this Doura, why was she hanging around a

degenerate poser like Prince High, and how was she involved in this murder?

I pulled up in front of the parking garage at the *Chronicle* building.

"What are we doing here?" Sailor asked.

"I'm dropping you off so you can pick up your motorcycle. I'm going home."

He looked rather dumbfounded.

"Were you planning on sleeping over with me?" I asked, feeling a sort of generalized exasperation with the male sex. I let out a deep breath and rubbed my temples, trying to ward off an incipient headache. I needed some willow bark tea. "Go on now, Sailor. I promise I'll be home all night like a good girl, and I won't go out until you come get me in the morning."

"Why should I believe you?"

"Because I don't want to get you into trouble with Aidan. Lord only knows who else he might send to harass me. Speaking of which—do you know a woman, she's a witch or some other kind of practitioner, named Doura?"

"Who is she?"

"She came by the store yesterday and warned me off Malachi's case. And I just saw her in the black abode with Prince High."

Sailor looked suddenly very serious. "She's not one of Aidan's."

I wondered about that when I saw her with Zazi, but I was never sure how these alliances worked. I thought she might have multiple loyalties, or be with Prince High for some kind of supernatural espionage of her own, even while answering to Aidan.

"How sure are you?"

"Very."

"Isn't Aidan in charge of the witch folk around here?"

"In general, but I wouldn't say one hundred percent."
He slipped out of the van. "Remember, straight home."

"Yes, Dad."

That evening I got busy with my cauldron. I harvested
dozens of fresh herbs and roots from my terrace pots,
stripped and crushed them, and created a protective
brew in which I soaked a talisman specifically against
Aidan, just in case. But just as when I was creating conjure balls with Aidan yesterday, I could sense something
else with me, something over my shoulder, restraining
my power. Everything I did required more effort.

Even Oscar's presence didn't help.

I managed to prepare a health tonic for Gregory,
whether he wanted it or not. If he could bring himself to
trust me, I knew I could help. Maybe I could convince
Rebecca to offer it to him, and while I was at it talk to
her about taking her husband back. But was this any of
my affair? I had spent so much of my life trying to avoid
close personal connections, but now that I was Bronwyn's friend, the web seemed to be growing: I loved
Imogen, so I wanted her daddy to be okay. It radiated
out, like beams from the sun, like a corona around a
moon.

Then I prepared a constellational talisman according
to the instructions by Albertus Magnus, scratching Serpentarius's symbol into a smooth blue-gray river rock.
After seeing all those snakes at Prince High's house, I
thought it was better to be safe than sorry.

Finally, I created a circle of salt, lit candles at the four
points of east, west, north, and south, and sat down with

the sumptuous silk gowns Nichol Huffman had given me.

Like the ones in Malachi's apartment, the gowns had fitted bodices with dozens of tiny buttons, true whale-bone structures in the bodices, and yards of billowing fabric. One cream-colored dress was studded with hundreds of seed pearls; a ruby red brocade was trimmed with gold embroidery. There were tassels, ruched neck-lines, and lace galore. Gorgeous specimens, in incredible shape.

I sat, modulated my breathing, subsumed myself to the powers . . . but still, I sensed very little. Like the dresses in Malachi's apartment, these gowns had been magically cleansed at some point. Holding them in my arms within my pentagram, I could feel the excited sensations of Nichol and her friends, I presumed, those who had worn them recently. But the older vibrations were still, motionless. Had they been cleansed on purpose? Was someone trying to remove all traces of what had gone before?

The only truly strong image I had while holding the dresses was that of Doura's face. Was this the red bro-cade she had worn to Malachi's last dinner? Or was she simply on my mind?

Something else was bothering me. It dawned on me that while Nichol seemed so young and sweet when she hugged me, she wasn't really an innocent at all. She was guilty of shoplifting that bracelet from my store. It seemed like a small thing in some ways, but it was a vio-lation. I should have felt some sign of the breach of trust when I held her. Could she be some kind of practitioner herself, or simply someone who truly did not know right from wrong?

By the time I looked up at the clock it was nearly two in the morning. As Aidan pointed out yesterday when I was in the cloister, time was relative, especially when in a trance.

As I was brushing my teeth I realized that I had gone the whole day and still hadn't spoken with Carlos Romero. I wrote a note to myself to call him tomorrow.

I went to sleep and dreamt of Malachi, an hourglass, snakes, and Doura.

Chapter 14

I was late getting started the next morning. Maya arrived before I finished my store cleansing rituals, or even went for coffee. I did manage to call and leave a message for Carlos, however, asking him to call me back.

"Are you sure you're okay?" Maya asked. I was usually more on top of things than this. "And is Bronwyn all right? I haven't wanted to ask anything too detailed."

"Her daughter has some problems."

"That's a nice way of putting it," she said, her eyebrows raised. Rebecca's occasional swooping down on us at the store hadn't endeared her to any of us.

I smiled. "You know what I mean. I guess she and her husband have been having some difficulties." I didn't really want to air Bronwyn's issues; she was usually open about them, as with everything, but that should be up to her, not me.

I started sorting through the clothes that had come into the shop over the past week. One Hefty bag held a nice stash of 1950s dance dresses; there were several with voluminous skirts and poofy crinolines that would re-

quire special attention in the wash. A bag of sweaters revealed that many of them had been moth-eaten, which
was a shame. No way to fix that. Finally, a battered cardboard box revealed a treasure of early 1980s disco clothes.

"Hey, check this out." I held up a gold-spangled, bell-
bottomed, one-piece jumpsuit. The outfit was so absurd
it made Maya laugh out loud.

"Bet you it'll sell by Friday," she said.

"I imagine you're right," I said as I tossed it into the
growing pile destined for dry cleaning. The wildest, least
wearable items seemed to fly off our racks. I put it down
to the Bay Area's wonderfully wacky populace.

"So, did Max ever find you yesterday?" Maya asked.

"He did, yes."

"And . . . ?" Maya's eye brightened with interest. "So
what did he say? What happened?"

"I decided I shouldn't see him anymore. I made a
resolution."

"Oh, that's no fun." She flipped the sign on the front
door to OPEN. "Was he being a jerk?"

"Sort of. Not totally. I don't know." I started inspecting the lace on several sets of 1950s baby-doll negligees.
"But I was pretty darned determined right up until he
kissed me."

"He *kissed* you?" Maya came over to the sales counter and leaned toward me. "Like, a little peck or down
and dirty?"

"Um . . ." I shouldn't have brought this topic up, either. I was just as confused about Max today as I was
yesterday. "You know . . ."

"Then it was down and dirty. Hmm."

"I have the willpower of an ant," I said, slapping my
forehead.

"Actually, ants have a great deal of willpower. They're famous for their determination. Ever hear that ant and the rubber tree song?"

"Oh, *please* don't sing it," I pleaded. Not only was I getting fed up with my lack of any normal popular culture references, but not long ago I had dealt with a magical music box that played a children's ditty incessantly. Took me a week to get it out of my head. "Okay, an ant was a bad example. I have the willpower of a marshmallow."

"A limp noodle maybe. Or a dishrag."

"Thanks," I said, tossing a crinoline at her head. "I get it."

"Anyway," she continued with a laugh, "why *should* you have much resolve around Max? He's a sexy, interesting, smart man, and you're both single adults. What's the problem?"

I realized that while Maya was my friend, she was still somewhat in the dark about my magic. She had been raised in the Baptist Church, and still attended occasionally. Though she had seen my magic in action, it was hard for her to reconcile both worlds. I wasn't as aboveboard with her as I had been, say, with Bronwyn.

"The problem is that I'm a . . . witch." I swallowed hard. It still took a lot for me to just come out and say it.

"You mean—"

She was cut off by the tinkle of the bell on the front door. We both swung around, as though we were naughty schoolchildren caught talking during an exam.

Sailor stood in the doorway, shadows under his eyes, looking even grumpier than usual. I had to smile.

"I take it you're not a morning person?"

He just grunted.

"Duuuude," said Conrad, who lingered behind him,

as though worried Sailor might pull a sawed-off shotgun out from under his trench coat. Given the look on Sailor's face, and the long gray trench coat he was wearing, it wasn't that off base of an assumption.

"Conrad, this is my friend Sailor. He's okay. Sailor, Conrad," I introduced them. Sailor held out his hand and they shook.

I was pleased that Sailor treated Conrad like a man, rather than the gutter trash that so many others did. The Con might be dirty, homeless, and addicted to illegal substances, but he was a sweet soul who meant no harm to anyone. Sailor seemed to understand this instinctively.

While I was at it, I introduced Sailor to Maya. He nodded hello, then slumped into a large chair by the dressing room and proceeded to scour the room with his usual glower.

Just then Bronwyn walked into the store, her two grandchildren in tow.

"Looks like we have a full house this morning," I said, pleased to have so many friends under one roof.

Bronwyn pulled me to the side while Imogen and James were distracted, chasing Oscar through the aisles and under racks of clothes.

"Rebecca and Gregory are getting together to talk. Were you able to find out anything?"

"Nothing definitive," I said. "But it sounds as though the police were interviewing everyone who was at the dinner. Inspector Romero hasn't called me back yet, but I doubt a simple overheard argument would be enough for them to pursue him for homicide."

"That's what I thought. My dear daughter does tend toward the histrionic."

"I'll try to get hold of the inspector today and see what he has to say. I'm glad to hear that Rebecca and Gregory are talking, though," I said, watching as Imogen stopped chasing Oscar in favor of the black cat. She picked it up, and it purred, contented in her arms. "That reminds me—I brewed a tonic for Gregory last night—it's in the fridge in the back room. I thought you might bring it to Rebecca and see if she'll pass it on to him. I believe it would help calm him, replenish his energy."

"Thank you, Lily," Bronwyn said, enveloping me in a bear hug. "For everything. Oh! I remembered to bring the algebra workbook as well," she said, bringing it out of her massive tapestry satchel.

"Oh, goodie."

"But you've been improving, and it's been ages since we worked on it," Bronwyn pointed out.

"I'll help you, Lily," Imogen piped up. "I like math."

"You see, Lily, the eight-year-old is offering to help you."

"This is so embarrassing," I said.

"There's nothing embarrassing about self-improvement," Bronwyn said. "We all have our own journey."

"My current journey's down to the café for coffee drinks," Maya announced. "Kids, want to come with me? Bronwyn, Lily, the usual? And, Sailor, do you want something?"

"Don't be too nice to him," I teased. "He'll never leave."

Like the cat, I thought. I looked over to see Imogen still cradling the animal to her thin chest. I sneezed. Oscar snorted, in what I presumed was a piggy version of "Gesundheit."

It was wonderful—*magical*—to see Aunt Cora's Closet full of friends. Customers started to arrive. I worked my way through three more bags and boxes of clothes, marking items for repair and special hand washing, and Bronwyn sorted her herbs. Sailor inadvertently sold a dress by giving the woman a blatantly interested once-over when she came out of the dressing room to look at herself in the mirror. A teenager with multiple piercings came in looking for a truly unique prom dress—she decided on a lemon yellow chiffon, circa 1963—and a transvestite came by looking for size thirteen women's shoes. In a wonderful feat for a second-hand store, he unearthed a pair of brilliant fire engine red pumps. Perfect.

As the hours passed, I decided that if I tried hard enough, when surrounded by friends and vintage clothes, I could almost ignore the memories of the black abode, and Doura, and the visual of Malachi Zazi dead upon the table, and the feel of Max's mouth on mine. If I tried very hard.

The bell over the door tinkled as a tall blond man entered.

"Atticus," I said. "How nice to see you. I thought you were Oliver at first."

"I get that a lot," he said with a smile. Then he glanced around the shop. "Would it be possible for me to speak to you in private?"

"Of course. Maya, I'm going in the back for a minute. Would you watch the register?"

I led the way to our small back room and we sat at a jade-colored vintage linoleum table.

"Would you like a cup of tea?"

"No, thank you," he said, glancing around the room. He cleared his throat. "Look, I don't know how to say this. . . ."

After a moment's hesitation, he reached into his pocket and brought out the silver-link bracelet I had seen on Nichol yesterday. He laid it on the table.

"She . . . Nichol's had a problem with this, as I'm sure you've heard. Shoplifting. But she confessed it to me herself, and she feels terrible. Look, I know it's not fair to ask, but could you let it go, just this once? I promise I'll get her back into counseling, and keep her out of your store. I'm happy to pay any damages, any—"

"Don't worry about it, Atticus," I said. "I appreciate you bringing it back."

"You won't be pursuing charges?"

I shook my head. I was more than willing to go above and beyond when it came to prevention, but punishment was something else altogether. I'd rather leave that to karma. "I've got the item back, that's what matters."

"She's truly sorry."

I nodded, though I thought that if Nichol were truly repentant, she might have come herself rather than having her brother do her dirty work.

So much for my attempts to forget the mystery surrounding Malachi Zazi. Had Nichol really come to Aunt Cora's Closet to find a dress for the Art Deco Ball, and was this just one more coincidence?

After seeing Atticus out, I couldn't stop thinking about going back to Malachi Zazi's apartment once more—but this time, with Sailor at my side. Since he was sticking with me anyway, I might as well put him to work. Just one more look in that bad luck apartment, and then I would drop this case. It really wasn't my problem, anyway, so long as Gregory wasn't charged with any crime. I would tell Carlos Romero—who still hadn't deigned to call me back—the little I had managed to unearth and let him piece it all together. But first, I had to be sure I wasn't missing some massive magical quandary, something orchestrated by someone with power, like Doura. I couldn't let Carlos walk into that sort of thing by himself.

And unlike my enthusiastic but limited familiar, Sailor was a powerful psychic capable of contacting the beyond. I had seen him in action.

Unfortunately, Sailor wasn't likely to do this sort of thing as a simple favor . . . and it was probably best not to spring such a plan on him on an empty stomach. Maybe a nice home-cooked meal and a beer would loosen him up a bit.

"Do y'all want some lunch?" I asked the assorted crowd a little after noon. "I have some leftover gumbo; I could make a salad to go with it."

"Oh, thanks, Lily, but I brought lunch for me and the kids."

"And I'm running out to meet my sister for Kashmiri food," said Maya.

"How about you?" I asked Sailor. "Do you like gumbo and corn bread?"

"My people are from Louisiana."

"They are not!"

"Atchafalaya."

"Seriously?" asked Maya. "Maybe you two are cousins."

Sailor graced her with a rare smile. "Maybe we are at that."

"Anyway, you've never tasted my mama's recipe. And it's been sitting for a couple of days, so you know it's good."

He nodded. "Takes a day or two for that sassafras filé to settle in. You make it with okra?"

"Of course," I said, returning his smile. Oscar snorted from under a rack of frilly bridesmaid dresses. The little critter could put away a whole lot of food in that little belly of his. He had been angry that I'd insisted on putting away the gumbo leftovers the other night.

"You two go on and take a lunch break," said Bronwyn, one arm around each of her grandchildren. "My two helpers and I have got the store, no problem."

I led the way across the sales floor and through the rear storage room to the narrow stairs that led up to my apartment. But as I started to climb the steps, I started to feel nervous about bringing Sailor into my inner sanctum. I knew he was reporting to Aidan ... I tried to think ... did I have anything lying out in the open that Aidan couldn't—or shouldn't—know about?

I wondered whether Sailor had felt this kind of apprehension the first time he allowed me into his apartment. Our type is nosy beyond measure, and we have insights that other regular folk don't share.

"You know how I told you I couldn't read your mind?" Sailor asked from behind me.

"Yes," I said, slowing my pace.

"That might not be entirely true."

Trepidation surged through me. "What do you mean?"

"Well now, let's see ... At the moment you're thinking: Should I really bring this guy into my apartment? What if he sees something incriminating and tells

Aidan? Has this all been some elaborate plan to get into my inner sanctum? What if he's after my virtue, just like my mama said all men were? What if—"

"Very funny," I said, resuming my climb up the stairs.

He gave me a derisive chuckle. "Had you going there for a minute."

"Until you brought up my mama. That was a dead giveaway. She didn't give me advice concerning men . . . unless you count: 'Get married young and start having babies as soon as possible.'"

"Sounds like good advice. Might have kept you out of trouble."

"Oh, somehow I doubt that. Anyway, it's not easy to find a husband when everyone hates you."

"Seems to me you have too many admirers, rather than too few. Frankly, I don't know what they see in you. You're crazy as a loon and you're not all that good-looking."

"Oh, thank you so much." I wasn't sure if he was kidding or not. It didn't seem like it. "Maybe I'm just not your type."

"I guess that's it."

I opened the door to the apartment and stepped inside, seeing anew the mirror that reflected evil back outside, the sachets of rosemary and eucalyptus leaves, the protective amulets hanging over the doorways and windows. The tiny foyer opened onto a short hallway, which opened, in turn, to the large kitchen and cozy sitting room. French doors led out to a tiled terrace, planters now lush with the bushes and herbs I had planted upon moving in. My garden was essential to my brews and potions.

I might be a dead loss at scrying, and I can't talk to

ghosts worth a damn, but I'm an expert at botanicals. Not coincidentally, I also happened to be a darned good cook.

I set down plates of tuna fish for Oscar and the cat, and while I brought out covered dishes of gumbo and dirty rice and heated up the corn bread, the animals ran to their respective places—since Oscar didn't transform in front of company, he hopped onto the sofa in porcine form and took up his napping pose, chin on the armrest. The cat stalked the perimeter of the apartment before meandering out onto the terrace.

Sailor and I ate at the kitchen table. He added generous splashes of Tabasco sauce along with a pinch of habanero flakes. I put out cold beers for the both of us. Sailor grunted in appreciation, but mostly we ate in companionable silence. Given that he was spying on me, it felt remarkably comfortable.

I couldn't help it. What with the food and the animals and not having to pretend to be something I'm not, it felt just a little bit like family.

Sailor caught me watching him over the lip of my beer bottle.

"What?" he asked before taking another large bite.

"I have a favor to ask."

"No freaking way."

"You haven't even heard what I'm asking yet."

"No need," he said with a sigh as he leaned back and wiped his mouth with a napkin. "I know it's something I don't want to do. I *wondered* why you were being so nice."

"I'm being nice because, for some unknown reason, I like you."

He grunted again.

"I want you to go to Malachi Zazi's apartment with me."

"This is the place Aidan told you to stay away from?"

"Maybe."

"I repeat: No freaking way."

"Why not?"

"You're insane—you know that? Certifiable." He took another swig of his beer. "You don't just go up against someone like Aidan, Lily. If he's told you to stay away he had a good reason."

"He had a reason, but whether it's good or not . . ." I shrugged. "Anyway, you're always going on about how I don't know my own talents. Maybe I'm just as powerful as Aidan."

"Terrific. Just what this town needs, a battle of powers. No, thank you."

I watched him for a moment.

"I could force you, you know. It wouldn't take much. A sleeping potion, a confusion spell . . . a threat. Maybe I've already put something in your gumbo."

He stopped chewing midbite.

"I'm kidding. Eat hearty. But if you don't come along and help me, I'll be sure to lose you and you'll have to explain it to Aidan."

His mouth tightened at the corners. I won this round.

I might be crazy, but like my mama always said, I was crazy like a fox.

Chapter 15

"We have to get past the doorman."

Sailor and I watched the front door of Malachi's apartment building from the car. As a concession to my grumpy companion, I left the van, and the animals, home. Instead, we had taken my vintage Mustang convertible. I even let Sailor drive.

"A diversion, maybe?" I suggested.

"I take it we're not supposed to be here? Aidan's not the only one who wants you to keep your nose out of it?"

"Maybe not exactly, no."

"'Not exactly'? Are we 'sort of' supposed to be here?"

"Okay, no. No, we're not supposed to be here. Don't give me that look—am I supposed to believe you're Mr. Law and Order all of the sudden?"

He snorted. "That's the problem, my witchy friend. I haven't exactly been on the straight and narrow. I can't afford to be caught breaking and entering by the SFPD."

"You've got a record? Really?" Now I was intrigued. "For what?"

"None of your business. Why don't you do that thing you did to the manager at the Fairmont that one time. That mind control thing."

"It wasn't *mind control*," I protested.

"Sure looked like it."

"It's a persuasion charm. Most people want to please you, especially people in the hospitality industry. The charm just enhances their helpfulness. Enhances it a lot, in some cases."

"So use one of those."

"Aidan says I'm not supposed to use charms for minor things. He says it dilutes my power."

"You didn't seem to be holding back when you were threatening me earlier."

"Yes, well. That was then. This is now." This was one of my mother's expressions that never made any sense but shut me up as a child.

"So honestly, Aidan told you not to use your powers for small things?"

I nodded.

Sailor grinned.

"What?" I asked.

"And you *believed* him?"

"Why wouldn't I?"

"Because it's Aidan Rhodes we're talking about. Look, Lily, magic doesn't work that way. Even I know that, and I'm sure as hell no witch."

I just looked at him.

"It's not a finite power supply that gets used up. In fact, quite the opposite. The more you use it, the stronger you grow. If Aidan's telling you not to flex your magical muscles, it's for his own reasons, not on your account."

"Seriously?"

He just raised his eyebrows and smiled. I needed to talk this thing out with Aidan, and soon.

"Oh, all right. I'll use the dang charm."

I always carried supplies in the trunk of my car. Basic herbs, oils, roots, and resins: lavender, Deer's tongue, Devil's Shoestring, rose hips and petals, cinnamon, angelica, Queen Elizabeth root. I mixed these together with some Van Van oil, put them in a small black silk bag, charged it with a mumbled chant, and was ready to go.

The doorman on duty was the same one I had seen two days ago. Thinning gray hair cut short, a broad face, chubby, the veins on his rather bulbous nose indicating a close relationship with the bottle.

I reached out to shake his hand with my right hand, cupping it with my left. I could feel the charm humming in my pocket.

"What can you tell me about Malachi Zazi?"

"Poor guy," he said, shaking his head. "He was an odd duck, that one. Never went out during the day."

"Any idea why not?"

"Said he had a sun allergy. If there was any daylight, he'd wear sunglasses, a hat, a scarf, and long coat and gloves, no matter how warm it was."

"Was he a friendly guy? Chatty?"

"Nah, but it's not like we had a lotta interaction. He basically stayed in his apartment; people brought him things."

"What kinds of things?"

"Whatever he needed, I guess. Probably groceries and all, I never saw him go out for things and come back with bags, for instance. But the man had a lot of friends coming and going all times of the day and night."

"Did you recognize any of them?"

He leaned forward as though to speak in confidence. "Some of 'em were pretty big names."

"Really? Like who?"

"Garrett Jones, the mayor himself. And Mike Perkins, the antiaging guy? I think I saw Paris Hilton once, too, but that mighta been the light. Hard to say. A lot of 'em wore sunglasses and hats, too, like they didn't want to be recognized. Hey," he said, his soft hazel eyes lighting up for a moment. "One time I seen that girl from the vampire movie, that Nichol Reiss gal?"

"Do you know anything about the Serpentarian Society?"

"The what's-it?"

"The Serpentarian Society? Zazi held a dinner every month?"

"Oh, right. The dinners. Sure. I'm usually on during the day, though. The night guy would mostly see them, unless I was here late. That's when he had those dinners, for some reason. I was here late on Saturday, though."

"You were? So on Saturday, all the dinner participants left on time? No one lagged behind?"

"Some left earlier, some later. I already told the police. One of 'em came real late."

"Which one?"

"Hard to say. A man. But they were all wearing hats and things, like they didn't want to be recognized. Like it's a secret society. Like Malachi always did."

"You didn't talk to him or anything? So you wouldn't be able to say who it was?"

He shook his head.

"Anything else odd or out of the ordinary?"

"Only other strange thing is, I could have sworn I saw him today."

"Saw who?"

"Mr. Zazi."

"Today?"

The doorman nodded. "I mean, I know it couldn't've been him. But it sure looked like him. Wearing sunglasses, all wrapped up the way he did, even though it's a nice day outside."

"He came in here?"

"Sort of hovered at the front door for a while. Like he wanted to come in but couldn't make up his mind or something. I was on the phone with Ms. Franklin, up in 5C, and by the time I got to the door to talk to him, he was gone."

I tried and failed to ignore the chill that ran up my spine.

"Okay, thanks," I said. "My friend and I are going to go up and take a look at the apartment, if that's all right?"

"Oh, I don't think so. Police won't allow it."

I fixed him with my gaze and concentrated.

"But it will be all right just this once, won't it?"

"It'll be all right, just this once."

"Thanks."

"Thanks," he repeated.

The elevator was an old-fashioned one, open to the stairwell that wound around it. Sailor pulled the grate closed behind us and pushed the button for the penthouse.

"Was he telling the truth?" I asked Sailor.

"I would imagine so. I didn't sense anything out of the ordinary. He responded to your 'power-diluting' charm." He chuckled at his own joke.

As the elevator clanked slowly upward, I closed my

eyes halfway and forced myself to put Aidan and Sailor out of my mind, concentrating instead on the vibrations, the wisps of energy humans had left within these walls through the years. I may not be any good at meditating over a black mirror, but I could subsume myself to historical sensations like a pro.

The sixth floor held a humming of strife and intimate violence. Domestic abuse, several years old.

There had been a suicide, I would guess, on the seventh.

Sailor met my eyes. He could feel these things as well as I could. Again, there was that sense of kinship. It was nice to have someone by my side, feeling what I felt. Made me feel like less of a freak.

I sensed something as I passed the tenth floor as well; something had happened in the stairwell: a fight of some kind. And a natural death or two.

But again, in historic buildings there were always ghosts in the walls. Spirits afloat. They didn't frighten me; very rarely were they malevolent, or even active. Usually they were just energy traces, the echoes of human life and energy left behind in the structures we inhabit.

Most of what I felt within these walls was positive: the vibrations of everyday life, of hopes and dreams and strivings. The rich, dense velvet of human life as it plays out, moment by moment, upon the earth. I had always found these feelings comforting; they allowed me to connect with humanity even when I was living in my self-imposed exile, without friends or family.

The elevator finally stopped at the penthouse level: the thirteenth floor . . . which wasn't called the thirteenth floor.

The crime scene tape sealing the door was already torn.

"Somehow I don't think we were the first ones here."

"I think you're right about that."

He tried the knob. "They locked it back up, though."

"Can't you open it?"

"I'm a psychic, not a wizard."

"Seriously? You can't, you know, jimmy the lock or something?"

"I'm no locksmith."

"I know, but you seem . . . I don't know, rather criminally inclined. I thought you'd be able to break into a simple lock. There's not even a bolt on it."

"'Criminally inclined'?" He smiled and shook his head. "Want to go back down and ask your buddy the doorman for the key?"

"I don't think so. He wasn't all that cooperative, when it came down to it."

"You're the damned witch. Can't you do something to open it?"

"I could, but it would take a while. I've got some stuff in here." I realized I should have brought the Hand of Glory, a rather gruesome souvenir from an earlier supernatural case I had gotten involved in. The Hand allowed the carrier to enter locked doors, and even lit up the dark. It was disgusting, but awfully helpful. Kneeling, I pawed through my bag and laid out a piece of stiff wire, a thin flat piece of metal, a screwdriver, and a wrench.

"That bag of yours reminds me of Mary Poppins's bottomless carpetbag. Remember when she pulls out an entire lamp?"

"I never saw that movie."

"You never saw *Mary Poppins* when you were a kid?"

"No. Was it good?"

"You never saw *Mary Poppins*." This time it wasn't a question, but a statement. A statement that said much more than five simple words.

I shook my head. I could feel him staring at me but refused to meet his eyes. I'd had just about enough of his incredulous expression for the day.

"Were your folks Holy Rollers or something?"

"Something. Let's get to work, shall we?" I said in my sweetest voice, the one that meant I was on the verge of losing my temper. A voice that wouldn't melt butter, as my grandmother would say.

Ten minutes later Sailor finally managed to get the door open. I acted as lookout, but since Malachi's apartment was the only one on the floor, no one intruded.

"I wouldn't suggest breaking and entering as your next career move," I said.

"Cute."

"I take it your trouble with the police was over something else entirely?"

"I don't want to talk about it. But if that charm has worn off your buddy the doorman, we might not have much time. I am not talking to the police about this, you get me?"

"Got it. Let's go."

We entered slowly, wary. As before, the ladder was set up in front of the door. I squeezed past it, in order not to walk under it. Sailor did the same.

The space felt different now, without the frenetic energy of emergency personnel bouncing off the walls, quite literally making my teeth hurt. Now there were only muted sensations, primarily attached to the earlier workers.

But the apartment was superheated. Had someone accidentally left the heater on? Within minutes I felt a bead of sweat roll down my back, and saw the sheen on Sailor's forehead as well.

"This is pretty bizarre," said Sailor, taking in the broken mirror, open umbrella, and upside-down horseshoes.

I stood in the center of the room and concentrated. Sailor did the same.

"Anything?" I asked.

He shook his head. "Not right off the bat. It feels as though someone performed a cleansing."

"Why would they bother?" I asked. "It's not as though the average homicide investigator can feel such things. How could they have known a witch like me would be involved in the investigation?"

A horseshoe, hung upside down over the front door, fell. It clanged against the aluminum ladder as it went down.

I jumped, letting out a squeak.

"Don't faint, Lily," said Sailor. "It's a stupid horseshoe. It doesn't mean anything."

I swallowed hard, and nodded. He was right. I was jumpy, on edge.

I went into the kitchen and looked through the cupboards and refrigerator. There was nothing, no food at all. That last Serpentarian supper must have been catered. Would the police have cleaned things out for some reason, or did Malachi simply not eat? In the closet, I found a whole collection of sunglasses, and lots of wide-brimmed hats. Did the man really have a sun allergy? Was that why all the windows were closed, and so thoroughly?

Gregory said he thought he saw Malachi walking around, as though risen from the dead. And now the doorman. The very idea was ridiculous ... but then again, what did I know? I hadn't gotten to the "vampire" section of Aidan's library.

"Sailor, you don't believe in ... in vampires, do you?"

"Is this a joke of some sort?"

As soon as the words came out of my mouth, I realized how ridiculous they sounded.

I shook my head. "Sorry. Never mind."

A door led off the back of the kitchen. I unlocked it, then eased it open.

It led to a back utility stairwell. The little landing held a mop, a broom, a bucket. Wooden stairs led both down ... and up. I peered into the darkness above.

Chapter 16

"Go on up," said Sailor from right behind me.

I startled again. "Stop *scaring* me."

"So stop being so jumpy. Some witch you are. C'mon, let's check out the roof."

"Do you sense something?"

"Not particularly. But it's suffocating in here, and I like rooftops, ever since I was a kid." He glanced down at me. "I'll bet you're going to tell me you never snuck up to a roof and drank cheap wine from the bottle when you were a teenager."

I shrugged. He shook his head.

"Your folks have a lot to answer for."

"Don't I know it."

He led the way up the dark stairs to the door at the top. Light came through the bottom crack in a bright beam. When he opened the door, light streamed in to show the stairs were just what they were supposed to be, nothing sinister about them at all. A cobweb-strewn access route to the roof.

The flat roof was made of tar and gravel, with a series of air vents and aluminum pipes sticking out, seemingly willy-nilly. One huge old antenna, a holdover from the days of broadcast TV, lay on its side in one corner. The building was asymmetrical, the roof shape irregular. A few beer cans in one corner gave silent testimony to an earlier party, like one of Sailor's younger trespasses, no doubt. Other than being litterbugs, I could hardly blame them—if I were Malachi Zazi, I would have spent a lot of time up on this roof.

And not just for the incredible view. But the gargoyles.

They were perched at the corners, and upon approaching the edge you could see several more, marching down the odd roof angles. Approaching one from the rear, I could have sworn it shifted a little to look back at me. I paused, then continued toward it, reaching out—

"Check this out," said Sailor.

I looked around. In an opposite corner, there was a small planter box filled with flowering shrubs and surrounded by a bench. And smack-dab in the center, as though in the place of honor, was a large stone sculpture of a man wrestling with a giant snake.

"Why would someone with a supposed sun allergy set up a little outdoor garden?"

"Maybe it was some other tenant's weekend project."

"I doubt it. That sculpture is Serpentarius. Malachi named his whole dinner society after him."

"I take it he's a snake guy?"

"He's *the* snake guy."

"I don't like snakes."

"I don't mind them."

"It figures. You're an odd one—you know that?"

I smiled. "Yeah, I know that. Anyway, Malachi Zazi clearly had a little Serpentarius fetish. So here's the question: Did this statue give him the idea, or did he put up the statue himself?"

"Looks like it's been here a while."

"So has—had—Malachi. It's tough to tell with stone." True, there was dirt in the carved recesses, and signs of weather. But I imagined that San Francisco's climate, subject as it was to salt air off the ocean and bay, fog, and temperature swings, could be hard on a hunk of stone.

"Why would anyone develop a fetish for a Roman god?"

"Not sure. But he's not all that obscure—the American Medical Association uses him as their symbol."

"What's the association with snakes?"

"I think it's that they shed their skin and are reborn. As though they are eternally young, never to die."

"But they do die."

"We all do."

"Except for vampires."

"Very funny." I looked back at the gargoyle, the one I could have sworn shifted just a little. It now sat, glowering and unmoving, watching over the city. Backlit by the harsh afternoon sun, its silhouette was dark and hulking. "What do you know about gargoyles?"

"True gargoyles are just downspouts."

"Downspouts?"

"They were just decorations put on rain gutters and downspouts. The water usually came out their mouths, hence the name, 'gargoyles,' which comes from the French word for 'throat.' Like 'gargle.'"

"Are you serious?"

"Now it's my turn for arcane knowledge, I guess. I have a background in architecture."

"Really? You mean before . . ."

He nodded. "Before."

"You should get back into it. What with your abilities, you could read a building's aura and really keep your clients happy."

"Yeah, thanks for the career advice I didn't ask for and don't need. Besides, how could I give up on the opportunity to trespass in dead guys' apartments with you?"

"Thank you for coming, Sailor. Are you going to tell Aidan about this?"

He shrugged. I didn't suppose it mattered that much. If I were overly worried about being spied on, I wouldn't keep Oscar around.

"I remember seeing gargoyles in France," I said, thinking of them on the Notre Dame, as well as just about every remote country chapel one came across. "I always thought they were believed to be guardians of some sort, not just downspout decorations."

"Oh, they are. They're both, really. They were meant to scare off the evil spirits in the same way that traditional Chinese put up mirrors to confuse and scare off bad luck."

"You think that's what they're doing here on this building?"

"I think they're here as decoration. You can see them plainly from the street; this whole building is a pretty unusual construction. The metal bars emerging from the four corners is a traditional device as well, used to confuse the magnetic poles."

"To what purpose?"

"To keep the ghosts away."

I looked over at him, startled. He laughed.

"I'm kidding. They were probably used to enhance television reception, back in the days of antennas and broadcast signals. They might do double duty as lightning rods."

"Oh." I took another moment to feel for sensations. Nothing but a pleasant, contented hum near the garden. Nothing untoward or evil. I headed back toward the stairwell.

When we reentered Malachi's apartment, I felt something.

A curse.

I hadn't noticed it before. Was it new, or was the other entrance confusing us somehow?

Whatever it was, it was fully charged. I could feel it from where I was standing. It was low, below eye level.

I got to my hands and knees and started looking under furniture.

There they were: little wax balls in the corner.

Goofer Balls. *Powerful* Goofer Balls.

I scrambled back, crablike.

Sailor caught me as I backed into him and helped me to my feet.

"What is it?"

I blew out a breath. Got my bearings. It wasn't like me to walk up on something like that. I usually felt vibrational warnings. Everything was off-kilter in this place.

"Goofer Balls," I said. "They—"

"I know what Goofer Balls are," he said, a grim quality to his voice.

"I—"

Suddenly Sailor put his finger to his lips to silence me, gesturing toward the front door. He ducked into the bedroom.

Before I could follow him, the door banged opened.

Backlit by the strong light from the hallway, I couldn't make out the silhouette at first. But then SFPD inspector Carlos Romero came into focus, a furious expression on his face.

"*Dammit*, Lily—"

He cut himself off in midsentence. His eyes shifted to a spot beyond me.

"*Don't* walk under the ladder. I can explain. . . ." I noticed something glinting above the door. Marks. As though something had been written, or drawn, in a clear but slightly shiny liquid. And there were dirt smudges. Someone had cast a spell on the door. Would that explain why it was so hard to feel anything in here, while I felt it when coming in the other entrance?

Carlos unholstered his service revolver.

"Don't pull your gun, Carlos. He's okay," I said, glancing behind me and expecting to see Sailor.

But no one was there. Sailor was still hiding in the bedroom.

Then I heard something. A buzzing, shaking sound. Almost like the hum of the cicadas that filled the still summer air in my hometown.

"*Don't move!*" Carlos barked from right behind me.

I froze.

Carlos aimed, holding the revolver with both hands.

He gestured, ever so slightly, with his head, to the floor
near the fireplace.

A snake. Its fat brown-splotched body was coiled, the
tip of its tail pointing up and shaking madly.

Poised to strike. At me.

"Rattler."

Chapter 17

"Back away very, very slowly," Carlos said in a restrained voice.

"It's all right," I said, holding my hand out to Carlos. "Wait."

I inched my hand to my medicine bag, stroked it, met the serpent's shiny flat eyes, and started to chant.

"Lily . . ."

I held the creature's gaze, continuing to murmur. After a long moment, the furious rattle subsided. The snake uncoiled, its body landing with a thud onto the polished wood floor. It scurried away, whispering along the polished wood floor, disappearing into the bedroom.

"Out of this apartment. Now," Carlos demanded.

"But—"

"Now. I'll call in the exterminators. *Dammit.* How could we have overlooked something like that?"

"It was probably hidden. Asleep."

"Maybe." He locked up, making a series of phone calls before we even got into the clanky elevator. Down in the lobby, he nodded at the doorman as we walked past, steering me by the elbow out the front door.

"You and I need to have a chat," said Carlos. "Either informally here and now, just you and me, or I take you to the station for an official interrogation. Your choice."

"Um . . . informally?" I answered, wondering whether this was a trick question.

He led the way to a dim old-time bar two blocks down on the corner. Two old men nursed their drinks and a petite fiftyish woman was tending bar, but otherwise we had the place to ourselves. We slid into a booth with scarred wooden benches that smelled of stale cigarette smoke and spilled beer.

When the waitress arrived, Carlos ordered iced tea and a plate of nachos *con todo*. I asked for a gin and tonic. It was still early, but I wasn't above a little liquid relaxation.

Carlos was good at his job. Simply sitting under his demanding stare made me want to come clean, to spill all my secrets just to make him go away. He remained silent and brooding until the drinks arrived, which, happily for me, was not a long interlude. I was starting to squirm.

Finally, after a long pull on his iced tea, he started in.

"What were you doing in Malachi Zazi's apartment?"

"I needed to take another look."

He reached into the breast pocket of his leather jacket and pulled out a business card with his name, official status, and phone number. He plunked it down onto the table between us with a bang. Then tapped on it.

"You need to get into an active crime scene, you

call your old buddy Carlos. *Homicide* inspector Carlos Romero. Hear me?"

"I've been calling you, old buddy, twice today."

"I've been a tad busy, trying to solve a homicide."

"How's it going?"

He gave me a noncommittal shake of his head.

"You're right that I shouldn't have broken into Malachi Zazi's apartment."

"Damn right."

"But I have a gripe of my own I want to address. Did you know of my connection to Gregory Petrovic when you asked me to come look at the crime scene?"

His gaze shifted away from me. "Not at first. When I asked you to come originally, it was because of all the bad luck charms we found at the scene. It was only later that we took Oliver's statement, and brought Gregory in for questioning."

"And that's when you realized he was connected to me?"

"*Is* he connected? I thought I sensed some distance between him and his mother-in-law."

"Some, yes."

He looked at me for a long time. These were the moments when I thought this by-the-book homicide inspector was doing his darnedest to read my mind, or my aura . . . or both.

"The point is that no, I did not ask you to look at the crime scene in order to get the inside scoop on your employee's son-in-law. Is that what you're worried about?"

That was precisely what had worried me. I hadn't realized until now how much it meant to me that Carlos had asked me for help, to weigh in on the crime. I watched him for a moment before deciding to believe him. I felt relieved, as though a burden had been lifted from my shoulders. For some reason, Carlos's opinion mattered to me. A lot.

The waitress arrived at the table with a platter piled high with enough nachos to satisfy a football team: chips glistening with bright orange cheese, small chunks of grilled chicken, jalapeño rings, black beans, and a little bowl of salsa on the side. I had been so distracted by Sailor earlier that I hadn't eaten all that much gumbo. Now that the adrenaline from our Goofer Ball and serpentine encounter in the apartment was subsiding, I felt ravenous.

"First time I tried what y'all call nachos here in California, I didn't quite know what to make of them," I said, biting into a jalapeño. "Back home our 'nachos' were just chips with a little queso cheese—you know, the melty cheese product stuff?"

"'Queso cheese' is redundant," Carlos said, picking up a bean-laden chip and dipping it in the salsa.

"Yeah, I get that. I even speak Spanish. I guess back home we never really thought about how odd that was. It's just one of those words, like 'nekked.'"

"'Nekked'?" Carlos looked at me with that mix of irritation and amusement I was coming to expect from him.

"I was raised saying 'nekked,' meaning someone without clothes. When I read the word 'naked,' I thought it meant something different. I assumed it rhymed with 'baked,' or . . . 'raked,' or . . ."

"'Snaked,'" Carlos said. His voice dropped. "You want to fill me in on what in the hell just happened up in Zazi's apartment?"

"I really don't know. I know the god Serpentarius is

always shown with serpents; given the name of Zazi's dinner club and all, do you think he might have kept snakes as pets?"

"I went through every inch of that place; there was no aquarium, no place to keep such a thing. And I don't care how much you like snakes, you're not going to let a rattler roam around free in your apartment unless you've got a death wish."

"Rattlers aren't actually aggressive," I pointed out. "They avoid humans whenever possible."

"Uh-huh," he said and eyed me.

"Were you really going to shoot it?" I asked with a half smile. "You must be a good shot."

"Good thing I wasn't forced to test my skills. What was that mumbling you were doing when the snake was poised to strike?"

"Just a little . . . prayer. Sort of."

" 'Sort of.' " He nodded absentmindedly, studying me. Finally, he gave a little shiver, hiking his shoulders to his ears. "I hate snakes. They give me the willies."

"A big strong homicide cop intimidated by a little reptile?"

"It's the way they slither. Creeps me out." He bit into another cheesy chip. "I notice you didn't seem bothered by it in the slightest, though it was ready to strike you."

"Snakes never scared me much. Don't rightly know why," I lied, thinking of another close encounter with the creatures, so many years ago in my dusty hometown. "The sight of you bursting in through the door with a gun at the ready, though, *that* gave me a fright."

"Uh-huh. We haven't yet talked about what you were doing breaking into a crime scene."

"I needed to see it again. I was hoping I might sense something without all the other folks there, mucking things up."

"What about the man who came with you?"

"Man?"

"The doorman said a man arrived with you, and you two went up together in the elevator."

"He was just helping me get in," I said, feeling my cheeks burn. I'm really not great at lying. "On account of me not having the key. And then he went away."

Carlos's dark gaze fixed on me for a long moment. I blushed some more under the scrutiny. Time to change the subject.

"Did Zazi's autopsy show anything unusual?"

"Actually"—Carlos's eyes shifted around the bar—"there *was* no autopsy."

"Why not?" I stuffed another chip in my mouth.

"Because there's no body."

I froze midbite.

"No body?" I said around the chip. "What do you mean, 'no body'?"

He cleared his throat, took another sip of his iced tea before speaking. "It disappeared sometime last night. It was signed in, and the autopsy was scheduled for this morning. But it wasn't there when folks showed up for work this a.m."

"They lost the *body*?"

He nodded.

I remembered the horseshoe falling in Malachi Zazi's apartment, and thoughts of bad luck washed over me. *Don't be superstitious, Lily. You know that bad luck doesn't work that way.* I took a deep breath and finished off my drink.

"How did they lose the body?"

"Very hard to say."

But Carlos's vibrations, usually hard to read, shielded and coplike, were worried. Humming at a high pitch, not unlike the rattle of the snake. Defensive and on guard.

"Were there cameras in the medical examination room? Videotape?"

"There were. But the tapes were erased somehow. The cameras from the parking lot across the street might have something; we're working on it. So, you don't think . . . you mentioned from the start that Zazi might not be entirely . . ." He dropped his voice. "Human. With his sun allergy, and then the blackout shades, I know he didn't sleep in a coffin, but . . ."

"No."

He seemed to relax, digging back into the nachos.

"Someone must have stolen the body," I said.

He nodded. "That's the only logical explanation. Maybe his old cronies wanted it for some weird celebration of the moon goddess or something. Probably we'll find his burnt remains in some isolated section of Golden Gate Park. Isn't the solstice coming up soon? This is precisely the sort of thing I was hoping you could help me with."

So much for my warm and fuzzy feelings toward this particular homicide inspector. Not long ago Carlos had seen and heard some things that made him believe I was in touch with another dimension. Like a scientist, he was open to things he didn't understand if he saw that they were based in something real. I had been so flattered when he asked me to weigh in on Malachi Zazi's crime scene, but now . . . he asked for my help in one breath, and disdained me in the next. He was distorting the practice of witchcraft, and by extension, disparaging me and those I loved.

"Witchcraft has nothing to do with making human sacrifices to the moon goddess, or any other god," I said, my tone sounding flat to my own ears.

"Oh, right," Carlos said, picking up on my mood shift. The man was no psychic, but he was a good cop—he could read people. "I didn't mean any of your . . . type . . . witches. I mean that you—"

He blew out a frustrated breath, took a drink, met my eyes, and tried again.

"I apologize. I did not mean to imply that you, or any of the witches you know, in any way endorse human sacrifice."

I nodded.

"I apologize."

"Apology accepted."

"Why don't I see if the film from the parking lot cameras shows anything, while you try to figure out why someone would want to steal a body."

I nodded again. "Oh, by the way, what do you think of Senator Huffman?"

"Senator Huffman?"

"Oliver Huffman's father. I spoke to him yesterday."

"You spoke to him? How? And more important, why?"

"I went to his house. Gregory said Oliver was the one who told you about the argument with Zazi."

Carlos pinched the bridge of his nose, closing his eyes for a moment. "You're not a *cop*, Lily. I asked for your opinion on a case, not to pursue witnesses."

"I understand that, but once I realized that Bronwyn's son-in-law might be in trouble, this case became a little more personal."

He sighed, but nodded. "We spoke with Oliver Huffman—in fact, with everyone who was there that night."

"Did you speak to a woman named Doura? Lots of blond curly hair, about fifty?"

He shook his head. "There was no one by that name on the official guest list."

"I think she was a stand-in for Ellen Chambers."

"The woman in the hospital."

"Right."

Carlos let out an exasperated breath. "No, we didn't. I guess we missed one. No one mentioned her, interestingly enough. Though I have to say, there must have been a lot of drinking going on. No one really remembers the end of the evening with any clarity. Most of them seem to have left on the early side, at least according to their spouses and whatnot."

"There should have been six men and six women at the dinner besides Malachi."

Carlos pulled out a small notebook that was molded to the contour of his hip pocket. He flipped through and swore under his breath.

"What's this woman's name?"

"Doura. I have no idea what the last name is. But I saw her with Malachi's father, at the black abode."

Carlos stared at me for a long moment. "You spoke with Malachi's father. And the Huffmans. Anyone else?"

"That's about it. And Gregory, obviously. Speaking of whom, do you have anything on him? Am I allowed to ask that?"

"He's not off the hook entirely, but nothing's pointing in his direction except for that scuffle. And that's not enough to convict someone with. He's cooperated, given us a DNA sample, and even offered to take a lie detector test."

"Good. Thanks."

"Did your conversations turn up anything unusual, anything you think might be pertinent, no matter how trivial it might seem?"

I gave him a brief rundown of my visits to the Huffman family compound, and then the black abode. "All I can say is Senator Huffman seemed extremely upset about his children's association with Malachi Zazi, but he also seemed genuinely shocked to hear of the death. Nichol struck me as a little odd."

"In what way?"

"She shoplifted something from my store the other day, but I didn't sense any kind of remorse or guilt."

"Shoplifting's a ways from murder."

"I know that. It just struck me as odd. And she and Atticus were both protective of Oliver, but I guess that's normal under the circumstances. I didn't get much chance to speak with him."

"I have, several times. His story is consistent, and he left that night with Nichol, and according to their own security detail they went straight home, got there on the early side. I suppose it could be fudged, but I don't see much there. So what about with Malachi's father. Anything odd . . . besides the obvious?"

"Just, as I mentioned, the woman Doura. I . . . know this is strange, but I believe she's some kind of witch."

There was a long pause.

"You think Malachi was killed by a witch?"

"No, I didn't say that. But I think it would be worth talking to her. It feels as though the apartment has a spell cast on it. There was something over the front door—I think maybe she, or someone else with special talents, altered things. And I found Goofer Balls in the corners tonight."

"What are Goofer Balls?"

"Hexes."

"But you don't know what all this might add up to?"

I shook my head. Then I thought about what Nigel said the other day—that murder was more likely caused by greed.

"Who inherits Malachi Zazi's money?"

"Half of it goes to an arts foundation, and the other half to the animal shelter. Speaking of which—how's the cat?"

"Still officially homeless, but bunking at my place. I can't believe you suckered me in."

He grinned and gestured to the bartender for the bill, handing her a twenty.

"Lily, I want to be absolutely clear on one point: I know I started this by asking for your opinion on Malachi Zazi's murder, but you're not anything like a cop. You cannot go around acting like one, get me? You'll get us both into serious trouble."

I nodded.

"That being said . . . I need to ask you for another favor."

"Does this have to do with vintage clothing or police work?"

"I'd like you to go with me to talk with Mike Perkins."

"The pharmaceuticals guy? Would that help?"

"I'm not sure. It's a long shot at best. But there's something . . . *off* about the guy. I don't know what to tell you other than my cop's intuition tells me something's going on. The interviews with him have been less than satisfactory. I'd be interested to see what you think—what with Malachi's father investing with him, and several of the dinner guests working for him, and him coming to the dinners himself . . . I'd just be interested to see what you pick up, if anything."

"I'm not psychic, you know."

"I know that. But among other things, he's got some stuff in his office—like carnivorous plants. That's odd, right?"

"A little."

"There are other things, too. Like, for instance, a lot of snakeskins, serpent motifs."

Our eyes held for a long moment. "I guess there's a lot of that going around lately."

"That's what I was thinking."

"When did you want to go?"

"How about now? I'll make a call."

One more meeting. One more interview. I didn't know how Carlos did it; it took so much psychic energy, putting yourself out there, doubting everyone you meet and speak with, taking mental notes and comparing. But I was awfully curious to talk to Gregory's boss. The man who, apparently, thought he could find the secret to eternal youth.

Under the circumstances, I figured Sailor could find his own way home. He was a resourceful fellow. And since he'd driven us earlier, he still had my car keys in his pocket. I'd be lucky if he hadn't already taken off to Vegas in my beautiful vintage Mustang, happy to be rid of me and Aidan once and for all.

Chapter 18

Mike Perkins's office was located in the Presidio, across town. Not far from Malachi Zazi's apartment.

The Presidio is a graceful collection of red-roofed white-stucco buildings that used to be part of an old military base, surrounded on all sides by forest and the bay. Golden Gate Park is spectacular, but I prefer the Presidio because of the historic buildings. It must have been the army's version of Club Med: soaring eucalyptus trees, meandering paths through the wooded grounds, rolling lawns, all looking over the bay and the Golden Gate Bridge. The buildings were, by turns, either elegant or charming. I had been told that the only truly ugly building on the grounds was the old naval hospital, but that concrete monstrosity was razed a few years ago and replaced by new Lucasfilm studios, built in a style that fit in with the traditional architecture.

Perkins Laboratories occupied an older clutch of buildings. One former residence had been made into administrative offices, while an old health care facility was used for the research laboratories and production. By the time we arrived the late-afternoon sun barely made its orangey way through the multipaned windows. The aged structure gave the entire enterprise a homey, friendly feel. That sense was mitigated, however, as soon as I met Mike Perkins eye to eye.

Perkins had thinning blond hair and glasses, and was slightly bucktoothed. But there the nerdiness ended. There was a hard glint of intelligence in his gaze, a careful, guarded sense to his aura. He was cold. Calculating. Self-satisfied, self-assured, self-centered. And focused, but I wasn't sure on what, exactly.

"So nice to see you again so soon, Inspector."

"I appreciate you making the time, Mr. Perkins," said Carlos. "This is a special consultant working with us on this case, Lily Ivory."

He nodded at me, and we assessed one another. Perkins was so cold that I was feeling a chill enter my own body. In that moment I was thankful that I'm not able to read minds.

Carlos started going over the statement Perkins had given previously, asking a few clarifying questions. While he did so, I glanced around the office, noting the snake motif Carlos had mentioned: There were several snake sheds, a rattle, an entire serpentine skeleton in the shape of a giant "S." And if I wasn't mistaken, this corporate mogul was wearing a snakeskin belt.

What bothered me more, though, were the signs of spell work: protective charms here and there, the barely discernible signs written over the doorway, much like what I had noticed in Malachi's apartment.

"So you arrived around when?" Carlos was asking. "And left when?"

"I arrived about eleven, and left about two in the

morning. Those were the usual hours for one of Malachi's events, and Saturday was no different," said Perkins. Though he spoke to Carlos, his eyes followed me.

I noticed the plants that Carlos had mentioned. Venus flytraps and a few others that I didn't recognize. The oddest thing about them was their setting: Other than the carnivorous plants, Perkins's office had been decorated in a Zen garden theme, with bonsai trees, a little tabletop fountain, and one corner of raked gravel. Somehow Zen philosophy and carnivorous plants just didn't gel in my mind. I remembered a friend of mine telling me about a Zen retreat she stayed at, in which every guest room was equipped with a "bugzooka," a device that allowed you to suck up an insect so you could release it, alive, outside. I doubted a place like that would have a whole lot of Venus flytraps adorning the window boxes.

A fly buzzed, coming perilously near to the hungry plants. Attracted by their scent.

"I was wondering," said Carlos. "The other folks I've met who were at the dinner, they all seem younger than you. I'm surprised to see someone of your maturity and stature at such an event."

"Maybe I believed in the cause of rationalism. Ever think of that?"

"Is that why you attended?"

He smiled, seeming genuinely amused. "No. I was there for the publicity. Malachi Zazi was becoming something of a media darling, and I'm not too big to ride on his coattails."

"Forgive me," I interrupted. "I'm not from here, and I don't watch TV or do much of anything to keep up with the news. Was there some reason in particular you or your company needed good publicity?"

Now he laughed. As was rather typical in my life, especially with the male of the species, I seemed to cause an inordinate amount of amusement. For the life of me I couldn't figure out why. But since I was never much of one to fit in, I tried not to take it too personally. Maybe they didn't get out much. . . . One thing was sure: They didn't come across witches like me very often.

"My company is very high-profile. It's the nature of the business—I peddle beauty, not to put too fine a point on it. It's good for me to be pictured, in costume no less, with youthful, good-looking people. Lovely women, handsome, virile men."

"Oh, I see."

"Do you?"

"Let's get back to my questions," Carlos said, giving me a look. He started to go over a few other items regarding past dinners. Then he asked about Doura.

"I don't recall the name," Perkins said, now blatantly staring at me.

"I guess she has a lot of curly blond hair—ring a bell?" Carlos said.

"I'm not great with faces," Perkins said, tapping his temple. "I'm more about the mind."

"What kind of research do you do here, may I ask?" I butted in again.

"You're unfamiliar with Perkins Laboratories?"

"I've heard you're quite a big name, but as I said, I'm from out of town. I don't know much."

"Huh." He remained unconvinced. "We do a lot of different kinds of research—we're invested in projects all over the world."

"But here on this site . . . ? Your focus is on antiaging products?"

"Yes, we have the Ever Young skin care program, and the Re-Juve line of products as well. What's different about our products is that they're part of an entire regimen including vitamins and hormones, which will keep you young just about forever," he said, launching into his practiced sales speech. Then he sat back and smiled. "I imagine we'll be on your mind more in the next few years, as you find the elasticity of your skin diminishing in your later thirties. Crow's-feet at the corner of your eyes, laugh lines . . ."

I blushed under his scrutiny.

He came around the desk, looking at me under the harsh fluorescent light. He put his finger under my chin and raised it, as though to study my face.

I could hear the fly buzzing louder, as though struggling.

Perkins gave a muted *tsk*, lightly touching the corner of my eye, then the corner of my mouth. He had a surprising sensuality for such a nerdy fellow. Talk about creepy.

Carlos came over to stand next to us, edging his shoulder between me and Perkins.

"No need to make this personal," Carlos put in.

"I'm proud of my laugh lines," I said, pulling away.

"That's what they all say. Wait until they start compounding, working with an overall sagging of the flesh on the cheeks."

Perkins was not exactly the finest specimen of male pulchritude, either, I thought, but it seemed petty to point it out. Just that moment, the inevitable began to unfold: The fly landed on the sticky interior surface of the carnivorous plant, buzzing loudly in its struggle to escape. The clamshell began to close.

Perkins's eyes were on me, observing me as I watched the doomed insect.

"I understand Malachi Zazi's father is an investor in your company, is that correct?" Carlos said, trying to keep us focused on business.

Perkins nodded.

"Was there any connection between that fact and your attending his son's dinner parties?"

"No."

"Was Malachi aware of this relationship between you and his father?"

"There was no 'relationship,' Inspector. Thousands of people invest in my research. If you were smart you'd do so as well. This is the future, I guarantee you. People are willing to spend millions of dollars on curing things that aren't actual diseases: aging, sagging, erection problems, baldness. None of those are illnesses per se, yet people will spend much more on them than they will on a simple vaccination that saves the lives of countless children."

"So you do pro bono work, then use some of your profits to help children?" I asked.

He shook his head. "Why should the onus be on me?"

"I thought it might be on all of us, with some having more to give than others."

"I've worked hard to get where I am," Perkins said with a shrug. "I have nothing to apologize for."

"Could you tell me once more what's been happening with your employee Gregory Petrovic?" Carlos asked. "I understand he's had some difficulties in his laboratory research?"

"There were some questionable experimental protocols, which led to a number of incidents. But I don't discuss confidential employee files with anyone, Inspector, unless you've got a warrant for such information."

"Have you fired him?"

"Not yet. Believe it or not, I'm loyal to my employees. I get a lot of satisfaction out of providing people with jobs, with livings. Gregory is not only an employee, I consider him a friend. He has a wife, a family. I don't take those things lightly."

"A lot of the guests seem to think they've been suffering from bad luck, stemming from those dinners with Malachi," I said. "How about you? A lot of bad luck lately?"

He shook his head and smiled. "Zazi hoped to champion the cause of rationalism, but superstitions run deep, don't they? As you can see, I'm doing just fine."

"Well, I thank you for your time," Carlos said. "I'm sure you'd like to get home and relax."

"No problem at all. Always happy to do what I can for the SFPD."

Carlos and I saw ourselves out. It was late afternoon, and the sky had become overcast. Dusk would be falling soon. We both breathed deeply of the damp, eucalyptus-scented air.

"*So* creepy," I said.

"It wasn't just me, then?"

I shook my head and told him about the charms and witch's signs I'd noticed. "Plus, did you see his belt?"

"Somehow it escaped my notice."

"Snakeskin."

Carlos gave me a questioning look.

"A lot of people wear snakeskin belts where I'm from. But until Mike Perkins, I've seen nary a one since arriving in San Francisco."

"I can't exactly arrest the man for bad fashion choices," said Carlos.

"I just thought I'd point it out. Seems odd, is all."

"Can't argue with you there," Carlos said, unlocking his car. "He claims not to remember this Doura person. You sure about her?"

"I think you should look into it, yes. Prince High says she looks after his interests here at Perkins Laboratories, and I wouldn't be surprised if that was her handiwork in Perkins's office."

He gave a quick nod and started to climb into his car.

I felt agitated. The Presidio surroundings called to me—as they did to many. There were couples strolling, families playing, joggers passing by. I hardly ever took the time to walk in the woods, and I was the lesser for it.

"I'm going to take a little walk, enjoy what's left of the day. You go on."

"How will you get back?"

"I'll take the bus. I've been meaning to check it out anyway. If that fails, I'll call a friend to come pick me up. I can manage."

"You sure? 'Cause I've got to get back to the station."

I smiled. "Very sure."

Carlos looked torn for a moment, then nodded. "Watch your back."

"You bet."

Cool and fragrant of eucalyptus leaves, damp with the ocean fog, the air here was so different from the dry, arid atmosphere I was raised on. In my part of Texas the soil was red as the Golden Gate Bridge; here it was yellowish, sandy, sometimes almost white. An ocean breeze played with the leaves. Squirrels scampered up and down trees, busily hoarding their nuts. A hummingbird buzzed right over my head.

I walked, hoping the damp afternoon air would clear my mind. We witches feel an innate connection to the natural world. We're close to our mother earth; her spirit replenishes us. I should take the time to do this more, spend more time in the woods. Like most witches, I drew sustenance from the earth, the moon, and the ocean, and the five elements: earth, water, fire, air, spirit. Each was powerful. Each essential. It was in nature that they came together.

There were some important ritual days coming up. Since they were about pleasing and appeasing the forest folk, they were best conducted in the thick of the woods.

I passed a serene little pond full of lily pads, and just beyond it I came upon a clearing. Stones had been erected, in a similar construction to Stonehenge, though at a tiny fraction of the scale. The stones were a few feet tall, at most. It always amazed me that people were still trying to figure out places like Stonehenge, when their magic seemed so obvious to me.

The primeval forces of the earth were held in the memory of stones, which arose from the great pool of remembrance within the land. The pressure, the heaving molten lava, these processes were powerful reflections of the life force of the earth itself. When stones are laid out in spirals and labyrinths, forces emerge from them and surge through them.

They're called serpent energies, because the lines are not straight, but curve and flow.

The ground around the stones was overturned. It was a newly established ritual ground. Unused.

I supposed it could have been put together by New

Age types constructing a labyrinth based on ancient designs, without any real sense of what they were creating. It could even be the result of a bunch of kids fooling around, playing with stones and only accidentally creating a magnetic field.

Or it could be something more. It might be grounds for a worshipping group of some sort, Druids even. A coven perhaps. I didn't know any of the local covens, other than Bronwyn's. But the more I looked at it, the more I believed someone had placed these stones with intent. They formed a strong web of magnetic lines. When I walked among them I could feel the reverberations coming off my skin, through my teeth.

I should at least meet with some of the other local covens, get to know some of the other witches. Aidan was the one I should talk to about that; too bad he wasn't available to me these days. I wondered whether Bronwyn might know. Her coven was made up of nature-worshipping pagans, but perhaps she knew something of the other groups in the area? Were there witch associations, conventions, that sort of thing? I knew from my travels that there were a whole lot of politics among covens, and I'd always tried to stay out of such entanglements. But that didn't work for me anymore. Since I'd decided to stay in San Francisco and become part of this community, and to associate with the likes of Aidan Rhodes, I'd entered that world whether I wanted to or not.

I wished I knew a way to communicate with the forest creatures, the brownies, the imps. There were many such creatures, but to tell the truth Oscar was the first truly sustained relationship I'd had with an other-being. And even then, I wasn't sure where he'd come from, how old he was, or even where he had lived prior to working with me and Aidan.

While I walked, dusk began to fall. Pools of light from occasional streetlamps illuminated the darkening eucalyptus forest as I made my way back toward the parking lot.

Perkins's car was still parked in front of his offices: a champagne-colored Lexus with a personalized plate: UTH EVR. It took me a moment: youth ever. The search for eternal youth.

Staying forever young . . . the Fountain of Youth . . . Shangri-la. It was a dream that had plagued generations of humans. What would a genuine youth serum entail? Was Perkins simply an ambitious scientist, trying to push the boundaries of nature through creative chemistry . . . or could he be operating on a different level entirely? Could he have, for example, allied himself with someone who wasn't bound by the rules of nature?

Chapter 19

When I got back to Aunt Cora's Closet that evening after a bit of an odyssey riding the city's less than perfect public transportation system, Sailor was sitting on the curb waiting for me, with Conrad at his side.

Sailor looked angry, but his voice was surprisingly measured as he said, "Conrad needs to talk to you."

"What is it, Conrad? Are you okay?"

"I saw . . . something yesterday," Conrad said. "I think I did. I think it was real."

"What was it?"

"It was a man, all bundled up. It was like he was, *dude*, almost like he was trying to get into the store. I totally, like, told him you weren't open this late, but he sort of looked at me, but through me, if you get me."

"Could you see his face? What did he look like?"

"Nah, man, he had these totally dark sunglasses, like the kind the motorcycle cops wear? Dude, those things make me, like, nervous."

"Me too."

"And then I thought I saw him in the park last night."

"Did he do anything? Say anything?"

He shook his head. "Maybe . . . maybe it's in my head, man. I been thinkin' . . . you know, down at the free clinic sometimes they can help you get, you know, clean."

This was new. "I could help you, too, Conrad. I'd be happy to."

"Dude," he said, in a serious, thoughtful tone rare for him. "I'm, like, gonna think about it. I don't like seeing things like that."

"So you think you imagined it?"

"I dunno. Seemed real. But even so . . . it was like I couldn't do much about it, I was so out of it. Feels weird being high if you need to, you know, do something."

I just nodded and tried to emanate empathy and understanding. Even mentioning going straight was a big step for Conrad. I didn't want to scare him off by jumping all over the idea.

"All right," Conrad said as he stood. "This is good. Good. Good night, then."

"Want us to walk you to the park?" I asked.

"Nah, dude. I'm good. Thanks much." He ambled off in the direction of Golden Gate Park.

Now Sailor felt free to vent. "You left me in that apartment with a freaking *snake*!"

"Look on the bright side—I left you my car. Meanwhile, I've been riding buses for an hour and a half. And *you* abandoned *me* to the SFPD, I might point out." I unlocked the shop door. "Besides, that snake wasn't going to hurt you."

"And you know this how?"

"I have a kind of connection with snakes." I flipped on the lights. "Trust me."

"You're a snake charmer now?"

"Not hardly. I just ... I'm not afraid of them, is all. And sometimes I can sense what they're going to do."

"Snakes creep me out."

"What is it with y'all and snakes? I thought guys liked reptiles. Snakes and snails and puppy dog tails. . . ." I entered the store; Sailor followed. "Did you sense anything in the apartment?"

"Didn't have much time. It's been cleansed, obviously."

"What do you think about what Conrad was saying?"

"I think the poor kid needs to get clean."

"Malachi Zazi's body has gone missing."

"So?"

"The thing is, a lot of people—not just Conrad—think they've seen him. Walking around."

"Uh-huh. A lot of people think they see Elvis, too. Maybe someone stole the body. It would be just slightly more likely."

"Good point. So as far as you know, there's nothing like actual vampires or anything, right?"

"No. But why do you keep asking me this? I'm a psychic, remember, I don't know about this sort of stuff. Besides, it's not the same in my tradition."

"Your 'tradition'? You have a 'tradition'?"

"Sort of." He shrugged, uncomfortable. "I'm half Rom."

"Rom? As in Romani, as in Gypsy?"

He gave a curt nod. "On my father's side."

"Really?"

"I don't have much association with it. My father separated himself from it fairly early on. A lot of that stuff—it tends to be handed down by the women, and my mother's Scots-Irish. I was raised just like any other ethnic mutt in this country."

"You act as though your heritage is something to be embarrassed about."

"I'm not embarrassed. I just don't want to have to answer any damn fool questions."

"Do you know any Rom witches or healers?"

"Questions such as that, for instance." Sailor rolled his eyes. "You know what they say: *Ki shan I Romani, Adoi san'I chov'hani.*"

"What does that mean?"

"Loosely translated, it means we're loaded with *chov'hani*, or witches."

"Is that a bad thing, or a good thing?"

"Depends on whether people are paying you for your services, or burning you alive, or herding you into Nazi concentration camps."

Not to put too fine a point on it.

"So, are some of your family . . . ?"

He sighed. "My aunt is a Gypsy witch, yes. Is that what you want to know?"

"Wow. That's fascinating. Is she local?"

"I'm not having this discussion. I just came by to make sure you hadn't landed in jail. Now I'm going home." He surprised me by kissing me on the forehead. "Be good. If I can't get off this detail, I'll see you in the morning, bright and early."

Up in my apartment, Oscar was still trying to decide on a name for the cat, and the cat was now totally uninterested in knowing him. Since I was allergic, it saved all of its affection for me. I sneezed repeatedly, which Oscar felt duty-bound to respond to with a series of "gesundheits." I fixed them both something to eat, reminding myself, again, to stop and get some actual pet food soon.

Oscar would find it offended his dignity to eat it, no doubt, but it would probably be best for the cat.

"Oscar, when we were at Malachi Zazi's apartment the other day, you said something about gargoyles being practically family. What did you mean by that?"

He stared at me. Oscar was so talkative that when he went mute, it was significant.

"You don't want to talk about it?" I asked.

He shrugged and started picking at his talonlike toes, refusing to make eye contact. "Oh, Mistress! I forgot to tell you. There's a message on the phone. From that *man*, the cowan."

"Don't call him that, Oscar. It's not nice." I used it in my own mind from time to time, but tried not to say it aloud. "Cowan" is an archaic, derogatory word for a nonwitchy human.

"I don't like cowans."

"That's not true. You like Bronwyn."

"The lady, she's nice," he said in a dreamy voice. Bronwyn tended to slip Oscar snacks, and to cradle him in her arms and against her ample bosom.

"And Maya."

"Maya . . . ," he crooned. Maya sang to him when she thought no one was listening. And she also brought him doggie bags from lunch.

"And just about every customer that comes into the shop. Especially the female ones."

"Female customers . . ."

I smiled and turned toward the message machine. But then I hesitated. Part of me was glad Max had called, but the other part wasn't sure I was ready to hear what he had to say. Especially with Oscar watching me with those huge, intent eyes.

Saved by the phone.

"Lily, it's me," said Bronwyn. "I'm right outside. Could I come up and talk to you? It's important."

"Of course," I said, going to open the front door of the apartment.

This was perfect. I loved the idea of having friends just dropping by—made me feel downright normal. Besides, I'd love to use her as a sounding board, not just for all the craziness surrounding Malachi Zazi, but also with regard to Max Carmichael. I was scared to listen to the message he'd left me. Who was the coward now?

But the moment I saw Bronwyn's face, I knew it wasn't going to be a girls' gabfest kind of evening. She refused my offer of tea, and we took our seats on the sofa in my cozy living room.

"Bronwyn, is everything all right? Did something happen with Gregory?"

"No . . . sort of. Lily, I want you to stop what you've been doing. Rebecca has asked me to get you to stop looking into this . . . issue of Gregory's."

"Before, you and Rebecca both asked for my help."

"I know that. But when I brought her the tonic you brewed, it set off an argument. She made some calls, talked to some people. She seems to think that Gregory will be exonerated soon anyway, and having people like us involved . . ."

"'People like us'?"

She fixed me with a look, her soft brown eyes shiny with tears. "Witches. She doesn't want my name, much less yours, connected with them, with . . . any of them."

"Oh, I see."

"She doesn't mean anything by it," Bronwyn said. "Or . . . I guess she does, doesn't she? But still, I have to honor her wishes in this. This is my chance, Lily. I have to do what she's asking of me. I failed Rainb—Rebecca—as a mother, but now I have to try to make it up to her. You need to let go of this."

"How do you mean you failed her?"

"I was so young when I had my baby." Bronwyn pushed some loose lavender around on the coffee table, absentmindedly making the shape of a pentacle—a symbol of safety. "I tried . . . I really believed that unlimited love would be enough. But now I see that structure and security are important, too. She lacked all of that. I didn't give that to her. There were times . . . I even remember bringing her to parties—with all kinds of things going on. What kind of mother does something like that?"

Shame rolled off of her in waves. This was not the calm, confident woman I had come to love and depend on.

"Was she ever unsafe? Was she hurt?" I asked.

"No. But we were lucky."

"I think you need to cut yourself a little slack. It might not have been the ideal situation, but you loved her, you took care of her. And it's all in the past, anyway. She's a healthy, accomplished woman."

Bronwyn nodded, took a deep breath, and released it slowly. "I know. I know that. This whole thing has just been so hard. But you know the crazy part? In a way it's brought us closer together—she's looked to me for support. That's why I want to respect Rebecca's wishes in this. I want you to stop investigating."

I thought of Carlos saying insulting things to me about witchcraft earlier in the day, and how strangely threatening Perkins had seemed. And how Aidan had reacted to my involvement, and the malevolent energy of Doura. . . . Who was Malachi Zazi to me, anyway, that I should spend such time and energy on him? True, it was bewildering that the apartment—and the corpse—had been cleansed before we arrived. But given the man's unfortunate relations, it could have been done for any number of reasons. I wouldn't put it past Prince High to have stolen his son's body and conducted séances in the apartment—if he researched cleansing ceremonies, used the right ingredients, and truly believed, he could have managed to instill at least a temporary freeze.

And now Bronwyn, my dear friend, was asking me to butt out. I didn't have much choice.

"All right," I said softly. "If that's what you want."

Chapter 20

I tried to spend an evening like a normal person. I didn't brew, and I didn't read about ancient Roman gods, or flip through my Book of Shadows in search of new recipes it might have miraculously added. I didn't try in vain to scry in my useless crystal ball. I did my best to put all thoughts of Malachi Zazi and Prince High and the Huffmans and Gregory and Rebecca and Perkins out of my mind.

Finally I decided that if I was looking for distraction, Max Carmichael seemed the most likely candidate. We met at the pub not far down Haight Street from Aunt Cora's Closet.

"How are you?" he asked as we settled into a small table in a secluded corner.

"Could we start with an easier question?"

"That bad?"

I shrugged. He ordered margaritas, adding, "Make them doubles." A man after my own heart.

"How are things going with the Satanists?" he asked.

I had to smile. "I haven't seen them since we were last there together."

"Good."

"Could you tell me anything about Prince High, or his so-called Church of the Devil?" I had promised Bronwyn to stop investigating, but I just wanted to clarify a few things in my own mind. That's all. It would stop here.

"I don't think they've got an actual hotline to hell, if that's what you're asking. As far as I can tell, the 'Prince' milked the 'Church' thing for as much money as he could. When times changed he lost the shock factor, and then he faded out of sight pretty fast."

"Should I assume you don't think he has any actual evil powers, then?" That was a silly question—Max Carmichael didn't really believe in *my* powers, though he had witnessed them in action.

"I don't think a person needs to connect with any supernatural evil in order to perpetrate crimes upon humanity, Lily. We've seen enough through human history to document that fact, haven't we?"

I nodded and took a deep sip of my margarita. The broad glass was rimmed with salt, of course, and redolent of limes.

"I looked up Prince Zazi, or whatever it is he calls himself," Max continued. "He has a long record of inquiries from Child Protective Services when Malachi was a boy, including several ER visits. Anyone who could hurt a child, or expose him to the sorts of things Malachi was exposed to—that signals a perfectly human evil, in my mind."

"Speaking of natural evil, do you know anything about Mike Perkins?"

"The founder of Perkins Laboratories? A little. He's not a person to be messed with. More money than the queen, and less of a sense of humor. Why?"

"Oh, I don't know. I spoke with him and he just . . . he gave me a pretty strange vibe, to tell you the truth."

He chuckled. "Now you're sounding more California than witchy. 'Strange vibe'? Is that a technical term?"

I smiled and played with the frost on the outside of the margarita glass, drawing swirly lines.

"He's not someone to be crossed, though, I'll tell you that much," Max said. "He didn't get where he is now, as fast as he did, by being a nice guy. I wouldn't put much past him. And a meddling witch like you . . . that could be a recipe for trouble."

"Bronwyn wants me to step away from all this, to stop asking around."

"And you, of course, refused, because you know what's best for her."

"It's just—"

"You think you know better than she does. Than any of us do."

It was on the tip of my tongue to deny it. But it was true. In this one very particular area, I *was* smarter *and* more able. I understood witchcraft, was able to alter reality and affect the future, simply by using the talents that ran in my blood and the accumulated knowledge of my training. I was more than happy to admit my lack of knowledge about almost everything else—I hadn't even graduated high school. And my mathematical and inter-personal skills were decidedly challenged. But with witchcraft, yes, I was a star.

"I *am* better. More able. In the Craft."

His lips pressed together, just a tad, and he stared at me with eyes the color of the gray sky over the sea. Those eyes killed me.

"You should stay away from this if Bronwyn asks you

to, Lily. And I'm not saying this as someone who wants to keep you safe from people like Prince High and Mike Perkins. I'm saying it as a friend. She has reasons to ask you to back off, and as her friend you should respect those reasons."

"I know that. I already told her I would drop it."

"Then why are we talking about men with strange vibes?"

I smiled. "I just wanted your take on the subject, but that's it. Case closed."

"Good." We looked at each other for a long moment.

"Speaking of vibes . . . I've been doing a lot of soul searching lately," Max said, "as well as a lot of research into the world of the occult."

"Really. And what does your research tell you?"

He shrugged. "That it's a bunch of hooey, by and large. And yet I've seen too many unexplained things with my own eyes—always in your company. And . . . and I care for you, even though your entire being is invested in this idea of yourself as a witch. It leads me to believe that there has to be something to it."

"And?"

"Look, as you know, I screwed up, royally, with my . . . late wife. She's still with me, in a sense."

"You mean your guilt's still with you?"

He took a deep breath, let it out slowly. "Maybe. Yes. I loved her. I wasn't there for her when I should have been. I should have done more, should have done whatever I could. I think I still have 'work' to do in that area. I was hoping that for the moment, at least, you and I could be friends."

"Just . . . friends?"

He nodded. "Good friends."

"That was a very friendly kiss yesterday."

"I know, I was out of line. I couldn't help myself."

"I don't know, Max," I said, slowly licking salt off my lips. "I've never tried to be friends with someone when I wanted to . . . you know."

"What?"

I shrugged. "You know."

"I . . . are you saying . . . ?" His voice sounded just a tad hoarse.

I just stared at him for another moment, shrugged again, and left him to pay the bill.

I might not know much about male-female relations, but I was a quick study. If the man wanted to play games, so be it.

Two could play at such matters of the heart.

Haight Street was crowded with people in high spirits, bustling to and from dinner and drinks. I walked among them, past Aunt Cora's Closet, to Bronwyn's place.

It killed me to see her so upset, so full of self-doubt earlier. I counted on her to be a rock, a port in the storm. I would do as she asked, but . . .

I only hoped Carlos could figure out Malachi Zazi's death without my help. Because this man who had survived his father, who had loved a beautiful movie star, who had been afraid of the sun but who set up a rooftop garden . . . the late Malachi Zazi was growing on me. I hated to let the injustice of his murder stand, just because of Rebecca's ridiculous prejudice against witches.

Maybe I could talk to her directly. Maybe all three of us—she, Bronwyn, and I—could hash this out like grown women.

Bronwyn's second-story lights were still on. I let myself into the building.

Something was wrong.

I felt it the moment I walked into the foyer—there was a rank odor, as though the yeast in the neighbor's baked goods had gone bad. But that wasn't the problem ... it was something else. As I mounted the stairs, I realized the dread was not merely internal. I was feeling something bleak and wrong outside, as well as within me.

I slowed my pace. Took deep breaths, trying to stay attuned to the vibrations.

On the stairs. Right above me. What was it?

I paused, stroked my medicine bag, whispered a protective chant, and then crept up the rest of the stairs.

Finally, my eyes alit on something on the landing. Right in front of the door, on the woven hemp mat that welcomed all to Bronwyn's hearth and home.

The door opened. "Lily, what—"

"Stop right there!" I commanded. "Don't step over the threshold!"

Bronwyn looked startled, but did as I said. "What's wrong?"

I gestured to an ugly bundle sitting on her doormat. Three nails and three sharp needles, wrapped up in ribbons of black, and deep purple thread. Humming, alive with malice. Charged with wickedness.

The nails were rusty, old. Coffin nails.

"It's a hex."

Chapter 21

"A hex?" Bronwyn paled.

"A curse." I nodded, surveying the landing to be sure we weren't dealing with anything else besides the bundle on the doormat.

I looked above the lintel. I didn't see anything, but I sensed something. In the old days lintels were often arched or bowed, because the straight horizontal shelf created by standard doorways was an invitation for demons to perch. Bronwyn should hang an amulet there. In the meantime, just in case, I needed to make a sign that evil spirits weren't welcome here.

"Do you have any paint? Something red I can make a mark with?"

She shook her head. "I can't think of anything."

"No paint, lipstick, anything at all?"

"I don't use lipstick, but . . . the kids and I made red velvet cupcakes earlier. There's still a little batter in the bottom of the bowl. Would that work?"

I gave her a small smile, despite the tension. "Bring it here, let me see it."

It might have been rather unorthodox, but I was after color more than substance. I reached across the threshold to take the bowl from her.

"I thought you said not to cross the threshold," Bronwyn said. "What about you?"

"I *want* them to come after me. Their hexes are no good where I'm concerned."

Between being a natural witch, which meant I was guarded at all times, and the protective talismans and medicine bag I was carrying, I was like a mirror when it came to something like this. The Wiccans like to point out the rule of three, that any act of goodness comes back to you threefold; similarly, a hex set upon someone like me bounces off of me and reflects many times back onto the curser. I welcomed their hexes.

I scraped my hand along the edges of the sweet-smelling mixing bowl, then jumped up, slapping the wall immediately above the lintel. The mark of the human hand was powerful. The mark of a witch's hand even more so.

My handprint was clear, in deep red batter against the creamy white paint of the wall. It would do for now.

"Listen to me very carefully, Bronwyn. Don't let any part of your body cross the threshold, and make sure none of your animals do, either. I have to run to my place for supplies, but I'll be right back. Are you expecting anyone?"

She shook her head.

"Good. But if you hear anyone come in, warn them to stay downstairs." Keeping my eyes on the bundle, I started to back down the stairs. "Or better yet, have them wait outside. In the meanwhile, make yourself some tea."

"What kind?" she asked, eyes huge.

I smiled. "It doesn't really matter. It's just to calm yourself. Chamomile would be excellent. And light a white candle and say a protection charm, then pet your cats. I'll be right back."

I ran.

The three blocks might as well have been as many miles. My lungs burned from the exercise and the fear, each searing breath feeding my rage. Bronwyn was an innocent in all of this. Someone had gone after my friend. My *friend*.

I burst into Aunt Cora's Closet.

"Oscar!"

I heard a thump overhead, and then the sound of the door opening. "Mistress?"

Oscar sounded unsure. I never called for him like that, always coming up for him when I was ready.

"Grab my box of stones and bring it to me. Then crush some rosemary with the mortar and pestle, set it on the tray in the kitchen, and bring it down as well."

"Yes, Mistress," said Oscar, for once doing as he was told.

I crossed over to Bronwyn's herb stand, pulling a glass jar of crushed eggshells off the top shelf. Eggshells are potent. In the old days, it was said that if you threw your eggshell away haphazardly while cooking, a witch could come upon it at night, make a boat of it, and sail away wherever she pleased. That didn't sound like such a bad idea at the moment.

I also gathered cobwebs, three dead flies, and a coarse black cloth.

Oscar brought me what I had asked for. I told him to stay upstairs with the cat and not to open to anyone, no matter whom, except for me.

"Can't I help?" he growled.

"No. Stay here." The look on his face gave me pause, even in my haste. "I don't mean to be harsh, Oscar, but right now I want you to stay here, safe and sound, with the cat, so I don't have to worry about you two. Understand?"

"Yes, Mistress."

Then I ran back to Bronwyn's with my supplies. Upon hearing me come in the main front door to the foyer, Bronwyn opened her door.

"Stay there," I said.

I crept back up, slowly, to the top of the stairs. I coated the fingertips of my left hand in the pure white powdered eggshell and picked up the bundle with my protected hand, holding it away from me.

Still holding the charm in my left hand, I drew a pentacle in salt around the rosemary on the tray, set stones of malachite and jasper and marble at each point. I chanted a protective spell, muttering the words as a verbal talisman while I created the pentacle.

> *North South East West*
> *Spider's web shall bind them best*
> *East West North South*
> *Bind their limbs and shut their mouths*
> *Blind their eyes and choke their breath*
> *Wrap them up in ropes of death*

Finally I set the evil bundle at the center of the charged pentagram, adding the cobwebs, the flies, and covering it all with the black cloth. The lines of salt would bind the wickedness temporarily, keep it from attaching to me or anyone else.

I breathed a sigh of relief.

In Bronwyn's kitchen I washed my hands thoroughly with lavender soap and then checked her whole apartment for Goofer Balls or any other hexes. It was clean. Still, I performed another brief protective spell, and then Bronwyn and I swept the whole place from the back to the front, including the landing and the stairs, and I took the broom out to the front porch.

Afterward, I sat with Bronwyn at her kitchen table, drinking tea from handmade, brightly painted ceramic mugs. A big yellow platter held a dozen or so very sloppy red velvet cupcakes topped with white buttercream frosting. Coloring books and crayons were still scattered about the main room, but the children had gone back home with their mother.

Neither of us spoke for a long time.

"I'll take the hex with me when I go. Try not to worry about it, Bronwyn. I promise you, I'll get to the bottom of this."

"I don't want you to."

I met her eyes for a long moment. She shook her head. There were tears in her soft brown eyes.

"Please, Lily. I meant what I said when I asked you to stay out of it. I thought you were going to."

"I was, but not after this. Not anymore. I can't."

"You can. Rebecca says if we keep pursuing it, she won't let me see my grandbabies anymore. She said she'll cut me out, shun me, won't speak to me." Tears ran down her face.

I was speechless. I knew they weren't all that close, but ... Bronwyn's daughter didn't want to even acknowledge her mother? How could she? I thought of my own mother, who sent me away at the age of eight—albeit to a loving home with Graciela, but still—and who then put me at risk in a desperate attempt to normalize me. The mother I still sent money to, but who preferred I didn't call. The mother who was still friends with the hometown neighbors who had vilified me. What would I have given for a mother like Bronwyn: openhearted, generous of spirit, confident in the good of humanity?

"Bronwyn, I'm so sorry."

"How can she ask me to renounce what I believe in? It doesn't hurt anyone. That's our creed above all: 'An ye shall harm none. . . .'"

"I know."

She shrugged and tried to smile through her tears. "I was so young when I had her. I truly thought . . . I believed that with enough love, she would eventually love me back."

"Oh, Bronwyn." I wanted to tell her that Rebecca did love her, in her own way, but it sounded like a platitude. Instead, I reached out to envelop her in a hug.

I'm not really a hugger. Other than children or animals, I could count on both hands the number of times in my life when I've willingly hugged someone. But Bronwyn sank into me, and sobbed with a broken heart. I held her for a very long time.

As much as I wanted to please her, I couldn't promise Bronwyn not to pursue the case. Not now.

If the powers that be wanted me to drop this case, they had just succeeded in convincing me to do the very opposite. I would hunt them down, and I would do what I had to do in order to destroy them, or at the very least to drain them of power. No one went after someone I loved. *No one.*

I could no more keep from exacting revenge than I could stop being a witch. I wasn't sure how that would play out among the Zen-inspired Bay Area types, but it was my witchy nature, plain and simple.

I only hoped Bronwyn would understand. Someday.

After another restless night, I headed down to the café for coffee and breakfast.

I was pretty clear on how to deal with the hex left on Bronwyn's doorstep, but I wanted to double-check with someone more familiar with this sort of curse than I: Hervé LeMansec. Hervé was a voodoo priest and—at least last time I checked—one of my few remaining friends. His shop didn't open until eleven, though, and I was just as glad. I could use a little downtime in the shop this morning, soaking up the vibrations of the clothes and their history.

A charming, rather scruffy holdover from the Summer of Love, the Coffee to the People café was now peopled by pierced, tattooed, vaguely antisocial types rather than the original peace-and-love hippies. But its rebellious nature was intact; whatever the majority of the middle class wanted, these folks did not. Along with the head shops and secondhand clothes stores—for Aunt Cora's Closet was not the only vintage shop in the neighborhood—it was both a Haight Street holdover and a landmark.

While standing in line, I listened in on the conversation in front of me.

"It just seems like you're giving in to conformity, though, if you actually have the gender reassignment surgery and then start acting all masculine. I mean, would you even still be a lesbian if you're, like, officially, a man?"

It was the kind of conversation it was hard to imagine hearing in most parts of the world. I smiled to myself and tried to remember it to share with Bronwyn later. But as the thought occurred to me, I remembered how we left things last night. *Bronwyn*. It about broke my heart to hear her crying yesterday.

I reached the front of the line. Wendy was an ample, curvy young woman with a penchant for wearing in public what would have been considered bedroom attire back home in Texas—for that matter, it would have been considered lingerie in most parts of the Bay Area. Today she was dressed in a black fishnet jacket over a corset—both of which she had found at Aunt Cora's Closet last week—along with black leggings. But with her Bettie Page smooth black hair cut in dramatic bangs across her forehead, and the "don't mess with me" look in her brown eyes, she was more than an empowered woman; Wendy was a phenomenon.

"I hear you need to stop messing around with Bronwyn's deal," she said as she started to concoct a Flower Power drink for Conrad and a Chocolate to the People for me. When life was difficult, I opted for chocolate. This was much of the time lately. If I wasn't careful, I wouldn't be able to fit in my own vintage clothes much longer.

"Bronwyn's 'deal'?" I asked.

"She didn't want to go into details, but she asked the coven to help support you in not butting in. I mean, she said it nicer than that, but that was the basic idea. So"— Wendy caught two bagels as they popped out of the toaster—"are you going to drop whatever it is you're doing?"

I considered lying. It would be much easier, and frankly, not that uncalled for in this situation, in my opinion. I wasn't sure that this was any of Wendy's business.

On the other hand, she was a coven sister to Bronwyn, who had clearly confided in her. They had known
each other, been friends and fellow Wiccans, for much
longer than I had known either of them. I was the new-
bie, the interloper. As usual.

I opened my mouth to speak, but Starr, another member of the coven, beat me to it.

"Don't be such a hard-ass, Wendy," she said from behind the local free paper, the *Guardian*.

"Just looking out for what Bronwyn needs right now.
We take care of our own," she said as she slathered hum-
mus onto the bagels and added roasted red peppers and
kalamata olives. "No offense, Lily, but you're not a member of the coven. It's not the same. You're not a sister."

"Don't worry too much about it, Lily," said Starr. Her
voice was kind. "Bronwyn'll get over it soon enough."

"I never did like that stick-in-the-butt Rebecca," said
another woman, whom I recognized from the coven
meetings as well.

I appreciated their words, but it was clear their loy-
alty was with Bronwyn—as it should be. They had been
friends much longer than I, and shared the bonds of the
coven.

I, on the other hand, had asked for the coven's help
twice now, putting them in danger both times. Before
they met little old me, their coven meetings consisted of
benign prayers to the goddesses and rituals celebrating
the solstice, and nature in general.

I felt like an outsider, again. I thought I had found
friendship, a sense of belonging in this neighborhood.
But had I? Was it that easy, or was a lifelong loner unable to forge those bonds? It had only been a few
months, after all.

Would anyone even be talking to me anymore when this was all said and done? I felt a stab of regret deep in my belly. Not for the first time I considered hopping in my car and driving off, away, just abandoning the scene and starting anew. It's what I had done for the past decade or so of my life, and escape always beckoned. But I had to remind myself that this was my town now, my community.

Back at Aunt Cora's Closet, as though to hammer home that point, I looked up from my bagel to see several familiar faces coming into the shop. I loved the informal, casual friendships I was developing with the regulars. These were mostly neighborhood residents, but there were also a few artsy types who made it a point to check out new inventory every week or so, as well as a number of trendsetting fashionistas. I was lulled by the rhythm of their conversation and the swish-swish-swish of the hangers along the racks.

Sailor arrived and wordlessly took up his bodyguard station, sitting by the dressing rooms. He looked up at me in silent gratitude when I offered him coffee.

"Here's an impossible challenge for you," said one young woman I recognized as a student at the School of Fine Arts. Lagging behind her, as though he wished he were anywhere but here, was a young man wearing a faded Black Sabbath T-shirt and grungy jeans. "My boyfriend and I are going to a thirtieth birthday costume party, and the theme's the pirates of the Caribbean. I don't suppose you'd have some sort of matching costumes we could wear?"

"Nothing's impossible when it comes to vintage clothes," I said. "You won't be a perfect match, but I'm sure we can figure something out."

I spent the next half hour digging up everything from

leather vests to frilly Victorian bloomers. It was amazing to see the couple transform from sloppy artists into a swashbuckling duo worthy of, if not Hollywood, at least a community theater production. The young man claimed he had a collection of real swords and knives at home to finish off the outfits.

"Just be careful," I said, unable to help myself. They rolled their eyes at me, but were so happy with their new clothes I could imagine them wearing their costumes to more than just a single party.

I noticed Sailor watching me with a sardonic smile on his face, but I tried to ignore him. I supposed vintage clothing may seem silly to some, but I loved finding outfits that suited people and made them happy. I reveled in the vibrations, and the history, and the humanity of it all.

Bronwyn was on the schedule to start at noon today, but instead Maya walked in.

"Good thing I'm on break from school," she said as she hung up her sweater and scarf. "Bronwyn asked me to cover for her again today. Listen, Lily, I really think you should stay out of whatever it is that's going on, if she asked you to."

Apparently Bronwyn had spent some quality time on the phone since last I saw her.

"I can't, Maya. I can't explain why, exactly, but it's for her own protection. And for all I know, for your protection as well. Someone went after her because she's my friend, I'm sure of it."

Leaving the shop in Maya's capable hands, I grabbed the covered tray that held the ugly hex, slipped out the back door, and hopped into my car before Sailor realized I was gone.

Chapter 22

Hervé LeMansec had rotten timing. Unfortunately for me, he was out of town, visiting family in Southern California.

His wife, Caterina, gave me this unwelcome news when I stopped by his voodoo supply shop on Mission Street. Caterina was a beautiful woman with traditional tribal facial tattoos, long locks, and two young boys who were huge basketball fans. She was soft-spoken, and though this was now one of my favorite supply stops, we had never exchanged many words. But I knew she worked with Hervé, and ran the shop. I was betting she would know something about my ugly little package.

Upon lifting the black cloth from the hex, her nostrils flared and she reared back.

"This is a suffering root. Charged with a blood sacrifice. This is no small thing." Her dark eyes were shiny and untelling as mirrors. "It could be hoodoo, or it could be one of yours. Have you run afoul of any practitioners?"

"Not that I know of. Unless . . . have you ever heard of Malachi Zazi?"

She became very still. Her movements were careful, studied.

"I think you should speak to Hervé directly."

"When does he come back?"

"Next week, but you'll need to talk to him before that."

"I hate talking on the telephone."

"So does he. Call him anyway." She dialed a cordless phone, handed it to me, and gestured for me to take my call in the back offices of the store. I didn't appear to have much choice. Caterina may be soft-spoken, but I had the sense she had a will of iron. Not that I was surprised; from what I knew of Hervé, it made sense he would have chosen an equal as a life partner.

"What can you tell me about suffering roots?" I asked Hervé as soon as we had taken care of basic pleasantries.

"That they have nothing to do with roots, but I imagine you know that. They're not amateur hour—if it was charged properly, then it was done by someone with skills. Were you able to disarm it?"

"Yes. And I looked it up in my Book of Shadows; I was planning to perform a drowning spell to dispense of it permanently."

"Good idea. I'm sorry I can't see it in person; I might be able to tell you more."

"Let me ask you this: If a body disappeared from the morgue, what would you think?"

"That someone was trying to avoid an autopsy."

"So it wouldn't occur to you that he, you know, walked away? Kind of . . . undead style?"

There was a very loud silence from his end of the line.

"You think you have a zombie on your hands? And you think that because I am a vodou practitioner, I would know about it? That's a very unwelcome stereotype about my belief system, you know."

"I know. And I don't really think . . . I don't know. I'm just a little shaky."

"You really believe in such things?"

"Not really. But you do, don't you?"

"Not in any way that you're thinking." He laughed again. "Someone's been watching too many late-night movies."

"I guess you're right. How about this: Have you ever heard of Malachi Zazi? His father called himself the High Prince Zazi, had a—"

"*Him*, I know. If you're involved with anything that has to do with him, I'd stay away from it."

"What can you tell me about Zazi?" While we talked, I meandered around his back room, checking out his grinding equipment, jars, tubs, and boxes full of herbs and roots I had never heard of. And I thought I knew a lot. It was fascinating.

"It was before my time, but I've heard the stories about Prince High. He's a devil guy."

"Do you know any details about him?"

"Not really. Hasn't been particularly active for a while. I think everyone was hoping he'd aged out of it. Still lives in the same place, though, as far as I know, at least I assume so. It was a house out in the Richmond District, on California. Painted it all black. If he'd moved, the new owners would have painted it, I feel sure."

"Yeah, I met him the other day. The house is still black."

"You met him? How did that go?"

"Um . . . okay. He's a nut, obviously, but there were no overt threats."

"Well, that's something, anyway."

"Do you know anything about his son, Malachi Zazi?"

"All I know is that when he was a kid his father did a big public baptism. Had a naked woman draped over the altar, and hailed the devil."

I braced myself.

He said nothing more.

"That's it?"

"Kind of a freak show."

"They didn't hurt the woman?"

"I don't believe so, no. It was mostly theatrics. They filmed it."

"And they advertised this to the world? Sounds like he's more of a showman than a serious practitioner. I mean, if they're serious, don't these people keep things sort of on the down low?"

"Like you?"

"And you."

"I would think. But it was a little wild back then, or so they tell me. It was before my time, which I think was just as well. I don't like that stuff."

I perused Hervé's bookshelves while he spoke. Voodoo was such a different system from mine; there was a lot of root work that overlapped, but it dealt much more with dirt and powders.

"But let me say this much: You shouldn't be messing with Prince High. Leave it to the police, or whoever's involved."

"This feels more like my area of expertise. Someone left that suffering root bundle to hex my friend. And a snake for me. I'm getting the sense it's personal."

"A snake?"

"A rattler at the scene of the crime. Whoever it was couldn't have been a witch, though, right? Or they would have known it wouldn't bother me."

"Oh, I don't know about that. Plenty of witches are bothered by snakes. We vodou types use snakes all the time, of course. The eggs, blood, heads, flesh, sheds, bones, and skins of all species of snakes are used in our magic. Then there's always Goofer Dust and Living Things in You poison."

"What is Living Things in You poison?"

"You really should know more about snakes than you do. This isn't only hoodoo—you use it in your system as well. In jinxing and crossing—you do hexes, don't you?"

"My grandmother never cared for snakes," I said. "She trained me, so I guess we just overlooked all those bits. And then I never quite finished my training." I hesitated, refraining from telling him what happened with me and snakes, back in the day. What was done was done, and the link I had with serpents now seemed like a handy thing, all things considered.

"With the Living Things in You poison, powdered eggs and sheds are mixed into the victim's food, along with the appropriate incantation. The target feels as though a creature is wriggling around in his body. It causes pain and distress, and has been known to drive men insane."

"Ew."

Hervé laughed, a deep rumble that I appreciated, but which made me a bit apprehensive at the same time.

"You of all people should know, Lily, the Craft is not for the faint of heart."

"That's for sure. One more question: Do you think Aidan Rhodes could have anything to do with this?"

"The murder, or the hex, or the snake?"

"I really doubt the snake would have been placed by anyone who knew me; they would know it wouldn't be a threat to me. But the murder, or the hex . . . either or both?"

"How well do you know him?"

"Not well. He's been training me a bit."

There was another pause on the other side of the line. This was one reason I didn't like talking on the phone—I couldn't tell what it meant.

"What do you mean, training you?"

"I never finished my training with my grandmother."

"And you're having *Aidan* train you?" Echoes of Sailor.

"Why is everyone so afraid of him? And why won't they tell me what the secret is?"

"For that very reason: fear. What does he think about you working on this?"

"He's"—I thought of his face the last time I saw him, the shimmering, powerful anger that emanated from him—"perturbed."

"Look, Lily, Aidan isn't my master. But we have an understanding. He's left me alone, and I'd like to keep it that way. And . . . I doubt I should be telling you this, but there was an agreement. Some kind of pact. It was established before my time, but it's very clear. The voodoo practitioners, the witches, the devil folks—we keep out of each other's way. We don't tread on one another's territory."

"Do you mean there's a figurative, unspoken pact, or a pact pact?" I had heard of such supernatural covenants, but I'd never actually witnessed one.

"You'll need to get the details from Aidan. As I said, it was before my time, and since I don't trespass, I haven't had to worry about it. Listen, you're in my office?" he asked. "There's a blue jar on the edge of the shelf nearest the window. Take a chunk of three fingers root. And some cemetery dust. Keep some in your medicine bag. It will help. And I have plenty of snake products if you need them as well."

"Thank you."

"You're welcome. Look, Lily, my mom and dad just showed up. I can't talk about this anymore."

"They're not . . . into the same thing you are?"

"They're good churchgoing Catholics."

"Really?"

"What can I tell you? I found my own path. Anyway, I'm sorry I can't be there to help you with this. It sounds as though you should have a magical ally, just in case things ratchet up. Do you know anyone else who might be able to stand with you?"

My stomach clenched. I had relied on Bronwyn's coven before, but clearly that wasn't an option this time. Aidan was angry at me, and Hervé was out of town. Sailor wasn't much help with this sort of thing.

But then something occurred to me. Sailor had mentioned he had someone who might be able to train me— had he been referring to his aunt, the Rom witch? It wouldn't hurt to ask. Lately I could use all the friends I could get, especially friends who knew how to kick some supernatural butt.

I thanked Hervé, hung up, took a piece of three fingers root, a pinch of cemetery dust, and helped myself to some snake sheds and eggs from Hervé's supplies. Just in case.

That night I found my way back to the little pond I had seen in the Presidio, not far from Mike Perkins's office.

I had surrounded the suffering root with sulfur, as my Book of Shadows had instructed, and mixed in some of Hervé's Goofer Dust while I was at it. Then I filled the tray with garlands of flowers and a wineskin full of a fine Napa Valley cabernet.

Now I stood at the edge of the water, barefoot, wearing a long white dress, wet to the knees and muddy with the sticky muck of the pond. Chanting, invoking, I pushed the tray—and all its contents—out into the pond. I called upon the water spirits to take the curse within their midst, where it could do no harm, and to take my offering in exchange.

As the tray floated out, I fell to my knees in the mud, lifting my hands to the skies. I felt the tingle of my powers, the rightness of my intent. I stayed like that until the candles had burned down to stubs, flickered, and died out.

I caught my reflection in the water: ethereal, otherworldly. It was one of those moments when I could stand outside myself and see how odd I seemed, as though I had been plucked from another time, another century. This was right, as it should be. I was a conduit for my spirit, a step in the never-ending cycle of nature, con-

nected to all those witches who had gone before—
powerful, persecuted, burned, and reviled. And loved.

Weary, as I often was after complicated spell casting,
I made my way back down the dark path toward the
entrance of the park, where I had left my car. Lucky for
me, I had excellent night vision. There was little moon-
light tonight, and I hadn't brought any modern conve-
nience like a flashlight, or even an ancient one, like the
Hand of Glory, to light my way.

A snap sounded behind me. I whirled around.
Searched the shadows.

Nothing.

I continued walking. But then came the muffled but
unmistakable sound of a footfall on eucalyptus leaves
and pine needles.

Someone was following me. I stopped and turned
around, taking a stance on the path. A vague silhouette
slipped behind the trunk of a large cypress.

"Who is it?" I called out, stroking my medicine bag.
Don't jump to conclusions, Lily. It could be anyone.

No answer.

I turned and walked some more, then whirled around
in time to catch a glimpse of someone wrapped in
scarves, and a hat, and sunglasses despite the dark of
night.

My breath caught in my throat. I walked faster. Then
I ran.

I didn't know this place, these woods. Many
witches—my grandmother Graciela included—came to
know their local forest or wild locale like the backs of
their hands: every cave, hollowed-out log, clear-running
creek. And along with it all, the forest folk. They fled to
them for safety.

If only I had that familiarity now. I would be able to hide, and the elves and brownies might step in, help me to escape. But here and now, they were making themselves scarce. I hadn't even seen signs of faeries since I moved to San Francisco, and everyone knew how curious *they* were.

The man chasing me managed to get in front of me. I had to turn back, farther into the woods. Toward the clearing I had noted when I walked here, the circle of stones.

I stopped short when I felt it: power emanating from behind the grove of trees, from the circle. I looked behind me, tried to quiet my harsh breathing. I was no longer being followed. Had I been chased here on purpose? Quietly I crept along the path, happy my sneakers were living up to their name, letting me sneak up without being heard. The otherwise still night air was filled with rhythmic chanting, the group intoning, calling on their spirits. I peeked out through the shrubs toward the circle of flickering torchlight. There were thirteen people forming the circle, their faces obscured by dark hooded robes.

Power surged along my skin, like ants marching. I tried to shake it off, stroking my medicine bag and mumbling my own charm to keep their magic from touching me.

I shouldn't be so frightened to happen upon a coven meeting, I thought. I was a witch, for heaven's sake. But I had seen Bronwyn's Wiccan coven in action twice, and neither time had I felt this sort of power. This was strong, tangible . . . and malevolent. It was impossible to make out what was at the center of their circle.

Could I stop this coven from performing some sort of

animal sacrifice? I thought of the black cat back at my apartment, feeling a surge of protectiveness. But whatever was here, within this group, was already dead. There was nothing to save, and even if I'd wanted to, the odds were not in my favor. Thirteen to one. Even *I* wasn't that arrogant. I needed to get myself out of here before I was spotted. I could call 911 from the safety of a nearby restaurant.

Too late. I looked up to see the coven breaking the circle, disbanding. The participants were talking, excited by their spell casting. I heard a distinctive baby-doll voice. Doura?

Remaining very still and stepping off the path into the forest, I willed them to pass me by. To my great relief, they seemed to be gathering on the opposite side of the opening.

But I hadn't counted on the watchers.

In the old days, covens had been forced underground. They began to employ sympathetic outsiders to keep watch for them while they were in the circle, absorbed in their casting. The watchers made sure the coven wasn't surprised by interlopers.

Tonight, here, I was the interloper. And I had been spotted.

Chapter 23

For the second time that night, I ran.

But unlike the earlier scarf-clad apparition that had trailed me, these were regular, unencumbered men. Men with longer legs than mine, who ran faster than I. One bald, the other dark-haired, they were gaining on me, coming inexorably closer.

The path forked up ahead. With no time to think, I veered to the left.

Wrong choice: There was a Cyclone fence in front of me, with a locked gate. I slipped into the woods, but the leaves and twigs made sound underfoot. And the fence made a forty-five-degree turn, trapping me. I was cornered.

I started chanting, murmuring under my breath, even though I knew full well that any protection spell I cast—without being able to brew and concentrate—wouldn't be strong enough. This was why witches didn't simply escape during the witch hunts. Most of us didn't have that kind of power. We relied on time, and focus, and plenty of both.

The men reached the end of the path. One shone his flashlight into the woods to the right, the other did the same to the left. Toward me.

A twig snapped on the other side of the path. There was a quick flash of light. Both men whirled around toward it, searching. I had a reprieve, a few seconds while they were distracted.

Think, Lily. Then I remembered an obscure spell I had come across in my Book of Shadows one lazy Sunday as I flipped through, just for fun: a Daphne glamour spell. When the god Apollo was in love with Daphne, he pursued her relentlessly; finally, she escaped by turning herself into a tree.

I felt a surge of confidence and regulated my breathing. Slowly and silently as I could, I backed up against the smooth trunk of a great eucalyptus tree. I squeezed my eyes shut, trying to remember the words of the spell, but more important, their meaning: I was merging with the tree, feeling its energy, piggybacking on its life force. I subsumed myself to it, concentrating on creating a glamour, a temporary cloak of invisibility. I willed myself to assume the texture, the brown and gray tones of the bark.

Glamours were tricky. If I maintained it too long, it would stick.

The bald watcher turned back toward me, the beam of his flashlight passing over me as he searched the thick woods.

He was looking right at me. I had to stop my mumbling, but I wasn't ready. I couldn't hold the spell. The cure hadn't set; I could feel it slipping away. I might blend in some, but the glamour was flickering, not whole.

The bald man squinted as he looked toward me, as though he had spotted something but wasn't sure. I held on, unable to murmur a charm, feeling as though the bark were sinking into my skin. He cast his flashlight beam my way, peering as though he wasn't sure what he was seeing. He crept closer. . . .

Someone jumped him from behind. The men tussled briefly, both hitting the ground and rolling. The other watcher ran to help, but yet another man jumped out in front of him, swinging. Both watchers were subdued quickly.

Vaguely, I heard coven members screaming from afar.

I dropped the glamour and stepped away from the tree, but my energy had been sapped. I fell to the ground.

Arms reached for me.

Atticus Huffman?

"Are you all right?" Atticus was asking me. "Lily? Lily, are you hurt?"

I shook my head, trying to snap out of it.

"No, I'm . . . okay." I felt dizzy, spent from the spell and the fear. But I wasn't hurt. "What are you doing here?"

"They had Nichol," he said, the look on his face grim. "She's been drugged. These people are crazy. Sick. They're like a . . . a bunch of witches or something."

"Is she okay? Is Oliver here as well?"

"I don't know where Oliver is. In fact, I was looking for him out here—some woman saw him here and contacted me. I know he takes up residence here in the woods from time to time, to get high in private. Ever since he used to work for Mike Perkins. That's how he lost his job in the first place."

"What woman?"

"What?" Atticus was distracted, worried.

"Who told you to come here? What did she look like?"

"Some woman called me. She sounded a lot like Minnie Mouse, like a little girl almost. Anyway, that's how we came upon the . . . whatever it was. The devil worshippers, whatever they call themselves. And they had . . . they had Nichol. I don't understand how, why. . . ." Even in the darkness I could see the look of barely contained rage on his face.

"She wasn't hurt?"

"I think she's fine, but I'm going to take her to the hospital—are you sure you're okay? Why don't we have you both checked out by the doctor?"

"No, I'm okay."

Atticus looked worried, unsure, but anxious to get going—he wanted to tend to his sister.

"Go on, really," I said. "Thank you for being here. For finding me, for intervening."

He looked up at the other man, who nodded.

"Okay, if you're sure. James here will help you get home."

I nodded. "Thank you."

I recognized James as the young buff man who had met our car at the Huffman residence. He was pure muscle, for which I was grateful. I leaned on him so heavily I might as well have dropped the pretense of my walking for myself, and asked him to carry me back to my car.

"Are you certain you'll be all right?" he said in a low-pitched voice when we arrived at the parking lot. "I'd feel better if you let me see you home."

"I'm really fine," I said. "I think I had a bit of an adrenaline drop, is all. I'll be okay for driving once I catch my breath."

I drove away, but only went a couple of blocks before I pulled over at a tavern that sat right outside one of the entrances to the Presidio. Liverpool Lil's was crowded tonight, full of people in high spirits, watching a Giants game on the television.

I wove through the crowd and made my way into a tiny cramped hallway that led to the restrooms. I was sure Atticus had already called the police, but I used the pay phone to call 911 anyway. I wanted to be sure they checked the area for any sort of animal sacrifice, and to give my anonymous version of events. I didn't want to talk to Carlos directly, because I would have to explain what I had seen, and more to the point, what I hadn't: I had no idea who was involved. Except for a woman with a baby-doll voice and way too much permed blond hair.

Doura.

Chapter 24

Goofer Balls and a coven. I still couldn't quite wrap my mind around the idea that Aidan would be involved in this, much less orchestrating it, but finding Goofer Balls in Malachi's place right after I told Aidan how to make them, and then stumbling across this evil coven when all the local witches were supposed to be under his jurisdiction ... it was too much. I had been avoiding Aidan because I didn't want to deal with his anger, and his power, but I felt the storm gathering in my own power spectrum. When my anger was focused, I was a force to be reckoned with.

It was well-nigh time to visit the Wax Museum.

The attraction was open late for the tourists tonight, so I blew past Clarinda in the ticket booth, charged up the stairs, and went directly to Aidan's office. I threw open the door with my mind.

Empty.

But across the room, the door to the cloister was ajar. There was a soft glow of candlelight. I heard a scraping sound, harsh breathing.

Carefully, I approached. Peeking in, I saw what I

thought at first was yet another wax figure. But it was a man. Hunched over and twitching. When he turned, I saw that one side of his face had a shiny, melted-plastic look.

Severe burn marks. I had seen scars like that one other time: when I tracked down my father.

The man swung away from me, still hunched over, grunted, stood, and when he turned toward me again, he was back to his beautiful self.

"Aidan?" I whispered.

"Lily." He ran a hand over his face and blew out a breath. "You caught me unawares this evening. Looks like I'll have to talk to my familiar. She's supposed to warn me about this sort of thing."

Words failed me.

He stood tall and gorgeous and fixed me with those sparkling blue eyes. A long moment passed before he spoke again, and when he did, his normally playful voice was low and sober.

"Surely you don't think you're the only one with a past?"

"Is . . . is it painful? I might be able to help."

He tapped his chest over his heart and gave me a rueful smile. "It only hurts in here. What brings you here, Lily? I trust it's something important to interrupt my privacy."

We witches could heal ourselves better than average humans, but we scar just the same. It must take a great deal of work for Aidan simply to maintain the illusion of beauty. No wonder he needed so many minions to do his bidding.

"I . . . needed to talk to you."

"By all means," he said, closing the door of the cloister and moving back toward the center of his office. "What can I help you with?"

Just like normal. Just as though I hadn't just walked in on a wreck of a man, learned his secret: His beauty was a glamour, a trick.

"But . . . what happened to you?"

"It's not worth talking about."

"It must be difficult to maintain the façade that you do."

He shrugged. "I can't leave here easily."

"You come see me at the store from time to time."

"Perhaps now you'll understand that I pay you quite the compliment by doing so," he said and gave me his typical flirtatious smile. "So, I have to say I'm a bit surprised to see you here tonight. I had the distinct impression you weren't talking to me."

"I thought it was the other way around. You were furious with me last time I was here."

We were slowly circling one another, as though readying ourselves for hand-to-hand combat. Then his eyes dropped to my chest. He reached one hand out and slowly, deliberately peeled a paper-thin piece of bark off of the skin just under my collarbone.

His expression shifted once again, from flirtatious to . . . something else.

"Where have you been?" His voice was quiet.

"In the park."

"At this hour?"

I nodded. He studied me.

"I take it you weren't having fun, rolling around on the forest floor?"

I shook my head. "Show yourself to me. Your real self."

"This *is* my real self."

"It's not, though, it's a glamour. It's only as much as you're willing to show."

"We all maintain façades, Lily. You of all people should know that."

"It's not the same thing."

"Isn't it?"

"No. I want to see you as you really are."

And then something new: self-doubt. Just a flicker, a quick glimpse. He moved away from me, taking a seat in his leather chair behind the desk.

"What did you see tonight?" Aidan demanded, back to business.

"Funny, I was going to ask you the same thing. Do you know of a coven that meets in a stone clearing in the Presidio woods?"

He froze. When he spoke, his voice was quiet, controlled. "I told you before to stay out of this. You have no idea what you're getting into. Listen, Lily, here's the harsh truth: Ultimately, it doesn't matter who killed Malachi Zazi. He was marked for death long ago."

"How do you know?"

"Trust me."

"That's a tall order right about now."

"Trust me on this, at least. *Dammit*, Lily, I don't know how much longer I can continue to protect you."

"What are you talking about?"

"The devil folks, voodoo, witches—we agreed to leave one another alone. It was a pact we signed to. A blood oath."

"An oath to leave one another alone?"

"Yes, essentially. But it's also a code of conduct; certain things are not allowed."

"Such as?"

He took a deep breath, let it out slowly.

"Part of the agreement was that no magical practitioner would join scientists, for example, in pursuit of unnatural ends."

"Would that be a scientist such as Mike Perkins, for example?"

He nodded. "He has no power himself, but if he allies himself with someone, and they go after eternal youth . . ."

"That sounds bad."

"You have no idea. The only way to produce something like that, on a massive scale, is to leach youth from elsewhere. It could be disastrous."

I had to ask about something that had been eating at me for days.

"What about you? I saw a photo of you taken more than thirty years ago. It doesn't seem as though you've aged since then."

"It's different. It's a glamour, it's not real. Look, the only thing we have going for us right now is that the dark practitioners are terrible about forming alliances. When we formed the pact, back in the chaos of that era—it was a time of great opportunity and great risk, like any thinning of the veil." I thought of the solstice, of Samhain, or Halloween. "A lot of good people were hurt, on all sides. Needlessly. A lot of work went into forming the pact. If it falls apart now, there's no telling what will happen."

"And what was the agreement, exactly?"

"It was complicated, as only these things can be. You know how bureaucracies are. But the gist was that we'd stay out of each other's way. Now you've forced my hand."

"How so?"

"You think you escaped tonight through natural means?"

"But Atticus—"

"Atticus had help. He could never have taken on a coven under normal circumstances—you know that. I've had the forest creatures on standby for days, assuming you might just get yourself in trouble."

I thought back on the flash of light, and thought about the wood sprites and the brownies, the forest folk I thought wouldn't help me. Traditionally they were allied with witches. Of course. Aidan's minions. Even the tree—had I been able to invoke the Daphne spell in my moment of panic, or had it been Aidan's magic that I had piggybacked on? I remembered that surge of confidence I felt, right before the spell began to work.

"So the coven in the woods—who were they? Devil folk?"

"I'm not entirely sure. They certainly aren't any coven under my jurisdiction."

"Do they even have that kind of power?"

Pause.

"Not really, not the elder Zazi, certainly. But he has some powerful associates."

"The woman? Doura?" His eyes slewed away from mine, telling me what I needed to know. "What is she, some kind of renegade witch?"

"Something like that. She certainly doesn't answer to me, and since she signed the pact along with Zazi, I was just as happy to avoid her altogether. She declared herself his underling, so she's supposed to abide by his agreement. But clearly, things have changed. I now think she pretended to be allied with him in order to evade oversight from me."

"So where does that leave you, then?"

"I don't know. It's none of your affair, in any case."

"I think it is. Isn't that why you agreed to train me? To have one more powerful witch in your army?"

"I'm training you for many reasons, few of which you are capable of understanding."

"Try me."

"I did. You failed."

"What are you talking about?"

He ran his hands through his hair in a rare impatient gesture.

"The pact was disturbed by the death of Prince High's son. It was not prophesied thus. And your involvement . . ." His voice trailed off as he shrugged.

"Prince High didn't seem all that concerned by his son's death, I have to say."

"I doubt he was sharing all his inner thoughts with you. He's been going crazy. Running around wrapped up in scarves and wearing a hat, like his son used to do."

"That was him? Why would he do such a thing?"

"I think he's trying to keep the idea of his son alive somehow . . . who knows? I wouldn't be surprised if this has driven him out of his senses. He will never have a chance to make things up to his son—regret is a powerful emotion. In any case, now I have to figure out who killed Malachi. They won't rest until I do."

"I thought you wanted me to stay out of it."

"That was before they went after you. Have you felt your powers diminished?"

"Actually, I have."

He nodded, grim. "Since you disobeyed me in the first place, we now need a way to find the perpetrator, and fast. Perhaps now that you understand better my 'limitations,' you'll see why I can't just run around the city with you and track this person down."

"Is this why you have Sailor trailing me? As protection? But he has no magic."

"He can communicate with me if he has to. If the chips were down, I could be there. It would help if you'd actually let him accompany you, rather than slipping away like you do. Poor guy's having a heart attack trying to track you down. Besides, you could have used him in the woods."

Aidan's familiar jumped onto the desk, glared at me, and then purred so loudly I could hear it from where I was sitting.

"*There* you are, little traitor," Aidan murmured to the cat. He took her in his arms and stroked her long white fur. Then he looked back up at me. "For some reason Noctemus thought you should know my little secret. As she's usually right about such things, I'll have to trust her. And I hope I can trust you to keep my confidence."

"Of course. Just so I've covered all my bases, I have to ask you: Did you place Goofer Balls in Malachi Zazi's apartment?"

He gave me a disbelieving look. "You really think I operate that way?"

"And I don't suppose you know anything about a rattlesnake there?"

"Sounds like his apartment's something of a hotbed. All the more reason for you to stay away. The only thing I know is that Malachi Zazi chose that place because of a magnetic field of some kind. There's an arrangement of metal and stones on the roof that tends to cleanse the place of vibrations. But that has nothing to do with hexes or snakes. It has to do with trying to keep his father, and his father's cronies, away from him."

I thought about the roof. I remembered the metal rods, but there were no stones set up. There was that little planter, and the statue of Serpentarius, but no Stonehenge-like rock formations, however miniature.

Aidan got up and came around near me, hitching one hip up on the desk and clasping his hands.

"About what transpired between us a few days ago, in the cloister. You know as well as I do that there's something there, when our powers mingle."

"Yes." There was no point in denying it.

"You should know this sort of thing doesn't come up often for me."

"I would imagine you could seduce anyone you wanted, anytime you wanted."

"It doesn't come up. Believe me."

I looked into his eyes, those beautiful periwinkle eyes that sparkled, horrific burns or no. This part, at least, was no glamour. It was him, Aidan, the man.

"I want to ask you on a proper date."

"A *date*?"

"To the Art Deco Ball. I want to go with you. As your official date."

"I thought it was hard for you to be out in public, to leave here."

He smiled his aw-shucks grin and ducked his head. "I believe it'll be worth it. Please?"

It was the "please" that did it. I still didn't entirely trust Aidan, and I wasn't quite sure what he was capable of, or whether he had ulterior motives for asking me.

But he was being so ... decent, it was impossible to say no.

I nodded. "All right. You'll have to come by Aunt Cora's Closet and let us dress you up."

He grinned. "I can't wait."

"First things first, though," I said. "About Malachi's murderer ... I might just have an idea. I think I know how I can identify him."

"How?"

"By playing to my strengths. I'll brew."

Chapter 25

I made a phone call to Hervé to see if my idea was even possible. He confirmed that it was, but also told me what I knew: I wouldn't be able to pull it off by myself.

"Have you ever heard of a *chov'hani*, a kind of Gypsy witch?" I asked.

"Of course. That would be perfect for this sort of thing. The Rom are noted for their snake magic. Do you know one?"

"Not yet, but I'm planning to get to know one. Thanks for all your help on this. Oh, and have fun with your parents."

"We're watching reruns of *M*A*S*H*. Many, many reruns. I might not make it."

I laughed.

"I swear, next time I'm closing the store so Caterina and the kids can come with me."

"If you let me know in advance, I'd be happy to babysit the store for you. In the meantime, hang in there, big man."

Most evenings Sailor hung out at a club called Cerulean, off a side street in San Francisco's vibrant North

Beach neighborhood. He wasn't there when I arrived, so I ordered a dirty martini, extra olives, and took a seat at a booth. I figured if he didn't arrive by the time I was done with my drink, I would track him down at his apartment. But for now the throbbing bass of the juke-box and vivacious hum of the crowd was strangely comforting. Or maybe it was just the effects of the gin.

After what had taken place in the woods, and then with Aidan, I might just need another martini after this one.

Sure enough, Sailor strode in, big black motorcycle boots stomping on the shiny wood floor. The crowd seemed to part, men wary, women watching him surreptitiously from under mascaraed lashes. He was the classic bad boy: dark good looks, tall and broad-shouldered, dressed in black leather, overall bad attitude. Just seeing him cheered me up.

When he spotted me, he stopped dead, as though reconsidering his choice of establishment for the evening. A redhead in a short leopard-print skirt seated at the bar preened, smiled, and cooed, *"Hello there."*

Sailor rolled his eyes and came to sit across the small table from me.

"Where the hell have you been? I thought you weren't going to run out on me, 'buddy.'"

"Sorry. I needed a little time alone."

"What's wrong?" he demanded.

"Could I buy you a drink?"

"Out with it, already. We both know this isn't a social call."

"If I were to ask a big favor of you . . ."

He snorted.

"What would you want in exchange?"

"What, we're bargaining before I even know what you're after? Must be something really good."

"Name it. What do you want?"

He looked suddenly serious.

"All I want is to be free of Aidan Rhodes."

"Okay."

"*Okay?*" He gave a bitter laugh. "And just how do you propose to do that?"

"I can't say, exactly. But I'll work on it."

He gave me a disbelieving look.

"You yourself keep saying how gol-durned powerful I am. So why do you doubt I could go up against him? Especially if someone like your aunt is willing to work with me, train me."

"Wait just a goddamned second," he said. "My *what*? My *aunt*?"

"You mentioned her before, remember? Outside of Aidan's, you said—"

"I know what I said. But I also took it back. I told you, I don't want any part of that life."

"She's the real deal, though, right? Powerful?"

He nodded, still wary.

"All I'm asking for is an introduction, for you to set me up with her. I'll take care of the rest."

"And you're saying that if I do this . . . that you'll get me free of Aidan Rhodes, male witch."

I nodded. "I can't guarantee exactly when, but I'll find a way."

He held my eyes for a long moment. Cynicism was edged out, just barely, by something very rare for Sailor: hope.

He blew out a loud breath. "I don't have a lot of faith, but it's worth a shot."

"Thanks for the vote of confidence."

"Hey, that's about the best I can do."

"I know."

I picked up the phone to call Bronwyn and then put it down at least ten times that night. Partly because I don't like telephones, and partly because I didn't know what to say.

I hadn't seen or heard from Bronwyn since I found the hex, though Maya told me she had visited and Bronwyn seemed to be holding up well. I felt terrible that our friendship seemed to be slipping away, but I wasn't sure what to do. I simply couldn't accede to her wishes and leave her unprotected.

The next day was busy at Aunt Cora's Closet. Maya's mother, Lucille, had started making patterns based on vintage dresses, enlarging them and sewing reproductions for the more typical, larger-framed modern woman. They were selling like hotcakes. On my way to Coffee to the People yesterday I had seen two women on the street wearing a couple of the popular styles.

A mother in her thirties and her teenaged daughter were having a rollicking time trying on outfits—the daughter fit into the originals, and the mother into the reproductions. They each tried on sundresses, then skirt-jacket combos, all from the late 1950s. They were joking about wearing matching dresses to the girl's graduation and started laughing so hard they could barely speak. Their relationship warmed my heart.

That's it, I thought. *I'm calling Bronwyn.*

To my surprise, she didn't hang up on me. In fact, she assured me that she loved me and she knew I thought I was doing the right thing. In a way it made me feel worse than if she'd yelled at me; it was just so Bronwyn of her.

As I was ringing up the mother-daughter purchases, the teenager looked down at the glass counter display.

"Oh, those are so pretty! What are they?"

"Spirit bottles," I said, bringing a few out and setting them atop the counter.

The bottles were among the few nonvintage items I carried in the store, alongside talismans that I consecrated and charged with the New Moon; pentacles, powerful crystals and stones, and a few small totems. I had recently been inspired to make the spirit bottles out of a bunch of old items I found at a garage sale in West Oakland. Spirit bottles are embellished on the outside, then filled with herbs, oils, and rolled parchments full of thoughts and wishes.

I had no intention of becoming a supernatural supply shop, but I had to admit that with Bronwyn's herb stand in one corner and my growing display of witch-related items, I might be accused of such. Then again, along the Haight Street shopping district, with its head shops and hippie paraphernalia, Aunt Cora's Closet was hardly out of place.

"They're so pretty! What are they used for?"

"They're meant to draw and trap evil and negative energy."

"So they bring good luck?"

"Not exactly. They take away negative energy ... sometimes it seems like the same thing. In the old days they were filled with things like needles, urine, hair, and herbs, and buried under the fireplace hearth, or the four corners of the floor, or plastered into the walls. It was said that evil would be impaled on pins and needles, drown in the liquid, and be sent away by the herbs."

The mom picked up a blue bottle embellished with shells, spangles, and feathers. It was filled with dew I collected in the forest of Golden Gate Park.

"Ooh, I love that one!" said the girl.

"That's a water spirit bottle," I said. "Are you crafty at all? They're fun to make for yourself. There are all different kinds, incorporating different sorts of items, depending on what you're after. Moon goddess and sun altar bottles, prosperity bottles, earth elemental bottles . . ."

"But would it be really, um, *magical* if I made one myself?"

"Oh, yes. Creative energy is very powerful. For most people, making art and crafts brings up a kind of relaxed concentration, similar to meditation, allowing the positive energy to flow through your hands and into the item you're working on." This was the sort of state I couldn't manage to attain while scrying—or at least never had until Aidan worked his magic. But creating things like carved talismans and spirit bottles got me pretty close.

By now several customers were gathered around for my impromptu seminar, picking up the bottles and inspecting them.

"It's like wearing a hand-knitted sweater." I picked up a hand-knitted pale pink baby's sweater made of the softest wool, with a little pewter Winnie-the-Pooh button at the collar. "What child could wear something like this without feeling comforted? And that goes tenfold when an item's handmade by someone you love. You can't help but think of that person whenever you wear it, or use it, or look at it. That's a powerful spiritual connection, and it sets off a series of positive thoughts, ideas, sensations."

The mother and daughter wound up buying two dresses each and the water spirit bottle. They also suggested we start a craft day at the store, to teach people to make their own.

"That's a great idea," said Maya. "I could bring leftovers from school. We'd have a blast."

I agreed. We could make it a regular event at Aunt Cora's Closet. But first I just needed to prevent the dissolution of a supernatural pact so that Mike Perkins didn't set up a massive youth-stealing company by allying himself with an evil practitioner. How hard could that be?

Right after lunch, Sailor came by the store to tell me we had an appointment with his aunt. He left his motorcycle under Conrad's loving care, and we took the Mustang east across the Bay Bridge. His aunt's house was in the Oakland hills.

As we drove, I peppered Sailor with questions.

"Are there a lot of Rom around here, in the Bay Area?"

"Enough," he said with a shrug. "Maybe more than enough."

"But there are a lot of different types of Gypsies, though, right?"

"Plenty. My family's mostly Gitan, Cale from Spain."

"And the language? You speak it?"

He shook his head. "Just a very little bit. A lot of it's dying out, anyway. And even among people who speak Rom, a lot of the words are borrowed from the host country language, so much so that the different dialects can be unintelligible."

I found the whole Rom culture fascinating. I had met a lot of them as I wandered the world, in Spain and France and North Africa. I'd heard they were originally from India, but they'd been wandering for so many gen-

erations it was hard to say. Like a lot of wandering peo-
ples, they didn't recognize any particular governmental
authority. They often deserved their reputation for being thieves and liars—as far as I could tell, they did what
they had to in order to maintain their cultural integrity.
And if that meant breaking the law, then so be it.

We wound through nice large homes with well-
tended yards and expensive cars in the driveways before
pulling up to a two-story structure behind ornate iron
gates. The house was painted a bright bubblegum pink,
and a large hand-painted sign, decorated with curlicues
and flourishes, read: *Fortunes Read, Desires Fulfilled.*

When I pulled up to the gates Sailor leaned out and
pushed the buzzer for the intercom. "It's me," he said.
The wrought iron swung open slowly.

There was a line of salt across the threshold of the
front door.

"*Sastimos,*" Sailor said by way of greeting. "*Sar san?*"

"*Sastimos,*" said the man who answered the door. He
was short and stocky, wearing jeans, athletic shoes, and a
sweatshirt. His coloring was dark, Mediterranean. He
gave Sailor a manly backslapping hug and invited us in.
Sailor introduced him as his uncle Eric, though he didn't
look any older than Sailor, probably midthirties.

"Renna's just finishing up with a client," Eric said.
"Coffee?"

"Sounds great. It's Turkish coffee, really strong,"
Sailor said to me.

"I'd love some. Thank you."

Eric led us into the well-appointed kitchen, which
was outfitted with maple cabinets and filled with bowls
of fruit, painted china, and carved brass knickknacks. I

also recognized charms against the evil eye, along with bundles of rosemary. Everything carried the aroma of cloves and cardamom, and then of strong coffee as Eric brewed it in a brass coffeepot.

I noticed a copy of the *Guardian* facedown atop the counter. At the back, circled in red, was an advertisement for Renna's "Gypsy Fortune-telling" services.

"You have a lovely home," I said, making conversation. "Have you lived here long?"

"Long enough. Neighbors hate us."

"Why?"

He looked up from the coffee-making equipment, met Sailor's eyes, and smiled.

"Because we're Rom. And because we painted the house pink, I imagine."

I thought of Prince High's black abode. I was willing to bet those neighbors would be happy to trade one Devil's House for a pink structure owned by Gypsy fortune-tellers.

On the stool sat a very old accordion. It looked like an antique. "Do you play?"

"Would you like me to?"

"Really? I love accordion music," I said.

He picked it up in a practiced swoop, looped the strap over his head and adjusted the fit. Then he started playing, swaying slightly. The accordion is an all-body instrument.

He played what sounded like a flamenco tune. The music carried with it history, and dancing, and sultry nights. Suddenly I was transported to a summer's night, heady with the scent of grapes and the lingering heat of the day, in a little plaza in a village in the south of Spain.

I remembered a young man playing the accordion, a very old woman dancing, the crowd keeping time with loud, rhythmic clapping.

I glanced over to find Sailor's dark gaze on me. It made sense, somehow, that he had this blood running through his veins. Whether he wanted to admit to it or not.

Just as Eric launched into a second song, a door down the hall opened and a young woman emerged. It was clear she had been crying. She clutched candles and flowers to her chest as she hurried past us and out the front door.

Sailor's aunt appeared to be in her late forties, at least ten years older than Eric. She was curvy, ample, wearing a long skirt and a vest over a white shirt, and an elaborate multitiered necklace of gold coins. Her dramatic dark eyes were lined in kohl.

"Lily, this is my aunt Renna. Renna, Lily Ivory," Sailor introduced us.

"Welcome to my home," she said with a sweeping gesture, inviting me into her room. And then in a no-nonsense voice: "Eric, put the accordion down and finish building those shelves in the basement. And all that new equipment needs to be unloaded from the Honda. Sailor, make yourself useful."

He rolled his eyes but followed Eric.

Renna shook her head as she led the way down the hall.

"Try to get anything done around here," she groused. "A witch's natural enemy is time—or actually, the lack of time. You watch, you'll see. The need to share oneself drives us, but it takes from us as well."

As I walked into the room, I realized we were in her

bedchamber. I tried to cover my shock at how open Renna was, to allow clients into her sleeping chamber, her inner sanctum. The house was large; surely there was no necessity to meet in this room. I wondered if perhaps she gleaned some of her power from the intimacy.

There was a shallow bowl of water and flower petals on the dresser. Renna dipped her fingertips in it and invited me to do the same.

"Dewdrops and rose petals," she said, sitting on the king-sized bed, which was covered with a velvet faux tiger-print. "As the flowers bloom, so does the love and happiness of my clients."

I smiled as I dried my hands on a nearby embroidered tea towel.

"Are you in search of true love?"

"I . . . at the moment I'm looking for something else."

"Ah! You are afraid of true love," she said with a nod.

"No, not really, I—"

"Do you know love?"

"Of course. But . . . there are all kinds of love."

"I mean true love, romantic love, but real romantic love. Love to the point of sacrifice."

I thought of Max, our talk. About his wife, and what he was looking for now. We barely knew each other, really, but I was certain of one thing: If Max Carmichael were in love with a woman, he would stand by her no matter what. He would remain loyal to the point of true sacrifice. In that moment I finally understood why this was so hard for him, why he was trying to go so slow, to be sure of what he was doing rather than just jumping in. He had to know he was pursuing the kind of relationship that would reward such love.

"That . . . that is a tall order, indeed."

"You will need an amulet made of coins, four white candles, a garland of spring flowers, orange blossom honey, the sweetest slice from the center of a watermelon, and you take it all—"

"I'm really not here for a love spell," I interrupted. We didn't have the time for such things. But in part, I didn't want to think about it. I was holding myself back from casting my own love spell on Max—or anyone else, for that matter—and didn't want to be further tempted. It was hard enough to deny my own abilities.

Renna looked disgruntled at my outburst. Our mentor-mentee relationship wasn't off to the best start.

"Sailor tells me you are a witch. In what tradition?"

"I'm not entirely sure. My father's people were in the European folk tradition, I believe, but I didn't really know him. My grandmother, who trained me, comes from Mexico."

"Ah, the Mexicans," she said, nodding. "Good with botanicals."

"Yes, I brew."

She nodded some more, then passed her hand in a circular gesture over a human skull. A live toad sat, fat and brown, on the table.

"Sit, sit," she said, gesturing to the other side of the bed. As I sat, she began to sing:

> *I've seen you where you never were*
> *And where you never will be*
> *And yet within that very place*
> *You can be seen by me*
> *For to tell what they do not know*
> *Is the art of the Romani.*

She laughed, almost like a cackle.

The whole shebang—the skull, the toad, the cackle— would have impressed me, except that I knew it was an act. Like my friend Hervé, Renna made her living by peddling her magic to the general public. Paying customers seemed to get a lot from the impression that they were stepping into a sometimes frightening world of the unknown— perhaps such a setting helped them to open themselves to the magic. I could sense Renna had true powers, but she was also vested in the showmanship of her profession.

She sat, her perceptive dark eyes holding mine. Her vibrations were calm, confident. She was a powerful woman.

"May I see your hand?"

I hesitated. Then I held my hand out and she cupped it in hers.

She took a deep breath, still looking at my eyes. Finally she glanced down, but the smile fell from her face. Her gaze flew back up to meet mine.

"No lines."

"I have lines," I protested. "Just not fingerprints."

She traced my lifeline, her eyebrows raised.

Then she dropped my hand and tapped the stack of oversized, dog-eared Tarot cards sitting between us.

"Make the sign of the cross over the cards."

I hesitated, glancing up at the huge crucifix hanging over the bed. I wasn't familiar with any kind of witchcraft so closely allied with Christianity.

"Like this." She showed me, with one hand in the palm of the other. She made a slicing, chopping motion, then came down in a fist, then a slice again. "Three times atop the cards."

I made the sign: chop, fist, chop, fist, chop, fist.

She spread the cards before us in a practiced motion that produced a smooth arc.

"Think of your situation, and choose one."

I closed my eyes, took a deep breath, and concentrated on communing with Renna, rather than fighting her.

"Ask your question, and pull a card."

"Could you see who murdered a man named Malachi Zazi?"

I pulled a card from the center of the arc, and she took it from me with a flourish, holding it up to look at it, pursing her lips slightly, then setting it down. It was the Three of Wands.

She shook her head. "The cards cannot tell us this. Perhaps if you had something of the victim's—a tooth, fingernails, something like that. You could bring me something of his—"

"No, that's all right." It was a long shot anyway. I hadn't really believed she could give me a name out of the blue—if only all police work was that easy. There was another reason I had come to see her.

"Renna, I know this is probably unusual, but I'd like to ask you for your help. In finding a murderer. It entails casting a spell from afar."

She got up and spun a whirligig made of wooden spikes and crosses. Finally, she nodded, and sat back down on the bed.

"Tell me your proposition," she said.

"I have to identify a murderer. I want to use the Living Things in You spell. Do you know it?"

She nodded.

"I know that normally the brew would be put into

food, but since I don't know who he—or she—is, I have to tweak the spell a little."

"To cast from afar, you must use a poppet."

I nodded. I had thought as much. "I can't do it alone—I don't really understand poppet magic."

"If you get me something of the victim's, I could create a poppet of wax and wood. If you brew well, properly, you would then melt the poppet in your brew."

"And what about casting the spell without knowing the identity of the target?"

"The *mamioro* is a spirit that carries illness. We could call upon it to carry it for us."

"We could do that?"

"Yes, but it is only possible once."

"Why?"

She looked at me as though I'd asked her to explain rain. "The *mamioro* will do us this favor only once. When the sky opens and direct connection between heaven and earth is possible, I shall call upon the forest and the field spirits, woods folk, and faeries to keep us safe."

As I was thanking her and standing to leave, she stopped me.

"The cards have told me something else."

"What?"

"Someone has taken earth trodden on by you, they have spit on it and put it into an empty walnut shell and buried it in the garden of a dead man. You shall have no happiness until you find this, place it on a tray with a garland of three different-colored flowers, nine white candles from a church, and put it out to water with honey and a blood sacrifice. I can get all this together for you for a very small fee. Doing this shall cleanse you of all evil spells."

Much like I did with the suffering root. Another curse, another hex. I forced myself to breathe. "Couldn't I just cast an antidote spell and let the dirt mingle with the earth of the dead man's garden?"

Renna looked a little disgruntled. She shrugged.

"One more thing," she said. "Sailor is indebted to a man named Aidan."

I nodded. "He talked to you about it? I told Sailor I'd do what I could to free him from Aidan. I don't suppose you have any idea how to approach that?"

"'By a spell to him unknown, he could never be alone,'" she intoned. "A *vila* follows him about."

"What's a *vila*?"

"A kind of spirit. You must find the charm Aidan has hidden in Sailor's apartment to control him. If you find this, and bring it to me, I can lift the curse from Sailor. But this is important: Sailor must not know you are doing this, for he is bound to Aidan whether he likes it or not. This will serve as payment in return for helping you."

"What kind of charm is it?"

"This I don't know. It's your system, not mine. Aidan is one of yours"—she smiled, her gold tooth glinting—"whether you like it or not."

Chapter 26

I hadn't been back in Aunt Cora's Closet ten minutes before Carlos Romero walked in.

"Were you perchance the person who called in a 911 last night for something going on in the Presidio, citing possible animal sacrifice?"

"I . . ."

"The truth, Lily."

I nodded.

"Okay." He let out a loud, exasperated breath and passed a hand over his eyes, red with lack of sleep. "I'm going to need to get a statement from you. An official statement. And do I even want to ask why you didn't just call me directly?"

"I wasn't in the right frame of mind to talk to you just then. And I needed . . . it's hard to explain, but animal sacrifice is powerful. I couldn't just wait around until you came. It wasn't safe."

"You can say that again."

Something prickled along my neck. "What was it? What was the sacrifice?"

"If her brother hadn't shown up, it would have been one Nichol Reiss, née Huffman. But they did have another body."

"A body?"

"Malachi Zazi."

"They had it there, in the woods?"

"Yep. So, the good news is we got it back. This time they did an immediate autopsy on it. Turns out he is a human, thank you very much, so at least we can rule out the whole vampire deal. Death by stabbing, we pretty much knew that. They did find one interesting thing, though: The reason his palms have no prints is because they were burned."

"Why would he have burned his palms?"

He shrugged. "To avoid fingerprints, maybe? Lots of folks think they can get out of databases, that sort of thing, if they can't be tracked through fingerprints."

"Was he some sort of master criminal or something?"

"More likely it was some injury left over from childhood. I looked up the poor bastard's records—there were lots of allegations of child abuse, and this was back when you didn't get so much of that sort of thing."

"Poor guy," I said. "No wonder he was so close to his school friends. At least he had them."

"I guess that's true. I hadn't thought of it like that. Oh, by the way, you know that rattlesnake in Malachi's apartment?"

"Yes."

"We couldn't find it. Anywhere. Had the exterminators in there for a couple of hours, but no dice."

"That's odd."

"Isn't it? You can't think of any reason that might be? Didn't have a chat with it somehow, anything like that?"

"Very funny. But listen, Carlos, I think I can find out who killed Malachi."

"Isn't that what you were trying to do all along?"

"Well, sort of, yes. But this, if I do it right, is almost foolproof."

"Oh, yeah? What is it?"

"I can't tell you, exactly. But I need something from you."

"Oh, boy. I can hardly wait to hear this one."

"A lock of Malachi Zazi's hair, and a piece of that mirror from the crime scene. Preferably bloody."

Carlos stared at me for several seconds.

"I know it sounds weird," I said.

"Uh-huh."

"What can I tell you, Carlos? I'm a witch, as you know. Witchcraft is odd. I need a little part of Malachi Zazi to make the spell work."

There was another awkward pause, but I was losing patience. Carlos knew what I was. Why did I have to keep apologizing for being a witch?

"I'll see what I can do," Carlos said. He paused in the doorway as he was leaving. "It sure is interesting knowing you, Lily Ivory."

Presuming Carlos came through with the crime scene supplies, Renna would create the poppet. In the meantime, I had to find whatever charm Aidan was using to control Sailor. And I couldn't let him know what I was doing.

I had to break into Sailor's place.

Most nights he spent at the bar. But how could I be sure? I considered sending in Oscar to find out, but a miniature potbellied pig couldn't just saunter into the crowded Cerulean bar without creating a ruckus. A cat or a dog, just maybe, but not a pig. This was one of those things that would have been easier back in the old days, the burning times. Back then, witches' familiars often spied on people—a cat could wander through a village, even in and out of homes, and come back to inform on the populace. But in our urban existence, things had changed.

Then again, even if Oscar were a cat, I imagined Sailor would have recognized him anyway. Guess I would have to take my chances.

On the way to Sailor's apartment, I tried to think up a story in case I found him at home. *I wanted company,* I thought, *I needed a friend.* They say the best lies were half true, and I guessed that was so. Because the part about wanting a friend was true enough.

Sailor lived in an apartment on Hang Ah Alley in Chinatown. There used to be a perfume manufacturer here, so the area retained the ghostly scents of flowers and musk. The heady aroma floated on the chilly evening air.

Cars weren't allowed in the alley, so I parked on Sutter Street, around the corner. Oscar was supposed to keep an eye out for Sailor, but I couldn't think of any way he would let me know he had seen him. By sitting on the horn, maybe? I didn't even know if I would hear it, so far away.

I walked past the dim sum restaurant, the mah-jongg parlor, and entered through a nondescript gray door in an even grayer building. Inside, the stairwell smelled like cabbage and spices. On the third floor, right outside of Sailor's door, was the ghostly remnant of a long-ago murder. Sailor claimed this was why his rent was so cheap, because no one else in their right mind would live in such a place. He also claimed it didn't bother him. Tough guy.

No one was tough enough to ignore that kind of despair day in, day out, I thought. I imagined it had a whole lot to do with his general attitude.

I knocked on the scarred wooden door. Nothing.

"Sailor?" I called out, knocking again.

Still nothing. I took out the Hand of Glory.

I hated this thing, but I couldn't deny it worked wonders. According to legend it was the left hand of a hanged man, cradling a thick candle in its palm. Upon lighting the candle, all doors before it swing open and it lights the way—not like a flashlight, but bright as day.

The apartment door swung open in front of me.

Sailor's place was a studio apartment, certainly nothing fancy. It was also a terrible mess, with books and newspapers and old coffee cups stacked everywhere. There was a bed under the windows that looked out over Hang Ah Alley, a tiny table and two straight chairs, a small chest of drawers. It smelled great, though, of exotic spices and perfume.

Where to start? I was a nervous wreck. I took a deep breath to steady myself. I was trying to help him, after all. Even if Sailor found me, I could explain it to him. Surely he'd see I was doing it for him.

I searched his bureau, the tiny closet with the bare bulb. Then I stood and looked around. There wasn't much more. The kitchen cabinets were bare—really bare. I found a half-full box of Triscuits and checked—stale. A single plate, fork, and knife were in the strainer. A bottle of tequila and a glass. It reminded me of Malachi Zazi's kitchen. Was it the sign of something wrong, something supernatural, or simply the style of a bachelor, depressed and sad?

I dropped to my knees and looked under the bed. Plenty of dust bunnies, but no charm.

But then I felt something. It was on the bed—I started tearing back the covers. And there it was. Sewn into the pillow. I could feel it. Using the pocketknife, I picked at the stitches. It was a packet sewn with crinkly, stiff fabric, decorated with spangles. . . . How could Sailor not have felt it? Was it disguised by some sort of glamour? Surely if Aidan was strong enough to concoct a charm to keep Sailor, he was probably strong enough to hide it from him. Still and all, it seemed odd to think of Sailor sleeping on this thing each and every night and not noticing. Not exactly a princess-and-the-pea type.

I put the packet in my satchel, but then realized that I was leaving Sailor's pillow torn open. That would be a tough one to explain. I couldn't imagine a fellow without a bowl would have a needle and thread lying around, but a quick look wouldn't hurt.

I opened a couple of drawers in the kitchen and found some miscellaneous odds and ends—soy sauce packets from takeout, disposable chopsticks, a couple of old keys, twist ties, double A batteries—but nothing of use. Then I remembered my mama used to keep her needles in the refrigerator on the theory it made them easier to thread. Further, she kept the thread in there with the needles, on the theory that when one needed needles, one needed thread.

I peeked in. A couple of white to-go containers, a half bottle of orange juice, three bottles of beer. A jar of mustard that looked several years old, and three bottles of hot sauce. Not a single needle, much less thread.

"Hungry?"

I screeched and whirled around.

"Sailor. Lord, you scared me!"

He tossed his keys onto the counter, then looked around, wary and apprehensive, as though checking for accomplices. Assured it was just little old me, he stared back at me.

"May I ask what the hell you're doing in my apartment?"

"I can explain."

"Start talking."

"I wanted to see you. I feel . . . lonely and wanted to be with a friend."

He let out a harsh laugh. "You're not leaving here until you tell me what's going on. Did Aidan send you?"

"No, of course not. Quite the opposite, in fact. I'm working on what I promised, trying to free you from him."

"I take it you've come up with a plan? Did it include absconding with my fingernail clippings or cuff links or something? Because I gotta tell you, Lily, you're sort of growing on me, but I sure as hell don't trust you. I'd rather you left me out of your witchcraft altogether, if it's all the same to you."

"It's nothing like that. I'm not brewing and casting . . . I was looking for something rather specific. Something you don't even know you had."

He looked at me intently, but didn't speak.

"Your aunt told me Aidan is using a kind of amulet to keep you under his thrall. She told me if I could find it, I could free you from Aidan's debt."

"And you *believed* her?"

"Um . . . yes?"

"Are you crazy? I think she may have been in league with Aidan in the first place to set me up."

"Why in the world would she do that?"

"She always wanted me to use the powers."

"I don't understand. I thought you weren't born with psychic abilities."

"I wasn't. But I'm the direct descendant of a great psychic, on my father's side. My aunt wanted to train me when I was younger, to develop what she was sure was lurking there somewhere, but my mother wouldn't allow her to. Still, apparently I had the inner capacity somewhere."

"So how did Aidan bring it out?"

"It's none of your business."

"Please tell me."

He turned away and grabbed a bottle of tequila and a shot glass down from the shelf. He poured two fingers' worth in the glass, downed it, then filled it again. Finally, keeping his back to me, he spoke.

"There was an accident. A car accident." He took another drink. "It wasn't my fault, but I was driving. I walked away without a scratch, but my wife, Amanda, was hurt, badly. In a coma. The first time I met Aidan, I was in the waiting room, distraught. He promised he could help, he could cure her, if I would pledge my allegiance to him. I didn't believe him, of course, but I wasn't about to give up any hope, however small. I agreed."

"Just like that?"

"It wasn't quite that simple. There was a ceremony. Smoke. Blood. I don't remember it all. But afterward, I had these ... powers. This curse. True to his word, Amanda came out of the coma. Recovered at a miraculous rate. It was so astounding, one of her doctors wrote up her case for inclusion in a medical journal."

"Where is Amanda now?" I asked, thinking of his sad, solo occupancy apartment.

"She left me. Couldn't handle this 'gift' that Aidan saddled me with. Or maybe she just couldn't handle how I reacted to it, which wasn't positive. I can tell you that. I spent a lot of time and energy keeping away from the Rom magic, and then here I was, thrust back into the paranormal world more than ever."

"But why would you even think to introduce me to your aunt if you don't trust her?"

"I don't completely trust her, but if she wants something, it's because she thinks it's for the best. She's arrogant, because she's more in touch with the other realms. So she tends toward the paternalistic. Rather like you."

"Like *me*?"

"You think you know what's best for everybody, and you sure don't mind meddling."

"I usually *can* help, though, when it comes right down to it."

Sailor grinned and took another swig of tequila. "Like I said."

"So whatever happened to Amanda?"

He laughed, more a cynical snort. "She married a dull, steady systems analyst and moved to Danville. Just popped out her second kid. Meanwhile, I'm stuck for life. Sold my soul. And that article you found in my pillow is the only thing keeping Aidan in check, thank you very much. I paid dearly for it."

"*You* put it there? What is it?"

"None of your business. But it's mine."

"Do you know why someone as powerful as Aidan needs so many minions?" I asked, wondering whether Sailor knew of Aidan's injuries.

"He has his limits, like anyone else."

"Do you know anything about his background, or maybe how old he is?"

He shook his head. "I can't read his mind any more than I can yours. He's a mystery to me, and I'd just as soon leave it that way. This place is safe from Aidan and any of my family—I've made sure of that. So give my charm back to me and I'll banish you as well."

"Please don't."

"Why shouldn't I?"

"I apologize. I was wrong. I should have spoken with you."

"Damn right."

"You're my only . . . lately I seem to be dropping friends at an alarming rate. I wouldn't want . . . I don't want you to banish me."

"Well, I got news for you, little witch: You and I aren't exactly friends."

"Then what are we?"

"We're a couple of misfits without the ability to make friends, is what we are. And we're each out for ourselves, so at least we can trust each other, up to a point. Sort of. So where's my charm?"

"In my bag."

The satchel was sitting on the counter, nearer to him than me. He reached out to undo the metal clasp, then jumped back, cradling his hand.

"*Ow!* What did you do? That thing's *hot*!"

"Promise you won't banish me."

He glared at me.

"No matter what you say, I think of you as a friend. In fact, lately you're pretty near the top of the list."

"Must be a short list."

"You have no idea." I looked at him, beseeching. "Promise, and you can have it back."

He shrugged. *"Whatever."*

Not exactly a declaration of devout and loyal eternal camaraderie, but beggars can't be choosers.

Chapter 27

My cauldron had been washed in rosewater and lemon verbena. My massive Book of Shadows lay splayed open on the counter beside my *athame*, a length of blessed rope, Sorcerer's Violet, and a jar of powdered snake sheds. Another jar held powdered snake eggs, and a rattle, two fangs, and a tiny vial of venom. My familiar looked up at me, huge bottle-green eyes full of fascination and trust in my abilities, ready to facilitate my powers in slipping through the otherworldly portals.

I was ready to go, but I hesitated.

This sort of witchcraft—casting hexes on strangers—was the sort of thing my kind was forever being accused of. It was for precisely this kind of power that so many of my ancestors had forfeited their lives. But as far as I could tell, my friends were in danger. I wouldn't let that stand. I couldn't let that stand. I would brew, and I would cast, and I would let the chips fall where they may in the full knowledge that no action exists in a vacuum. There would be consequences.

Besides, whoever murdered Malachi deserved it, I

thought. Or did they? How did I know? Who was I to judge?

I *wasn't* the final judge, I reminded myself. Whoever it was had the right to be judged by a jury of their peers, in the decidedly normal court of law. The spell would reveal the murderer and make him or her wildly uncomfortable, even temporarily insane, but it was reversible. I would brew the antidote along with the curse.

Before beginning, I asked Oscar to put the black cat—now named, at least temporarily, Beowulf—out on the terrace. For me, brewing was a solitary art, the witch's familiar being the only exception. For some reason the feline presence interrupted my spell casting, yet another reason to find him, or her, a new home.

I centered myself, putting myself into the almost meditative state of stripping and crushing herbs, measuring and counting out ingredients, and chanting as the brew began to boil. I had never used snake ingredients before, other than the occasional shed here and there. Now, upon including them in the bubbling cauldron, memories washed over me, heightened by the steam and transformation of the elemental brew. The snake magic felt natural to me. And I supposed it was no wonder.

Snakes had once saved my life.

My father had some kind of special relationship to snakes. And ever since I was very small, I had the sense that this was one trait I had inherited from my father that scared Graciela, the only thing I can ever remember making her nervous.

My mama and most of her family are members of a snake-handling church in my hometown. They truly believe that if their faith is strong enough, the snakes' poisons cannot hurt them. How many times had I heard the story of my uncle Boyd, bit by a cottonmouth, who was cured by a laying on of hands in front of the entire congregation? As a healer myself, I wasn't about to deny the possibility that with enough faith, miracles could be brought to fruition.

One day, when I was seventeen, my mother begged me to go to a church meeting with her. She never asked anything of me—in fact, she rarely wanted any contact with me after sending me away to live with Graciela when I was just eight. Afraid, but unable to deny her, I agreed.

So on that sweltering summer day, air so thick it was hard to breathe, much less move, I entered the huge tent with my mother.

I had barely set foot inside when rough hands grabbed my arms. I was lifted off the ground and carried to the makeshift stage. My struggles were useless against the strength of the grown men who held me. They laid me on the floor and strapped me down, then placed their fat rough hands upon me. As though to cure me.

And then they opened the boxes that held the snakes. The reptiles wound around me, up and over my chest, encircling my arms and legs.

The preacher chanted:

"In my name shall they cast out devils, they shall speak with new tongues, they shall take up serpents, and if they drink any deadly thing, it shall not hurt them; they shall lay hands on the sick, and they shall recover."

Over and over, they all said the words. *They shall take up serpents*. Chanting swirled around me. I was surrounded by our neighbors: men in John Deere baseball caps marked with salt rings, their workingmen's jeans caked with the red dust of our west Texas earth; determined, frightened, thin-lipped women wearing embroidered cardigans and wedding rings; kids from school, pimply and spiteful, scared but driven to change me. Alter me. Or kill me, if need be.

They were exorcising me.

Their fear and rage swirled about me, invaded my soul. My fright turned to sheer, blind rage. Aluminum chairs started to cast about. The keys flew off the small keyboard they used in lieu of a proper organ. The preacher's Bible was wrenched from his hands.

The snakes turned on my tormentors.

By the time the screaming and near riot ended, there were twelve snakebite victims. I tried to do what I could, but several in the congregation covered my mouth to keep me from chanting. I still recalled the acrid taste of the dirty rag shoved in my mouth, a faint scent of axle grease.

In the end, two men and one woman perished that day. Old Mrs. Lockmiller, my third-grade teacher—the only teacher who had ever been kind to me—died from a cottonmouth. A man who ran the gas station when his farm went bust succumbed to the venom of a rattler. Another, a man who had been terrible to me, vicious even, died an excruciating death from a water moccasin.

Though I had not enchanted the snakes, nor wished death upon any of my attackers, they were out for blood, for vengeance. In the chaos I escaped the church and ran to hide in the woods, not wanting to endanger my grandmother.

Still, the townspeople marched on Graciela's house that night. I surrendered myself to police custody to keep myself—and Graciela—safe from the mob. One by one the witnesses dropped away as I sat for weeks in that filthy, sweaty jail cell. Then the county prosecutor fell ill, victim of some strange, unexplained malady. I knew it was Graciela's doing, though she denied it. In any case, the official charges were dropped, but the town's populace wasn't going to let it go at that.

Graciela packed my bags and sent me away in the middle of the night in her rusty old Ford truck, with a change of clothes, her old mortar and pestle, my crystal ball, and four hundred dollars, along with the directions to the home of a good friend of hers, a powerful *curandera* in Chiapas, Mexico.

Instead, I went in search of my father. Graciela had forbidden me to go to him. She was right, as usual.

"Mistress," I heard Oscar growl, waking me from my reverie, "it's ready."

The brew was giving off the distinct aroma that signaled it was ready for the next step in the process. The most important step.

Earlier today Renna had sent Eric over with a box, wrapped and bound eight times. In it was the poppet, in which Malachi's lock of hair and piece of bloody mirror had been enveloped in black wax. It was an evil-looking doll, featureless, crude.

I mumbled my spell as I wrapped the figure in red thread, for the life force, and black thread, for the death shroud. I bathed him in Tabasco sauce, letting the capsicum of the peppers begin its magic. The murderer was in the hot seat, so to speak.

> *What is evil and death is nigh, take*
> *this poppet through and through*
> *As serpents twist on high, so the*
> *snakes shall live in you*

I dropped the poppet into the cauldron. There was a great bubbling up, and a burst of steam that filled the space just below the ceiling as though it were a cloud.

But it didn't connect. I could tell. My helping spirit did not come to me. I looked at Oscar, who stared back at me. It was just like what happened in Aidan's place. Had I lost something? Or was this the effect of the curse Renna told me about, the dirt in the walnut shell?

I thought I might know where the shell was. And I realized, also, that the brew would most likely work if I could place it where Malachi Zazi lost his life, to mingle with the energy of the victim. What there was of it. Was this why the place had been cleansed, so no one could piggyback on the energy?

My conscience nagged me. I had promised Carlos Romero I would call him if I needed to get into Malachi Zazi's apartment again. I called and got his infernal voice mail. I told him where I was headed, confessing ahead of time to breaking into an active crime scene. Sometimes it's better to ask forgiveness than permission.

I decanted the still-hot brew into a special, wide-mouthed, heat-tolerant mason jar. Oscar helped me to pack up my white cloth, the *athame*, the Sorcerer's Violet, and the blessed rope in a hemp bag. I brought my satchel already full of a variety of oils and herbs, the Hand of Glory, and a small can of sterno to heat the brew.

And as an afterthought, I stuck the Serpentarius stone into my large pocket. Just in case.

Oscar was angry with me, once again, for refusing to let him come up to Malachi's apartment. But this time, my refusal had more to do with his safety than any worries about polite company. I wasn't sure what I would find up there, and I had a premonition it wouldn't go all that smoothly. A witch's familiar is usually her best ally in such circumstances, but the truth was that other than his helpful energy while brewing, Oscar wasn't very good at being a familiar. He was about as helpful in most things as the black cat. Speaking of which, what was I going to do with the poor feline?

The doorman was not at his post, so I brought out my Hand of Glory and unlocked the front doors. I let myself in and rode the clanky elevator up to the penthouse, on the thirteenth floor. Crime scene tape hung limply on either side of the door. Once again the Hand of Glory worked its magic, opened the lock, and lit the way.

I crept in carefully, but the place seemed empty.

I made my way through the kitchen, to the back door that led upstairs. To the little roof garden that Malachi Zazi had made for himself at the foot of Serpentarius. God of eternal life, eternal youth. I dropped my bags and extracted the items necessary for the spell.

After opening the jar of brew, I set it on a wire grill over the little sterno can on the tile surrounding the little raised planter.

I started to dig into the soft dirt. After several minutes I unearthed a walnut shell. This was the hex; I could feel its sinister hum. I split it open, spit on the contents, and applied a drop each of rosemary, orange, and cinnamon oils. I murmured an incantation to reflect the hex back on the sender, though I could feel that my enemy was strong, and protected. Finally, I mumbled a quick cleansing spell, let the soil spill back into the garden patch, and dug it in with the rest of the earth.

The jar of brew started to boil, the steam ascending to a point about six feet over my head, where it stayed in a cloudlike puff. I started to chant, invoking the spirits of the witches that had gone before me, my ancestors, and my spirit guide. With a flash of light, I finally saw the amorphous, barely-there face in the steam. My guardian spirit. I could feel that the spell had taken. It was done.

"What do you think you're doing?" said a woman's high-pitched voice. It was Doura.

I fell back on my butt. "Just casting a quick spell," I said. My eyes went past her to see Tracy. Behind her, looking befuddled, as though under a spell, was Claudia.

What was she doing here?

I took a deep breath, trying to keep my calm. If my anger cast about without control, I could end up making the situation worse. At this point I wasn't entirely sure what I was dealing with, but I knew one thing: Doura was trouble, with a capital T.

Her blue sunken eyes moved past me to the planter box. She smiled. "Found the walnut?"

I nodded.

"Told you we should have kept watch," Tracy muttered.

"This is between us, Doura. Why is Claudia here? What have you done to her?"

"She's okay—we saw her at your shop the first time we were there, remember? She mentioned she lived in Malachi's building. I figured she might be useful to have along. You go after me, she gets hurt. Like your buddy Bronwyn."

I felt rage surge through me, but I clamped down on it with everything I had. I breathed deeply, trying to remember—and channel—the feeling of Aidan's power wrapping around me in the cloister, helping me to focus on seeing the unseeable. This was no time for my powers to cast about, uncontrolled. I needed to figure things out, come up with a solid approach. Keeping Doura talking seemed like the best plan for the moment; I imagined she'd love to brag about her own abilities.

"What would Prince High think of all this?" I asked her.

"The High Prince of Hell? He's a putz. He works for us, not the other way around."

"Oh?"

"He used to bring in good money with those books of his. But lately he's back to playing the Wurlitzer. He's still useful as a cover, but not for much else."

"How could the Church of the Devil act as your cover?"

"They all thought he was nuts, that we were just the background. No one pays us any attention—once they figured out he was just for show, they didn't worry too much about him. Besides, it keeps your darling Aidan out of our hair. If he wants to respect the pact he has to leave us alone, go through the Prince for everything."

"So you still act according to the pact?"

"Oh, sure, we did. But you're the one who broke the pact, *sister*." She chuckled, low and sexy. "Hands off each other, remember? Then you went and got messed up in this whole Malachi Zazi deal."

"I wasn't the one who killed him."

"Of course not. Heaven knows who did the actual deed, but it was useful in any case. We were just as glad he was dead, frankly, weren't we, Tracy? He was starting to drive Nichol nuts, wouldn't leave her alone. I guess he really fell for her."

"What does Nichol have to do with any of this?"

"She's in training. She's surprisingly gifted, and malleable. Quite the little actress. And she has marvelous connections."

I thought of Atticus "saving" Nichol from the ceremony in the woods. Had she been there of her own free will? Was it an indoctrination ritual?

"But the Prince flipped out when Malachi died. Who knew he even *liked* his son that much? He started running around town imitating his son, of all things. People started asking questions, snooping around, not least of all, you."

"But why would you even care about Malachi's death?"

"There's the ironic thing: Malachi actually had some talents. Must have gotten them from his mother's side of the family, is all I'm saying. So I thought I might as well tap into some of his energy, since I was already having such fun with his dinner companions."

"What about them?"

"The Serpentarius Society, and 'bad luck'? *Please.* They were the perfect power source for our research over at Perkins Laboratories. Leaching just a bit of vitality each time. Turns out they were a bunch of superstitious folks after all. They never figured it out—felt like garbage, got jittery, and created their own messes."

I looked over at the mannequin-like Claudia. She swayed slightly on her feet, but seemed unharmed. Tracy kept one hand on her upper arm.

"Anyway," Doura continued. "Malachi's death turned out to be useful because it's a legitimate reason to dissolve the pact. That way Aidan can't come down on me for working with Perkins, and it's not even my fault. So we cleansed the place, snatched the poor guy's body so we could pretend to bring it back to life. I'm telling you, the Prince doesn't have much sense of what does and doesn't work. But now for the fun part: Since we've come this far, we might as well righteously avenge the dissolution of the pact."

She smiled and came to stand very close to me. I had to force myself not to back away. She picked up a lock of my hair, as though feeling it for softness.

"You'll do nicely."

"For what, exactly?"

"Eternal life, youth. We're not quite there yet, but Perkins's scientists are getting closer all the time. Only problem is that apparently, the only way to attain eternal youth is to drain the energy from others. And the only way to do that is through the Craft."

I felt Tracy come up behind me. I thought of how much she reminded me of an elf the first time we met. If only she *were* an elf, maybe I'd have a shot. I haven't known all that many witches in my life, but there was always a part of me that hoped there might be more of a natural sisterhood. Apparently, I was wrong.

With Tracy behind me and Doura in front, I could feel their energies connecting, challenging and weakening my own.

"So what's next?" I asked, making a play for more time.

Our intense face-off was interrupted as a man burst through the door from the stairs, out onto the roof. *Atticus*. I couldn't believe he arrived to save me a second time.

But then he cried out. He yanked his tie off his neck and frantically reached into his clothing, all the while making a high-pitched squealing noise, as though there were a hornet down his shirt.

"What is your *problem*?" Doura asked, aggravated. "Whatever you're on, you should consider rehab. Seriously. Is Nichol with you?"

"There's something in me!" he yelled. "Something . . . ! Aaaaaah!"

Tracy laughed.

While their attention was distracted, I fled.

Unfortunately, there was nowhere to run. Everyone stood in between me and the door, temptingly ajar, that led to the stairs. And there was Claudia to consider—I couldn't leave her here on the roof with these two. But I had to put some distance between me and Doura in order to concentrate, to find my center. Otherwise, I would be useless to anyone.

I ran toward the corner, where one grand spire rose high above the roofline. The moldings acted like thin makeshift steps. Hugging the main part of the spire, I edged out on one of the lips, a shallow stone overhang.

Doura just arched one tweezed eyebrow and curled her lip. "Just where do you think *you're* going?"

"Not sure yet," I said. "I'm sort of thinking on my feet."

"Tracy," Doura barked, gesturing with a quick nod of the head.

Time slowed again, and I felt that strange, nightmarish sensation of moving through water, or worse, molasses. When Doura and Tracy spoke and moved, it was almost normal speed, but Atticus's laments became drawn-out, eerie, slow-motion cries.

A black cat meandered by the nearby rooftop crest. Was that *Beowulf*? All I could see was the black silhouette against the sky. When the breeze blew over the feline and toward me, I sneezed.

"Gesundheit," came a whisper.

I froze. That was Oscar's gravelly voice.

Frantic, but trying to appear nonchalant, I cast my gaze around the gargoyles. Until I finally spotted a small one I hadn't seen before. Big, batlike ears. Clawed feet. Funny grimace on his face. *Oscar.* I closed my eyes in gratitude. Never had I been so happy to see a gargoyle.

Speaking of gargoyles, the big hulking one nearest me shifted. I was sure of it this time. Then another, the funny smiling one from halfway down the main roof. And the one atop the spire I was hugging.

They moved slowly, so slowly it was almost imperceptible. But with Tracy's time spell, even normal conversation seemed warped and laborious. If the gargoyles' movement was barely perceptible before, now with the slowing of time it was nearly impossible to detect.

The gargoyle seemed to hold its arm out. I sensed more than saw it move. But one thing was sure: There used to be no place to go, but now there was.

I grabbed the arm. It was cold and hard, stonelike, under my palm. Just like one would expect from a gargoyle. The only odd part is that it had moved—unusual behavior in a stone object.

I inched my way over, pulling myself onto its shoulder. Just putting more distance between me and Doura felt comforting, allowed me to breathe more deeply and channel my energies.

"C'mon now," said Doura. "Don't be difficult. Thanks to you I still have to find out who killed Malachi in order to calm the Prince down. Or maybe I'll just tell him you did it, and we got revenge for him. Poor guy, I feel kind of bad for him."

"I can tell you who killed Malachi," I said.

"How do *you* know?"

"I cast a spell. To determine who might have done it."

"Liar. You're saying you saw someone while scrying?"

"No. I brewed. And then I cast from afar."

She looked at me silently for a long moment. When she spoke her voice was skeptical, but intrigued. "You can do that?"

Atticus quite literally threw himself at Doura, falling to his knees in front of her.

"I'll do anything you ask. Just make it stop!"

"Get up, for the love of—*Tracy!* Take care of this!"

Tracy looked miffed, but she did as she was told, coming to grab Atticus from behind. She hooked her hands under his arms and drew him up and toward her with remarkable strength.

The slowdown ended.

"And just where is Nichol?" demanded Doura of Tracy. "Does she have to be late to every damned thing? Wasn't she with Atticus? We need the three of us to complete this."

The gargoyles shifted again. I didn't know what they were capable of, for better or for worse, but I was certain that Oscar would intervene. I didn't know how much he could do, and I didn't want him to get hurt, but it was heartening just to know that I wasn't all alone. I could feel their elemental stone energy; it helped center me, calm me.

I looked over just as a snake slithered through the open stairwell door. It came toward me, still unnoticed by any but Oscar and me.

As it passed Doura, I met its flat reptilian eyes. Concentrated.

It paused. It coiled. It struck.

Chapter 28

Doura cried out.

Tracy ran to her side.

"It bit me! It bit my leg!" Doura cried, falling to the tar-and-gravel rooftop. The snake was still attached by its fangs, still pumping its venom into her leg.

Tracy grabbed the snake with her bare hands and ripped its head off. Blood spewed on her. The energy of death tingled along my extremities when I cast out my senses.

Doura fell over, crying and holding her leg.

Tracy was gearing up for something big; I could feel her rage.

"I can save her!" I yelled at Tracy. "I have the Serpentarius talisman to heal poisonous bites. I can save her."

Tracy's freckles showed red against her pale skin. She looked around, clearly at a loss. She was powerful, this much was clear, but I had the sense that, like me, she had not had the best upbringing or education. She had latched on to Doura as her friend and ally, and would go to great lengths to protect her. Doura was the brains of the operation. Now, on her own, Tracy was at a loss.

"Doura! Talk to Tracy, tell her to let Claudia go, and I'll help you. Do it now, or it might be too late."

Still sprawled in the gravel of the rooftop, holding her leg and gasping, Doura met my eyes. Her blue ones showed pain, but I barely twinged. She had hexed Bronwyn. Lord knows what she had planned for me, and for Claudia. No, I spared no love for Doura.

Still, I don't hold with taking human life, no matter the crime. It was in my power to save her, and I intended to do so. Just as soon as I got what I wanted.

"Do it, Tracy, let Claudia go," Doura said. *"Now!"*

Tracy mumbled an incantation, and Claudia awoke, looking around her, fearful and confused.

"Claudia, run back to your place and call 911," I said. "And tell them there's been a rattlesnake bite. They'll need to have serum on hand. Now!"

I climbed off the spire, my arms shaking from the fear and effort of holding on. Using one of the old beer cans, I dunked it in the rain barrel and rinsed it out as well I could. Then I began to wash the Serpentarius stone in the barrel, invoking while I did so, scraping the stone with my fingernail, mumbling and chanting.

I scooped water into the beer can and brought it to Doura.

"Drink."

"That's disgusting," she said, pushing it away. I could hear a hitch in her breathing, as though it was becoming labored. Her lower leg was swelling, the area around the bite showing bruising even in the dim light. "That can's dirty."

"I rinsed it out," I said with a shrug. "Anyway, it's your funeral. I won't be losing any sleep over it."

She glared at me, but grudgingly accepted the can

and held it to her lips. Grimacing, she took a ladylike sip.

"Drink all of it," I said, knowing full well that it wasn't necessary for her to drink the entire can. I was being mean. I would do my best to save her life, but I was nowhere near in a forgiving mood.

I knelt by her side and brought the talisman to the site of the wound, and held the cool wet stone to the fang marks. Doura jumped and tensed when I touched her, crying out again.

This time my heart did go out to her. Humans were so fragile, so fallible. I had no idea what her story was, but once upon a time Doura had been an innocent. Like all of us.

Holding the stone against the ugly wound, I started to chant again. Doura either relaxed or fainted.

"Tracy, come and hold her upper body in a sitting position. Don't let her lay down."

Tracy seemed relieved to be told what to do. She knelt behind Doura and held her from behind.

"Keep her heart above the wounded area," I said. I was worried that Doura wasn't responding more quickly to the Serpentarius talisman. I had never used one before, it was true, but the magic felt right to me, I could feel its hum, as though its magic were slipping through the portals as it should.

"Tracy, let's carry her downstairs to the apartment so I can see what I'm doing."

Once we were down in the apartment, I flung open the windows to let some of the stifling heat escape. A sparrow came flittering in. Death was in the air. I tried to ignore it as I held the Serpentarius charm to Doura's leg and chanted some more.

Atticus sat in the corner, whimpering and twitching.

Nichol walked in, her beautiful eyes flickering about the room as she took in the scene.

"Atticus! Why did you run away from me? What's wrong with you?" Nichol looked down at Doura and grimaced. "What's wrong with *her*?"

" 'Bout time you arrived," Tracy muttered. "Doura got snakebit."

"I'm trying to save her," I said.

"Save *him*," Nichol said, shoving Atticus in my direction. "What's wrong with him? Did you do something?"

"He'll be all right," I said softly. "It will wear off."

"You did this, didn't you? Yes, okay, all right already, he killed Malachi. But it wasn't his fault. I saw the whole thing. It was an accident."

"Make it stop!" Atticus cried out. "What's happening to me?"

Atticus. The big brother who was so protective of his sister, his baby brother. The one who intervened on their behalf, who supported their father's career and wanted him to thrive. The one who tried to cover up Oliver's drug problem and Nichol's shoplifting past.

"It was an *accident*," Nichol repeated. "I just wanted Malachi to stop with the curses and the crazy talk, the photos and the publicity. He wouldn't leave me alone. And then Oliver was beginning to think he was truly cursed."

"But the curses weren't Malachi's doing, they were . . ." I glanced down at the witchy woman sprawled on the couch before me. "They were someone else's."

I heard far-off sirens, growing louder. I was hoping the paramedics would get here quickly. Though the Serpentarius stone had helped, the rattler had given Doura quite a dose of venom.

"Come on." Nichol was trying to get Atticus to stand. "Let's get out of here before the cops come. Come *on*."

"He's a lost cause until the spell wears off, Nichol," I said, not mentioning the antidote I had up on the roof with my supplies.

She glared at me. "I'll pay you back for this, so help me."

And with that she abandoned her tortured brother and ran.

Tracy, Doura, and I all sat in silence for a few minutes, the fluttering of the sparrow and Atticus's sniffling and moaning the only sounds within the apartment. But outside, the sirens grew deafening before petering out as they pulled up to the building.

"What do you want?" Tracy asked me.

"What do you mean, what do I want?"

"In exchange for saving Doura's life?"

"I want y'all to stop making animal sacrifices and conducting evil spells. Stay away from Mike Perkins and any of his research. If I find he's advancing on his projects due to magical intervention I'll come after you. And *stay away* from my friends, and me."

She nodded, looking down at her companion, who had now passed out.

"And I want the bird," I said, watching as the sparrow finally flittered out of the open window.

"What bird?"

"In the black abode, y'all have a poor little sparrow caged up right next to the snakes. It's cruel. It must feel in danger all the time. Besides, a sparrow in a house is a sign of death, y'all should know that."

"Okay," Tracy said with a sigh. "I guess you can have the stupid bird."

*   *   *

I gave a statement to Carlos Romero, gathered my spell-casting items, and then gave Atticus—who was more than anxious to confess to the SFPD—the antidote to my terrible spell.

On the way back home, Oscar transformed into his natural state, but remained mute. He held the cat in his lap, stroking its velvet-soft coat.

"Oscar, I'm going to ask you a question, and I want you to answer me. What relationship do you have to gargoyles?"

"Relationship?" He looked at me, eyes huge.

"Don't you trust me? You can tell me."

"You won't make fun?"

"Of course not."

"I was looking for my mother."

I waited a beat. "Your mother's a gargoyle?"

He shrugged a skinny shoulder and looked out the window.

"I don't understand: Are you a gargoyle come to life? Can stone do that?"

"They're not stone, at least not all of them. That's where it gets confusing."

"I can imagine."

"Some of them are descendants of forest folk who are under a curse, and they turned to stone. They only come out of it under very particular circumstances."

"So you're not actually a goblin at all?"

"Halfsies."

"You're half a goblin?"

"When my mother was in her walking time, she laid an egg. My father found it, and took it to the faery circle and hatched me."

"Gargoyles are born from eggs?"

"*Duh*. Where else—ooooh. *Yuck*. I've heard of that. Cowans grow them on the inside, like a tumor. That kind of weirds me out."

So says the half gargoyle born of an egg in the faery circle, presumably fertilized by a goblin. I didn't want to think too hard about the mechanics of that one, either.

"Just FYI, it's not only cowans who have babies like that. All of us humans do. Even witchy folk."

"Yuck. Anyway, so's I'm like a whattayacall, a half-breed. The other forest creature kids used to call me a gobgoyle."

I smiled.

"It's *not* funny."

"I'm sorry. You're right. I know what it is not to fit in." Once when I took Oscar to the cemetery, he had hopped up on a crypt and tried to scare the passersby. I guessed it made a certain kind of sense that he had gargoyle-ness in his genes.

"Now I look for my mother's face whenever I see gargoyles. I don't know where she ended up, but gargoyles live just about forever, so I think that she might be out there somewhere. I keep looking for her."

"I never really knew my dad, either."

"Do you look for him, too?"

"Not really. It's not exactly the same kind of relationship. I did meet him once, but ... he's not someone I want in my life. I reckon if I did see him, I'd end up running the other way."

We rode in companionable silence for a moment. Then I sneezed.

"Gesundheit."

"Thanks. And, Oscar, thank you for being there for me on the roof."

"I disobeyed you."

"That's true. But you and I don't exactly have a traditional witch-familiar relationship. I think we should just accept that about ourselves."

Oscar gave me his version of a smile, which looked a lot like a grimace.

"Awesome," he said.

Chapter 29

"Dudettes, there's, like . . . a bird in a cage out here on the stoop," said Conrad.

Two days had passed since that nightmarish evening up on Malachi Zazi's rooftop. Carlos had informed me that Doura had gotten to the hospital in time, was given an antivenin serum, and then left against medical advice. Atticus, still shaky from his experience, had given inspectors a full confession. Nichol was nowhere to be found.

Mike Perkins had also fled town, with the results of a few crucial experiments disappearing along with him. Carlos had confided in me that even if they could track him down, they might not have any actual charges that would stick. They had no proof that he'd done anything wrong.

"Well, what do you know?" I said as we all came out to look at the ornate cage sitting outside of the front door of Aunt Cora's Closet. "Tracy came through after all."

I opened the little wire door. The sparrow chirped, flitted up to my shoulder, then flew away.

"Awww-ah," Imogen said, disappointed. "Why'd you let it go?"

"When a sparrow's not where it's supposed to be, it's a bad sign. An omen. But when it's out in the wild, it's a sign of hope."

"Duuude, that's like a . . . whaddayacallit? A metaphor. Yeah." Conrad returned to take his seat on the curb.

The rest of us—Sailor, Maya, Bronwyn, Imogen and her brother James, and Claudia—trooped back into the store. I carried the cage with me, figuring we could decorate it and use it for a store display.

Sailor took up his position as reluctant bodyguard, arms crossed over his chest as he shared the velvet bench with James. Apparently Aidan had told Sailor to keep an eye on me for a few more days, to make sure Doura was willing to play ball and there weren't any other renegade folks out there trying to dissolve the pact among paranormals. As he explained it to me, I was a supernatural magnet for trouble.

"So I just stopped by to tell you that it looks like the ball is definitely on, after all," Claudia said. "They found a new keynote speaker, and everything seems to be coming together well, finally. Lily, I really hope you're coming."

"I intend to. I have a dress picked out, and an escort, and everything."

"That reminds me," said Maya. "Mom brought your dress over, it's all set. You should try it on for us. Give us a little fashion show."

I glanced over at Sailor and felt suddenly shy. "Maybe a little later. Also, I need to find a man's outfit that's suitable for the dance. Suppose we could find something that coordinates with my dress, by any miracle?"

"Usually it's just a tuxedo for the men. He could rent one, presuming he doesn't own one," said Claudia.

"So Max is taking you after all?" Maya asked with a grin. "I figured, after that kiss . . ."

Sailor made a rude noise.

"Oh, I . . . uh . . ." My cheeks burned. Every pair of eyes was on me. "Not exactly. Actually, Aidan Rhodes is taking me."

Sailor made an even ruder noise and held his head in his hands.

"Aidan? He's back in the picture?" said Bronwyn with a smile as she straightened the jars on her shelves, turning all the neat little labels out so they were easy to read. "Your love life's hard to keep up with—you know that?"

"Thank you for coming back to work, Bronwyn," I said. "Frankly, I wasn't sure you'd ever be back after I went against your wishes like that."

"Oh please, Lily, I would never stop being your friend simply because I was upset with you. Don't you know that?" She gave me a warm smile, then lifted her eyebrows and teased: "I never thought I'd be accusing *you* of being a drama queen."

I just shrugged and blushed, unable to speak.

"Among other things, that GED is waiting for you. You might be running around the city, getting involved in murder investigations and what all, but that's no reason to avoid working on your algebra."

"This part's easy, Lily," said Imogen. "I can show you how if you want."

An eight-year-old was outdoing me in math. I groaned and looked at my feet. Today's Keds were white, but they had been adorned with painted flowers and glitter by Imogen and her brother James, as a special gift to me—a thank-you for their new black cat, Beowulf. Rebecca, reunited with her husband and thankful that their nightmare seemed to be coming to a close, had relented on her no-pets policy. She also seemed more willing to let the kids come by the shop to spend time with their grandmother.

James brought a book to read in the corner, but Imogen was already something of a vintage-clothes horse and enjoyed folding scarves and trying on every outfit even remotely in her small size. Better vintage than new, I always said.

"Hey, Maya, what's this?" I asked as I noticed a cardboard box full of baby clothes sitting at one end of the sales counter.

"Oh, this woman came in with a baby on her hip, and she seemed so desperate . . . I just couldn't say no," said Maya. "I know we don't carry children's items, so it wasn't a wise business decision . . . but she really seemed to need help."

"That's all right," I said as I started pawing through the box. I didn't get far before realizing that there was something dreadfully wrong. I held up an adorable little red-and-white-striped outfit, complete with footies, and concentrated on it. The vibrations were off.

I closed my eyes and let out a sigh. Cases involving children were always the most difficult to deal with. But deal with it, I would. And not by myself.

Back when I roamed the world, looking for a place I might fit in, part of me never really believed I would find it. Or even if I did, by some miracle, I never thought I would have a true home. But now, looking around Aunt Cora's Closet at Bronwyn and the kids, calm, loyal Maya, my "pet" Oscar, and even sullen Sailor, I knew I had stumbled upon more than just a safe harbor peopled by good friends. I was becoming part of a family.

And as I looked down at the suspicious clothing in my hands, there was one thing of which I was absolutely sure: Life in San Francisco would never grow dull.

This was one pitiful-looking mansion.

As I pushed open the heavy front door, an empty beer can rolled across the dusty oak floor, its metallic rattle echoing off bashed-in walls and broken bookcases. More cans, wine bottles, and an impressive assortment of power tools lay strewn about the floor. Half-filled cups spoiled the once-shiny black lacquer of the grand piano and littered the graceful sweep of the circular stairs leading off the octagonal foyer. A damp, salty bay breeze blew in through a broken casement window. I tried clicking on the overhead chandelier to shed some light on the dim interior, but either the fuse had blown or the electricity had been cut.

My former client lay sprawled on a worn black leather couch, a gash between his eyebrows still oozing blood.

I had warned him.

Long freckled fingers gripped a half-empty bottle of a local favorite: passion fruit–infused Hangar One vodka, brewed in an abandoned navy airplane hangar just on the other side of the San Francisco Bay. At least the fool had taste, if not sense.

I pried the bottle from his hand.

With a snort, Matt Addax opened red-rimmed bright blue eyes.

"Wha . . . Mel? What're you doin' here?" he asked in a British-accented slur.

"Your son called me," I said. "He was afraid that last night's 'Do-It-Yourself' remodeling party might have gotten out of hand."

"The lad's wise beyond his years."

"Mmm." I kicked at a stray piece of old molding, lying rusty nail side up, with the steel toe of my work boot. "What happened to your face?"

He sat up and raised a hand to probe the cut between his eyes. "Ah, *bloody hell*, I've got a photo shoot tomorrow. A piece of wood snapped off—the stuff that they used to put old plaster onto. What's that called?"

"Lath?"

"Yeah. I was prying off some lath and it snapped and beaned me. I loathe lath." He smiled. "Try saying that five times fast."

"You promised me you'd wear safety glasses."

He shrugged, looked me up and down, and lifted his eyebrows. "You always look like you're on the way to a fancy-dress party. Don't the boys tease you?"

"Not if they want their paychecks signed, they don't."

Provided I wore the proper footwear—my ever-present work boots—and knew my single-bevel miter saws from my random orbital sanders, the construction workers in my employ didn't much care how I dressed. Today I was wearing a multicolored spangled shift dress under a leather bomber jacket I had borrowed from my dad's closet as a concession to modesty and the weather. The carnival nature of the dress was a little over-the-top for a woman just a couple years shy of forty, and strangers on the street frequently mistook me for a Madonna groupie, but after years of wearing the "proper" faculty-wife wardrobe, I had sworn never to hold myself back. Besides, even in progressive California, people were so surprised to see a woman running a construction company, I figured the clothes gave us all something tangible to fixate on.

I sank onto the sofa next to Matt, held my hand out for the vodka, and took a little swig. It was barely noon, but the havoc that forty or so drunken amateurs had managed to wreak on this formerly gorgeous, if down-at-the-heels, Pacific Heights mansion was motivation enough for a quick drink an hour or three before happy hour.

Matt leaned his elbows on his knees and cradled his head in his broad musician's hands, his thinning sandy hair sprouting between his fingers. Looking over at him—and at the once-elegant mansion falling apart around us—I could feel my resolve melting away.

I had sworn I wouldn't get involved with Matt's scheme to flip upscale houses, trading on his celebrity and social connections to market to an exclusive clientele. But I liked Matt, and it wouldn't take that much for me to help him out. After all, remodeling historic homes is my business.

A lot of rich and famous people wind up growing abnormally close to their contractors. We camp out in their homes for weeks, sometimes months, at a time. We have no particular stake in their wealth or celebrity—though our rates might spike when we enter the poshest neighborhoods. But aside from obvious budget considerations, ripping the toilet out of a crumbling Victorian in humble West Oakland is essentially the same as ripping one out of the fanciest Pacific Heights Beaux-Arts mansion.

The very banality of this interaction can transform a good general contractor into a client's trusted confidante. There's nothing quite like a protracted remodel project to devastate a marriage or threaten family harmony, and since taking over my dad's construction business two years ago, I've mediated more than my fair share of domestic disputes. I respond to panicky calls about leaky faucets in the middle of the night and find myself hearing much more than I want to know about unfaithful spouses, shady corporate deals, and murky political alliances. I'm like a confessor to some of these people.

Matt Addax—whose long-haired, blue-jean-jacketed, guitar-playing image had adorned my bedroom wall in my teenage years—was one of those people.

"Anybody else get hurt?" I asked.

"I don't remember much past the . . ." He held his hand up toward the jagged shards of glass remaining in the smashed window frame and trailed off with a defeated shake of his head. "It seemed like a good idea at the time. Ya know that remodel show on cable, where they do their own demo?" Matt asked, his voice recovering its familiar upbeat tone. "Like Kenneth said, it always seems like a blast. He arranged to have a photog here from the *Chronicle* to document the whole thing. He thought it'd make a brilliant human interest story."

"Why am I not surprised that Kenneth was involved?"

"He means well."

I found that hard to believe. But as my mother used to say, if you can't say something nice, change the subject.

"I'm pretty sure that on TV they don't encourage participants to drink while using power tools," I pointed out, passing the bottle back to Max. "They also have professionals running things."

"You're right. I'm an idiot. I should have hired you to supervise."

"You called and asked me to, remember? I refused, because I'm smart."

"Right. Now I remember."

"Besides, Kenneth doesn't like me."

"He just doesn't like your rates."

"Believe me, he doesn't like *me*."

And the feeling was mutual. Kenneth had acted as project manager on Matt's kitchen renovation in Sausalito, but he kept insisting on cutting corners and fudging on little things like code requirements. I had finally walked off the job after an incident involving threatening words concerning the creative use of a jackhammer.

"I give up on this place," Matt said with a defeated sigh. "Will you fix it?"

"Which part?"

"All of it. I'm tired of it. I don't care what Kenneth says. Just take over the remodel. If you cut me a break on your fees up front, I can offer you a share of the sale price. We should still be able to make some good money."

"You're one week into a remodel and you're already tired of it? You might want to reconsider this house-flipping venture."

"We made a killing on the last place."

"One lucky sale is no foundation for such a risky line of business."

"Kenneth got this place cheap, though. Because of the haunting deal."

I was afraid to ask. But I couldn't stop myself.

"*Haunting* deal?"

"You don't know about that? People say this place is haunted. So we got it cheap."

"Seriously?"

"Previous owner had to disclose it in the sale."

"Let me get this straight: The owners have to tell you if they think their house is haunted?"

He nodded. "Real estate law. It's part of full disclosure and all that." His red-rimmed eyes scanned the disaster area surrounding us. "Maybe it really *is* haunted. Maybe *that's* what happened last night."

I held up the bottle of vodka. "*This* is what happened last night. These are all the spirits you need to screw up a construction project."

"At least I followed your advice on one thing: I packed up all the glass lampshades, a lot of the door and window hardware, and anything else that looked valuable or historical." Matt dug into the pocket of his faded jeans and brought out a chain with two keys, one small and one large. "The crate's in the garage. Could you arrange for storage? It's padlocked—here's the key."

"What's the other key for?"

"The front door. Say you'll save me."

"It'll be a huge job if we do it right."

"I know that."

"Pricey." Just wanted to be clear.

"I'll make the money back in the long run. This is Pacific Heights, after all. The sky's the limit. . . . Listen, Mel, I can't afford to look like an idiot with this one. I'm too high profile. I need to flip it—fast."

I looked at the living room, the entry, and the dining room beyond. Yes, there was trash everywhere, holes in the walls, cracked and peeling paint and varnish, and signs of dry rot along some of the windows. But I knew from my previous inspection that the all-important foundation was solid and the main wood supports were intact. And, like most historical structures, Matt's house had been built with more care, better skills, and finer materials than one would find in any modern home.

Indeed, the bones of the place reflected the grace and refinement of an era long past. Ceilings were high, with peaked arches leading from one room to the next. Wide-plank oak floors were dressed up with an inlaid Greek key border design. The crown moldings were intact, boasting intricate fleur-de-lis and acanthus leaves. The living room fireplace mantel, crowded at the moment with plastic cups and beer cans, was elaborately carved limestone complete with spiral columns and frolicking putti.

I could practically feel the people who had once come to this parlor for a cup of tea, hear the rattle of a newspaper, smell the aroma of pipe smoke, and sense the tinkle of laughter through the years.

Who was I kidding? I had fallen under the house's spell the first moment I walked in to do the inspection two months ago. The signs of its long neglect and recent abuse hurt my heart. I was already itching to get at it.

"All things considered, the damage looks pretty superficial," I said, patting Matt on the knee and giving in to my inevitable impulse to save the place. "Nothing a big fat check won't fix. As long as no one broke a water pipe or compromised a load-bearing wall, you'll be okay."

Matt's bloodshot eyes fixed on me. "You're a peach, Mel. I mean that."

"Let's go survey the damage, shall we?"

As Matt and I mounted the steps to the second floor, I bit my tongue, trying to keep from commenting on the vodka. It really wasn't any of my business.

I made it almost halfway up the flight of stairs.

"I thought you quit drinking."

"I'm in a new program. Booze isn't strictly forbidden as long as it's taken in moderation. Besides, my new neighbor brought over a bottle of eighteen-year-old scotch. Old enough to vote. What's a man to do?"

Sounded more like rationalization than science to me, but who was I to say?

I had to smile as we stepped into the master bedroom. A sheet of wallboard had been hung both crooked *and* backward. There were several nails placed, seemingly at random, in one multipaned window frame. And the pièce de résistance: a lacy red bra hung over a closet door.

If this was Matt's definition of moderation, I'd hate to witness his version of overindulgence.

As I stepped over an empty champagne bottle, my boot kicked something that clinked and skittered across the floor. I squatted and picked up a few of the small brass objects.

"Are those shells?" Matt asked. *"Bloody hell."*

"What exactly went down here last night, Max?"

"I'm telling you, I don't remember. My ex walked in with her new boy toy, and I started downing that great scotch. I'll admit, I lost it."

"Who was invited to this shindig?"

"Everybody. The A-list. Rory Abrams—the guy with that hot new restaurant in North Beach?—took care of the catering. Everyone thought the whole do-it-yourself demo idea was a scream."

"Oh, sure," I said, "brandishing Sawzalls and pneumatic drills and *handguns* while downing tequila shooters is a real hoot."

"It wasn't that bad. The photographer gave me the name of a guy to handle security at the front door, and he brought along a couple of friends to make sure things didn't get out of hand."

"Sounds positively sedate. You guys trashed the place, cut the lights, and someone had a gun?" My eyes scanned the floor for more cartridges. "Tell me, Matt— what would 'getting out of hand' look like?"

"Be kind to the man with a beastly hangover. Besides, those bullets could have been here for years for all we know. Maybe they were behind something, just got knocked about in the hubbub."

"Was there anyone at the party that I'd know? Who was the photographer?"

"A kid—Zachary something. He's new. Cute. Looks like a young Antonio Banderas, except, ya know, not Spanish."

I crossed over to the crooked wallboard and peered into the deep recess beyond. Because of the line of the eaves, there was more than the standard six inches of space behind the wall. A dark niche extended back several feet. The perfect hiding place.

"Hey, Matt, I think I see something back in here."

Matt wrinkled his nose. "I hate that—when they open up the walls. It smells funky."

"Are you serious? That's the fun part."

"It's the anthropologist in you coming out. The love of digging up old bones. I'm telling you, it's bad juju."

"I was a *cultural* anthropologist, not an archaeologist. I dealt with live people. And anyway, I relinquished my badge when I became a contractor, remember?"

"Once an anthropologist, always an anthropologist. You guys are like musicians. You can't shake it."

He was more right than he knew.

To me, old houses might as well be ancient pyramids. They hold secrets and messages from the past; I feel them whispering to me as I walk the hallways. Walls, attics, basements . . . Over the past five years I had found newspapers from the thirties, liquor bottles, old coins, address books, even the occasional stash of money or stocks. I once unearthed a button-up baby's shoe and a dress pattern book from 1916. I even liked the smell: the distinctive musty aroma of history, reminding me of used bookstores . . . promising the serendipitous discovery of the perfect novel or family relic or beloved treasure.

I dug through my satchel for my key ring, on which hung a miniflashlight. Holding the light with my teeth, I crouched, grabbed onto a stud with one hand for balance, leaned in through the hole in the wall, and reached.

It was frustratingly close, but my arm wasn't quite long enough. I stretched just a little more, managing to knock at the item with my fingertips. Unfortunately that just pushed it farther until it fell into a well between the floor joists. I couldn't see anything anymore, even with the flashlight.

"Darn it!" I swore under my breath. "I almost had it. . . ."

Behind me, Matt screamed.